Spellbound

NIGHT

ERIK CLARKE

Night
ISBN # 978-1-78184-744-2
©Copyright Erik Clarke 2014
Cover Art by Posh Gosh ©Copyright January 2014
Interior text design by Claire Siemaszkiewicz
Totally Bound Publishing

Published in 2014 by Totally Bound Publishing, Newland House, The Point, Weaver Road, Lincoln, LN6 3QN, United Kingdom.

Totally Bound Publishing is an imprint of Total-E-Ntwined Limited.

NIGHT

Dedication

To Tori, Sophie, Teague and Lana.

For always believing I'd finally get this finished, and riding my ass until I did. This one is for you guys.

Chapter One

"Seriously, Luke, I'm going to be late!" I called backward over my shoulder to the Dreamwalker, wherever the hell he was. Last thing I had heard was him mumbling something about needing to grab more papers to roll before he had disappeared to some other part of the apartment. I tossed the Xbox controller to the floor, leaving the game at the pause screen—I had *told* Luke that I needed to leave soon so I wouldn't miss my date. But he'd kept coming up with things to distract me, like showing me the new shooter I'd been dying to play for a week when he *knew* I didn't have time to be playing it, the asshole.

I wandered around the counter into the kitchen. I was about to go out to dinner so I didn't need to eat, and I had to drive back to my own apartment to get ready, so I wasn't going to be able to drink anything either. I still perused through the room, opening cabinets and drawers even though I knew exactly what was in each of them. I knew Luke's place better than my own, considering my organization-freak of a roommate, Jake, was constantly moving shit to make it more 'efficient' — whatever the hell that meant. It was a kitchen, for God's sake, how *efficient* did it need to be? I swung open the refrigerator door, staring mindlessly at the items looking back up at me from the washed-out fluorescent glow.

My date really was getting close, and since Luke was busy finding whatever it was he was looking for, I swung the door shut again with a plan to just shout a "*See ya*" over my shoulder on the way out. But just before the fridge sealed closed, a tiny glimpse of silver caught my eye. I threw my hand out to catch the door and managed to get my fingers thoroughly crushed for my efforts. That was me — Cole Turner, the epitome of forethought. With a muttered "Fuck," I reached blindly for the tiny vial I'd seen.

I pulled the glass tube out into the light and almost immediately dropped it when I realized how *warm* the thing was — it was like a tiny furnace, threatening to burn my fingertips. How could it have been that hot when it had been in the *refrigerator*? I rolled it over in my hands, watching as the mercury-silver fluid twirled beautifully in its translucent suspension, coiling and helixing like it had a mind of its own.

The sound of shuffling feet made me finally tear my eyes away from the show. Luke rounded the corner and stepped into the kitchen, his messy hair looking even more trashed than usual. He looked up from the joint he'd just lit with glazed-eyed disinterest — a look that shattered the instant he saw what I was holding. The Dreamwalker's eyes widened, making the green stand out even more poignantly as he froze in place.

"Luke, what the fuck is this stuff?"

His mouth opened and closed blankly for a second, and I couldn't help the smirk that was tugging at my lips. In all the time I'd known Luke, I'd never seen him actually *embarrassed* about something he'd picked up — which just made me want to know what it was even more. He squirmed for a half second longer before taking another drag and letting the smoke tumble out of his mouth lazily. "It's...just some shit I bought off a Were-shifter."

I cocked my eyebrow and stared him down, spinning the vial between my fingers. "Okay, but what *is* it?"

Luke shrugged noncommittally, but he couldn't hide the way his eyes refused to leave the little tube as I twirled it. "It's just...*stuff*, you know?" The Dreamwalker ran a hand through his hair. "It's called Night."

"Night, huh?" I took another look at the vial and the silver swirls it contained, then tossed it to Luke. He caught it reflexively, and I patted him on the shoulder as I stepped around him to head for the door. I wanted to keep pushing him for more, but I didn't have time. Besides, he'd tell me later anyway — Luke had never been good at keeping secrets from me. "Well, Mr Mysterious, I've got to head out before you make me even later tha — "

"I got it for you!"

I stumbled to a halt an arm's length from the door. I turned around in confusion, but Luke wasn't looking at me — he was staring seriously down at his palm, at the tiny coils of mercury that moved without a care. He looked up after a beat, nodding in a way that seemed more for his benefit than mine.

"For *me?*" I ran a hand through my hair, my brow furrowing. "Why?"

Luke scratched his head, coming around the side of the counter so he could approach me. "You..." The Dreamwalker paused, staring out into nothing for a second, and I honestly couldn't tell if it was because of the weed or — God only knew what, at that point. Luke shook his head, pulling back down to reality as he caught my gaze again. "You feel like you have no control in your life."

The words rattled around in my head for a few seconds, and I ran my hand along my other forearm as the truth of that statement really started to sink in. I'd never put it quite so succinctly, but after listening to my problems for seven years, Luke seemed to have found a surprisingly accurate way to sum it all up in ten little words. Before the barbed memories could hook in too tightly, I forced my face to crack into a smile, a lie that hurt more than I'd expected. "Tends to happen when you're a Seer who can See everyone's future but your own, I guess." My voice was light, but I couldn't stop the smirk from faltering as my eyes honed in on that little bottle. "Occupational hazard."

The Dreamwalker's expression softened and his thumb ran over the length of the glass for a moment before he extended his hand out toward me. "This'll give you control."

I stared at my best friend like he'd gone insane — because if he honestly thought whatever was in that tiny vial could fix the problems in my life, he really had to be nuts. But at the same time...

Luke had never lied to me before and, as stupid as he was sounding, I couldn't pretend I wasn't curious, even if I didn't have it in me to be hopeful quite yet. I reached out, gently picking up the warm bottle and looking up into his eyes again.

"Seriously, Luke, what the fuck *is* this stuff?"

The Dreamwalker smiled, his eyes a little clearer for it. "This is what makes an Incubus tick."

What? I took a half-step back, extending the glass out at arm's length like it was poison. The crazy shit *had* to be kidding—my brow furrowed as I looked back down at the vial and its contents. "You took this from an Incubus?"

"*I* didn't take it, Max did."

I didn't bother to ask who Max was and, for the sake of my stomach, I also didn't ask exactly what *part* of an Incubus the liquid had come from—much less how it had been collected. I shook my head, already holding it back out to him.

"Look, Luke, thanks for trying to help, but…"

Next thing I knew, his finger was over my mouth, shushing me to a halt. "Shhhhh…just…take it with you." He shrugged, smiling openly. "Never know if you'll change your mind."

I definitely *did* know if I would change my mind, and the answer was I *wouldn't*. But it'd hurt the poor guy's feelings if I didn't at least take the stuff. I barely stopped myself from rolling my eyes as I dumped it into my jacket pocket, instead flashing Luke a smirk.

"I'll, uh…keep that in mind." I pointed my thumb back toward the door. "But I really am gonna be late for my date if I don't head out."

Luke's smile faded and he leaned back against the countertop with his arms crossed. "Are you *sure* you want to go? The first time you met this Derek guy you told me he was a total asshole."

I shrugged, my hand already wrapped around the doorknob. "He is kind of an asshole. What's your point?"

Now it was Luke's turn to look at *me* like I was insane and, considering the words that had come out of my mouth, I couldn't really blame him. But I also wasn't about to tell him the real reason, so that one would have to do.

"Why would you go out with him then?"

I looked up to the ceiling and gestured mindlessly with one hand, trying to think of an answer fast enough to seem natural. I was sure I had failed in that regard, but as long as Luke didn't question me outright it would be fine. "I don't know... Nothing else to do?"

The Dreamwalker's eyes lit up, and a shy smile curved those full lips of his. "You could stay here — we'll order a pizza, get wasted, play video games till we pass out, just like old times! It'll be awesome." He looked at me so excitedly, silently pleading with me to just give in.

God, did he even know what he was doing to me? What that crooked little grin of his made me feel like? But that was just the point — he didn't, and he couldn't, since I wasn't about to tell him. The fake smile I flashed him burned, but I held it firm and turned the knob, shaking my head.

"Sorry, Luke, but unless they've made a game that can take care of *this*—" I gestured toward my crotch, stepping back through the door and into the hall. "I'm gonna have to rain-check. I'll see you tomorrow, okay?"

Luke sighed and slumped back, reaching for his joint again. He tried to keep his smile up, but I could see the way it faltered as he gave me a wave. "Have fun." The door snapped shut, cutting him out of view.

I immediately slumped back against the wall, scrubbing at my face. After a few seconds in the silence I spun the vial in my fingers again, watching as it twirled and swirled. I closed my eyes. "I would, if it was you on this fucking date instead of him." My reply was a whisper that only the Night heard, and for a brief moment I almost thought I felt it flare hotter for it. But by the next second it had already passed, and I slipped the tube into my pocket without another thought and headed for the elevator.

* * * *

It was going to be *perfect*. I had the entire thing orchestrated to a T. Derek would be at my apartment to pick me up any minute—he was a Dreamwalker like Luke, so I didn't even have to stress at the thought of eventually explaining everything, like when you date a human. We'd head over to Angelique's for our reservation, and provided that all went as flawlessly as I knew it would, I'd probably—maybe—*please God it's been so long*, get laid. *Fingers crossed.*

I checked myself in the mirror one last time. Blond hair spiked, blue eyes popping thanks to my rail-thin tie of the same color. Black dress shirt, dark jeans and my black 6.0s—everything was accounted for. I ran a hand through my hair to get the angles just right, then bent down to fix the cuff of my jeans.

Bam!

"Ow, *fuck!*"

I grabbed my forehead and stumbled backward, slipping on the rug and landing hard on my ass. Dull pain was throbbing dimly under my hand. I got to my feet to take a look at the damage in the mirror.

Shit... A thin line of blood now glistened on the right side of my forehead, with a rapidly growing, livid bruise swelling underneath it. How in hell did a twenty-three-year-old adult with twenty-twenty eyes misjudge a distance like that? I switched hands, pressing on the wound so I could look at my watch and let out a frustrated hiss when I saw Derek would be at the door any second. *Thank you, lack of Foresight...* I couldn't even warn myself before I cracked my head open.

Fuck it.

I cranked the tap to full and filled up my hands, splashing the water onto my hair until my perfectly constructed spikes were soaked, lying limp on my head. I grabbed the towel off the rack and assaulted my hair, tousling until it was mostly dry just as three knocks resounded from the living room.

"Damn it. Damnitdamnitdamnit." I shook my hair down over my forehead, swooping bangs across the bruise so he'd never have to know it was there, and pressed down the cowlicks rising up at the back as best I could. I made it to the door just as another set of more tentative knocks seeped through and I swung it open.

"Sorry, I was having issu—"

With a muffled thump my back was suddenly pressed hard into the door, and a hand carded into my half-wet hair. Mint seethed over my taste buds as Derek's tongue collided with mine. I pulled back and gulped in a breath in the half-second pause before he placed his lips on mine again, giving my overheating brain the blast of air it needed to keep me conscious.

I set a hand on the side of his neck and the other against the wall to help keep me propped up, standing as I was on my tiptoes. I pulled away for air and he moved down to lave kisses along my throat, brushing black hair along my temple.

If we actually were going to have dinner we didn't have much time, but the way his molten hot mouth was stealing over me, I wasn't sure I cared. I rocked my hips forward into him, closing my eyes at the solid press he gave me in return. Our lips scraped together again as I slid my hand under his shirt, sliding over — *fuck...yes* — six pack abs, dipping my fingertips into each indentation on the path to his jeans. I felt the lead edge of the elastic of his boxers, but just as I went to rip the button and zipper of his pants clean off, my hand was gripping empty air.

I jerked open my eyes to see Derek staring down at me grinning. He was done up like me, but at least I'd wreaked a little havoc on that styled black hair of his, making him look a little less collected. I tried to ask why he had stopped, but my brain was still crackling a little, too hot to form the words. Instead I shot him what could probably best be called a glare, to which he just smirked.

"We're gonna be late."

My brow furrowed as I took a step closer, pointing toward the door I'd just been plastered against. "Then what the hell was *that*?"

His grin split wider and I wanted to feel those lips brushing against mine, not watch them smile like an idiot. "Consider it a sneak preview," he drawled, setting a hand on the small of my back and leading me out of the door.

I shifted the growing bulge in my jeans as we went and found a smile matching his spilling onto my face. Maybe I didn't need Sight to know what was going to happen, after all.

Cole's getting laaa-iii-d, Cole's getting laaa-iii-d!

* * * *

"Ow, *fuck!* God *damn it...*" I clutched my fist to my chest, trying to kill the pain lancing through my fingers like knives. I hissed out a breath and brushed my thumb gently over my screaming knuckles, but the stabbing ache hit fever pitch in an instant, forcing me to sit down on my bed. The spider-web cracks my fist had left in my wall stared at me tauntingly with sightless eyes, mocking me.

At least my roommate wasn't there. He was still on vacation with his family back home, so I wouldn't have to offer any explanations for a while. I focused on my hand and closed my eyes, feeling backward in myself for the cool white that was my power. I gripped it gently and pulled, the threads inside me twisting and bending as the magic worked its way up to the surface. Then I let it go on my injured hand.

I may have been a Seer, but at the core I was still a magical being, and that came with some leeway. Healing magic was pretty easy—I wasn't able to do a very precise job, but the pain at least faded some as the bones and cartilage reoriented back to their normal positions, marks of soothing and restoration dancing under the skin.

So why did Cole the Master Dater punch a wall in the first place? The answer was rather simple.

Not five miles from my place, the tire had blown out on Derek's car. He didn't have a spare because he'd thought it "took up storage space"—I'd barely held back the urge to knock some sense into him and had told him to call AA while we walked the last two blocks to the restaurant. We'd lost the reservation and had to wait another hour to be seated. Once we had a table, I was told by Derek that he'd "liked me better when I was using my mouth for shit *other* than talking." Cue a nearby waitress to trip and spill an entire tray of booze down my back, and a few *Oh my Gods* and *I'm so sorrys* later, a fire in the kitchen had set off the sprinklers in the restaurant and drenched all of us. I'd ridden the bus home, soaked and smelling like a bar rag.

In other words, Luke was right. Even more so than he knew.

Normal people accepted that there were things in their lives—a lot of things—that they had no control over. Like tires blowing out, for example, or a drink being spilled. But I was different—I was a Seer. That's not how it worked, not for me, anyway. I was intimately aware of an infinite number of possible alternatives for every action that occurred, and as it just so happened, I knew which one would come to pass, provided no one who *knew* what would happen altered the stream. In other words, I knew the future, and by knowing it I could change it to an extent, then See what new events I had set into motion.

Our power was dangerous, and highly sought after—I could make anyone a millionaire by just spouting a list of numbers, for God's sake. The Council kept us in line to a degree, but it largely just came down to our own judgment and morality, which is why it was a damn good thing there were so few of us.

But more to the point, when something bad happened to, say, Derek, he got upset because he felt it shouldn't have occurred. When something happened to me, I got upset because I felt that I should have *known* that it would happen. I *was* a Seer, after all. But by some genetic fluke, I was Latent. I couldn't see any events that involved myself, leaving me as clueless as any other race. The odds of being Latent were incalculably rare—a Latent Seer just never happened. Except, of course, in the case of one Cole Turner.

The date was horrible. But what was worse for me was knowing that I *should* have known that it would be horrible. Instead, I just had to cross my fingers and hope, like everyone else, and it turned out like *that*. It wasn't *right*, damn it, and I was fucking sick of it! I had control over everyone's life except the one I actually had a right to affect — *mine*.

I was standing before I knew it, clenching my freshly healed fist in anticipation. I stepped toward the wall, pulling back my arm to land another punch, when I heard a clink of glass from my feet. I paused and looked down.

The little vial of Night had rolled out of the pocket of the hoodie I'd thrown on the floor, and I'd kicked it into the wall. I picked it up and swirled it, but the contents were fine, the silver still floating innocently in suspension, still heating up my hand like a flame.

Luke's soft voice whispered along my skin tauntingly.

"This'll give you control."

Fuck.

It didn't make any sense, but I'd been too hot for my date to ask Luke many questions. I couldn't see how some stuff from an Incubus would possibly help my situation, but right about then I didn't give a shit.

If it could keep something like the date disaster from happening again, I was willing to try just about anything. Besides, Luke was my best friend. He wouldn't give me stuff that would *kill* me or something.

I popped the cork off the vial and took a sniff, but there was no smell. I could only hope that the same went for taste. Cool air filled my lungs as I took a breath, then two. Without another thought I opened my mouth and knocked the vial back before slamming it down on my nightstand.

At first there was nothing as the clear suspension washed to the back of my throat, but in the next instant the mercury hit my tongue. It immediately began to effervesce, crackling into gas like a demented form of Pop Rocks. Cinnamon so hot I thought my mouth was going to catch on fire seethed over my taste buds, followed by a wash of syrupy sugar to soothe the burn. In another moment, all the flavor and the Night were gone completely. I waited a few seconds, but I didn't feel any different.

Oh, what the hell.

I closed my eyes and focused on myself, tugging at the threads winding through my core until I could twist them all at once. The spells rang out gently, a silent symphony of power weaving through me—the cold pulse of it rocked my body, rippling just under the skin like pins and needles that made the hair on my arms stand up. As the chill crept toward my fingertips, I bombarded my mind with every memory and image of myself I could dredge up, flooding my consciousness with a narcissistic display of self.

My hands tightened into fists as energy poured into them. The ringing in my ears had escalated from mosquito buzz to siren screech, and with one last inhale I released the pent-up magic.

Instead of images of the future, infinite white flared to life in my mind, showing me nothing…as usual. The magic fizzled to a halt in my body, leaving my muscles tight and clenched as I fell back onto the bed.

Whatever Luke had meant for it to do, apparently it wasn't supposed to help my Sight. That, or it just didn't work. I made a mental note to ask him how much he'd paid for it. It couldn't have made the situation any worse at least.

I needed to get undressed, brush my teeth, the whole deal. But I was just so damn *tired* after everything, and the fire sprinklers had basically been a shower, anyway. Sure, I still smelled like Tanga-Jack-dka-roq, but at this point a few layers of clothes weren't going to change that. I rolled onto my stomach, half dragging the sheet over my body as I did. I grabbed my phone to set my alarm, and saw that I had an unread text from Luke.

'How was the date?'

My thumb lingered over the Call button in the corner of the screen, and for a second, I almost pressed it. It wasn't like Luke would have minded—he may have been straight, but he knew everything about me, always had. But the shit that had happened that night...it had really gotten to me in a way I hadn't gone through in a long time, enough so that I was even willing to drink that crazy Night stuff. Add to it that I was always a little worried to talk relationships with Luke, because even though he never thought twice about the fact that I was gay, I was always afraid of saying something that I might regret. Like how, sometimes, at night when I was alone and frustrated... When my latest "relationship" had drilled itself into the ground, and Luke was there with his little smirk and his easy touches and that gravelly little voice of his that was still so soft...

No. Just...no. Thinking like that was dangerous.

I locked the phone and tossed it to the floor before I did something stupid. With a click I snapped off my light and settled into my warm sheets, trying to relax away some of the tension I'd built up. The next day, when the events of the night stung a little less, I could tell Luke about the latest travesty that was my love life if he still wanted to hear it. Maybe that way when I laughed about it, it would almost be genuine.

* * * *

Fuck. *Fuck.*

If I could just stop rethinking that same scenario for *one Goddamn minute* maybe I could get some sleep. But I couldn't stop. Every time I shut my eyes, I saw myself standing there on the side of the road, or having drinks dropped on my head, or standing soaked in the restaurant while sprinklers rained down, and for the life of me I couldn't think of what I'd done wrong to deserve the hand I'd been dealt. The night played on a loop in my mind, and with each replay I thought of new ways I could have stopped each of the little things that had gone so wrong, could have headed off the future if I just could've known what was coming... But it never made me any happier. At the end of all of the made-up saves and salvations, I had to face the truth again—that I was stuck lying there on my bed alone, smelling like booze and disappointment.

It was pathetic. And I was *sick* of being pathetic.

I pushed myself to my feet, scooping my phone off the floor and squeezing it into the pocket of my too-tight jeans with a little persuading. Not getting undressed had its advantages. I practically emptied a bottle of cologne on myself to try to cover the alcohol, and when my nose burned too much to smell anything, I figured it was close enough. The building was pretty dead, seeing as it was one in the morning, so I slipped out unnoticed.

* * * *

I lived in a college town, with all of the perks and let-downs that had to offer. We were bisected by the highway, with the university and most of the commercial and retail crap on the east side, and my apartment and the majority of the residential on the west. A little farther from the highway back in the more wooded land, there were the trashed remains of some amusement park that had tanked, but other than that our side was almost strictly housing.

People with magic weren't exactly common—if we were, it would have been a lot harder to pretend we didn't exist. That being said, though, like any group, we did tend to gather in the same areas naturally and Kelvin was just one of those places. People like Luke and I, the Dreamwalkers and Seers of the magic world, could hide like it was nothing. Our powers weren't obvious. Now, a clan of Vampires fueled by blood and sex...that could be a little harder to blend in. But that's where the college town atmosphere came in handy.

A ridiculously popular nightclub, catering almost exclusively to an entire town of drunk, baked college students, naturally bled sex like you wouldn't believe—and if the patrons *themselves* were occasionally made to bleed here and there when magic and a little booze could combine to keep anyone from remembering it in the morning...well, what was the harm? Hence why William Carraway's clan of Vamps had decided Kelvin was as good a place as any to set up shop. Magical beings watched out for each other, and seeing as I was a crystal ball for hire, I'd used my fair share of Sight to give Will and the business an edge here and there. As an added bonus to the cash, I could get the VIP treatment at Seethe whenever the mood hit me — and if you were looking for a good fuck, there was no better place.

A five minute trip across the highway had me pulling up at the main entrance of the club. The door was discreet, but the six-foot-six bouncers outside of it were a little less so. They were human, but Will had let them in on as much as they needed to know — specifically that there were certain clientele, like yours truly, who were to be treated appropriately no matter their looks or lack of cash. I hadn't gone there often unless it was on business, but the bigger guy seemed to recognize me, just as I did him. As soon as I got close he cocked an eyebrow and I held out my hand as though for him to shake it. Catching on, he did so, and as soon as his calloused hand engulfed my own, I felt his hand pivot so that two of his fingers could slide under my sleeve to touch my wrist. Needling heat prickled painfully there, and the bouncer pulled his hand back, expressionless, before opening the door with a nod.

I stepped inside, taking a second to pull my sleeve back enough to check out my wrist. The Mark denoting me as a Seer was standing out in livid black like a tattoo, the three organic lines and circle it was made up of warping slightly in time with my heartbeat. An occupational hazard that had been tagging along since birth, something only we Seers had to deal with, but at times like that it came in handy. I pushed my sleeve back down, too busy in my own little world to notice as I walked straight into the living wall in front of me.

"Where do you think you're going?"

The authoritative voice was low and loud, and I jumped backward so fast I almost landed on my ass. I was about to stutter out some kind of apology, try to explain myself to what I assumed must've been another huge bouncer in the hall. Then I looked up and saw who it really was and promptly shoved him into the wall as hard as I could.

"You ass!"

Adam Harkin laughed as he bumped against the wall, a testament to his comfort with me rather than my own strength — seeing as he was a Vampire, there was no way I could have budged him an inch unless he had let me. He smiled down at me, idly rubbing the spot on his chest where I'd pushed him, as if he could even feel it, the dick.

"Shoving your boss isn't such a good idea, buddy." Adam smiled, showing the trailing edge of fangs he didn't bother to retract in front of me. They suited his tall, dark, handsome look well anyway, stuck as he was in a twenty-something body despite an age almost four times that.

I grinned back, shoving him again for good measure. "I use my Sight for William. That makes him the boss, not you, *buddy*." I started to walk past him, heading toward the main floor of the club, when I was spun around and pinned against the wall faster than my eyes could follow. Adam leaned in against me, holding me tight between the wall and his body.

"Well, possession's nine-tenths, right? 'S gotta count for something..." he purred as the arms he had on either side of my head bent, bringing his flawless face closer to mine. I rolled my eyes.

"That's in property, not employment." Fucking Vamps. God forbid they not flirt for *one second*. At least the view wasn't bad while it lasted...

Adam's fingers trailed down my neck, dipping under my shirt to lightly trace my collarbone in a move that made my skin tingle longingly. "Well," his liquid heat voice swirled around me, "is Foresight the only...*service* you offer?" His hand came back up, fiddling gently with my hair as his mercury eyes poured visceral warmth into my pinned body. "Because I think that might *blur* the line a little... Say I wanted a...*personal* consult...off Seethe payroll, of course. Tonight." He bit down on the corner of his lip, again flashing a fang for a brief second before he blinked heavily. I felt the magic in the hall spike slightly, pulsing out like radiation that made my cock stir and my breathing shallow. It wasn't calculated per se—Vamp aura was a natural occurrence when they started to heat things up—but Adam sure as hell wasn't trying to hold it back either. His smile spread. "What would you say to that?"

"I'd say..." I moved in close, letting my lids grow heavy for a second as my lips neared Adam's. "Club owners can't play with the Seer." I pushed Adam back with a single finger in his chest, smiling slightly at his look of shock at being shut down. "House rules."

To his credit, Adam bounced back almost instantly, crossing his arms and pouting as he took another half-step backward. "You don't play fair."

I shrugged, trying and failing to reign in my smirk. "Hazard of working with the one Latent Seer on the planet. If one of you gets too close, I might not be able to See the club's future." I patted Adam on the shoulder. "Blame Will. Or genetics...depends on how you look at it."

"I'd vote for the latter." A rich voice called out from farther down the hall, and Adam and I turned to face the speaker.

Will was a solid six-foot-two, and everything about him exuded the kind of confidence that only came from seeing everything twice and still moving on. The way he walked, the controlled way he talked — it was all perfectly aligned to show that the guy owned his world and he knew it. It always threw me when I had to try to make all of that add up with the not-quite-thirty, fucking *hot* body it was all wrapped up in, especially since I knew he actually was already well past the century-plus milestone.

"It's always a nice surprise, Cole. What's the occasion?"

Funny, how a guy who lived off sex and blood and owned a college-town nightclub still came off as almost a little too formal. My reply had a lot less class.

"I need a good fuck."

To his credit, Will didn't even flinch. He just smiled, throwing an arm over my shoulder as he led me toward the dance floor, Adam trailing behind us. "I'd say you came to the right place, then."

Not five minutes later, I was locked tight in the middle of a grinding, groping mass of sweat dripping, drink toting sorority whores and ripped jocks. My ears were ringing, I could feel bruises forming from all the places where elbows and shoulders had slammed into me, and fuck if I didn't *love* it!

The bass dropped as the music got somehow even louder, and I jumped fanatically into the air with the rest of the crowd, shoving my fist skyward mindlessly. I squeezed my eyes shut, blocking out the strobe and laser lights burning across my eyes and focusing in on the sounds and the heat instead. I couldn't have told you what the song was, or if there even *was* a song playing anymore — all I could make out was the screaming white noise, the collective pounding of the hearts around me and the blood rushing in my ears.

I jumped up again, and someone slammed into my back, knocking me off balance. My foot came down on a bottle that shot out from under me, rolling my ankle with a punch of pain, and I realized I had maybe two seconds before I face-planted into the cement.

Strong arms abruptly came out of the crowd and caught me around the chest, pulling me into a pocket of empty floor amid the storm. The words "thank you" were barely out of my mouth before the guy was gesturing with his head toward the bar, his hands conspicuously still holding onto me. I gave him about the fastest once-over I've ever done—looked good, brown hair and eyes, and he had caught me, so he couldn't have been too much of a dick—and nodded, gripping his hand as we pushed through the throng toward the comparatively quiet bar.

* * * *

Fifteen minutes later I had the guy naked. Not bad for me, I gotta say, especially considering he'd insisted on at least a *little* small talk and a drink each before we could dip out. He lived in one of the apartments just outside of campus, so it was by far closer than mine. A little make-out session in the elevator later and we were in his one-room, stripping down as we made the stumbling path to the bed at the back of the place.

I was a little buzzed thanks to the vodka I'd knocked back at Seethe. The unashamed groping and desperate, sloppy kisses would seem to show that the other guy—his name was Zac, I'd found out at the bar—was either a little more sloshed or a lot more in need of a fuck than I was. Whichever it was, I had no problem delivering.

We hadn't really talked about who liked to do what, so I decided to just play it by ear. If he actually was as wasted as he seemed, then I didn't wanna deal with whiskey dick after the mental prep I'd need to psych myself up for if he wanted to top. My hands slid around his hips as I walked him backward toward his bed so I'd have a good grip if he tripped. He'd caught me, and since it looked like he would fall over any minute, it only seemed fair I be ready to do the same.

The back of his knees hit the mattress and he tipped backward, held in check by my grip on him so we went down slowly instead of crashing into a pile. I sidled up on top of him as he scooted back toward the headboard excitedly, putting extra focus into the way my shoulders rolled and my body arched as I moved over him. Sure, he probably wouldn't even remember any of it in the morning, but I didn't half ass things, sex included. With Derek I had played the shy bottom who would've turned out to be a freak in the sheets if we'd ever gotten that far. With Zac I decided to go for the old primal-top standby. Not exactly aggressive, but definitely in control of the positions, the angles, the this-hand-goes-theres.

I dipped my head to catch his mouth, trying to focus on keeping my lips moving in a way that would reign in the guy's slobbering attempts at kisses. His eyes were closed as he groped around my waist until he found the button of my jeans, the only clothing still on between the two of us, tugging so hard I thought he was going to break the damn thing. When a tug of his almost yanked me down flat against him, I bit down on his lip, just enough to make him gasp and pull back a few inches. My left hand pressed down into the bed behind his head to keep me up while I slid his hand out of the way, undid the button and tore the zipper down, and grabbed his wrist to move his hand back onto my crotch. To his credit, he got back with the program immediately, squeezing tight through my boxers before scrabbling at the elastic of the waistband. My back arched involuntarily, helping Zac's hand slide in so he could drag his fingers over my length teasingly.

"F-fuck..." The word shuddered past my lips and Zac swallowed it greedily as his mouth moved against mine again. His hand started to slide up and down my cock with as much dexterity as he could manage, and it surprised me how hard I had to fight to not just lose it right there—I hadn't been lying when I'd said it had been *way* too fucking long. But damn it, I hadn't gone all the way back to the guy's place for a quickie hand job. I needed to take control of this while I still could.

I shifted backward onto my ankles, keeping my body low over Zac's as I did. I slid my hands over his sides on the way down, and pressed soft kisses against his chest then abs as I moved far enough down him that his hand finally couldn't reach my aching dick anymore. He found new places to hold almost immediately, death-gripping my shoulder with one hand and twisting his fingers into my hair with the other. His head lolled backward as I blew on the throbbing head of his cock, a tease that made him groan then gasp when I followed it up with a scrape of my teeth along the underside.

Zac suddenly thrust up into my face, probably by accident, but all I knew was I got a pelvis slammed into my nose with no room to dodge. I grabbed his hip automatically to hold it down flat against the bed and tried miserably to keep my eyes from watering. Damn it, but that shit *hurt!*

Accident or not, no blow job for Zac!

I slid backward a little farther on the bed, rolling his legs up so that his knees were on top of my shoulders. I started to take my jeans off, but the position I was already in didn't leave much room for that... *Fuck it.* I shuffled them down my thighs just enough to make it easy and reached into my back pocket, slipping the condom out from between my pants and my wallet. Zac's eyes bore into me through their own watery haze as I brought the package to my mouth and used my teeth to hold it in place while I tore it open, one hand never leaving his hip.

Not ten seconds later I'd slipped it on and was in him to the hilt.

Drunk or not, Zac knew what he wanted. His fingers were white-knuckled into the sheets as he angled his hips upward, making every thrust slam into his prostate. I took it in stride, picking up the pace and twisting just enough to make his body shudder and to spark the white heat in my veins. He tightened around me with a delicious squeeze of warmth. "Fuck..."

I didn't bother to start slow, to work myself up to a rocking pace—honestly, this wasn't that kind of night. I wasn't here to cuddle and make love, I needed to *fuck*, and *come*, and that was exactly what I intended to do.

I took one of my hands off Zac's hip and grabbed his dick, squeezing tight at the base and slowly working my way up, helped along by the pre-cum that had already poured down it. Zac bucked upward, ramping up the friction as I moved inside him. The guttural moan he let out when I touched him was liquid pleasure, and I closed my eyes, focusing in on the sound of it, the feel of his overheating skin under my palms and against my groin.

In and out, in and out... It wasn't exactly beautiful, sure as hell wasn't the start of a relationship, but shit, it was working. I felt Zac tightening underneath me, getting ready to come, and the way it made him squeeze around me tighter, made him rock his hips down into me each time I thrust upward... I could feel the hot rush flooding my head as needles and pins danced across my cock.

I pulled out as far as I could without blowing right then and there and used the tiny moment of lucidity it gave me to focus on working Zac even closer to the edge. I moved my slicked hand faster and faster until the blatant groan I was looking for slipped out of his clenched teeth. I turned my hand, scraping my thumbnail ever-so-slowly over the flushed head of his dick, straight up to the leaking slit.

When I heard Zac cry out, felt his body lock down like steel around me, I slammed myself forward in him, knowing that the way I collided with his spot must've made stars burst in his eyes, because fuck if it didn't do the same for me. The air caught in my chest as the pulsing blackout that was my climax roared through my body and out of my ravaged vocal cords.

"Ah, fuck!"

The electricity jumping from muscle to muscle robbed me of any strength, dropping me flat against Zac's chest with barely enough self-control to pull out first. I was too tired to even be a little grossed out at the way my face had landed with a splat in a pool of his cum. So long as it didn't get in my eye, I really didn't care at that point. Zac seemed to agree, letting out a breathless sigh as he brought his arms around me as best he could, a move that ended up being closer to just having a guy drop his arms on my back than cuddling.

I'm not sure how long I laid there just breathing it all in, but it couldn't have been all that long—definitely not long enough to warrant the *snoring* that I clearly made out drifting down from above my head.

Fuck. Figured the drunk would be passed out.

I reached up tentatively, grabbing his wrists and lifting them off me gently. I slid myself up and backward, settling back on my heels between his legs before setting his hands back down on his own body. I couldn't help but cringe at the way the drying cum had tried to glue my fucking face to Zac's chest, and I took a second to scrape it off as best I could without a mirror.

I slipped off his bed as quietly as I could, not that it mattered. Zac was out. I found my shirt on the floor and started to tug it back on, but I couldn't shake the feeling that something was...*wrong*, somehow.

I'd danced, I'd drank and I'd gotten laid. It was exactly what I'd wanted to do with my night, though admittedly it had come a little later than I'd originally planned. But my mission had been accomplished—so why didn't I feel *accomplished*? I sat back on the bed, running my hand over my arm. I felt tired—and not because I hadn't gotten enough sleep. I felt sad, in a way I couldn't really place. I felt alone, even though there was a man not two feet from me whom I'd been *inside* less than five minutes earlier.

I felt...*empty*. And the worst problem was, I knew why—even when, given the answer, it would probably be best if I didn't.

* * * *

I pulled my hand away from the door, already starting to turn to leave when it swung open, revealing the very welcome sight of a very tired Luke Cowen, running a hand through his mess of hair as he squinted at the bright lights of the hall to his apartment complex. His sleep-shrouded eyes cleared when he finally realized it was me.

"Too late to play video games?" I tried with as innocent a smile as I could manage.

Luke smiled, but it seemed more like a concession than anything else. He tilted his head toward the living room. "Come on."

I shuffled through the doorway then angled for the couch, settling down into the familiar warmth of the cushions as Luke closed the door and moved past me into the kitchen.

I squeezed my eyes shut and tried to slip into the black as easily as Zac had, pointedly ignoring the way his dry cum was smeared across my chest, the way my underwear bunched uncomfortably in my jeans from the way I'd dragged them back up my legs in my rush to get out of the place before he might wake up. I smelled like every drink under the sun, with a healthy dose of cologne to top it off. I was pretty sure I had jizz in my hair, and even if I didn't, it had to look like hell. Put simply, I was a train wreck of the first degree, but Luke had seen me look worse and with less reason, so I didn't sweat it much.

A nudge to my shoulder had me opening my eyes, which almost immediately crossed as I tried to focus in on the glass of brown liquid being held less than an inch in front of my face. I grabbed it and extended it out far enough to get a better look as Luke settled down next to me on the couch.

"Chocolate milk? Seriously?"

The Dreamwalker leaned back, propping his feet up on the coffee table as he shoved the sleeves of his shirt up over his elbows. "Figured you didn't need any more booze."

I scowled over at him. "I've only had one drink, you ass. A chick spilt a tray on me at the restaurant, that's why I smell so bad."

Luke's smirk spread wider. "I know. If you had actually drank enough to smell like that, you would've shown up at my door in nothing but tube socks, boxers and a necklace that says 'Barbie'."

My cheeks flushed so fast I must've turned the color of a fire engine, and I shoved him in the shoulder for good measure before taking a swig of the milk. "*One* time, peanut gallery. One fucking time." I ran my tongue across my teeth. "Nesquik?"

Luke's eyebrow cocked. "Hershey's syrup. You're losing your touch."

I twirled the glass and took another drink before setting it down on the end table. "Outta practice, I guess."

"So what did he do?"

Damn. He'd gotten to the point a little faster than I'd wanted, but I hadn't really expected anything less. It wasn't like this was the first time this sort of thing had happened. I ran a hand through my hair as I tried to figure out how to phrase it.

"Derek...didn't really do anything." I shrugged. "Didn't get the chance, honestly. The world in general was a little too busy fucking with me."

Luke's warm hand settled on my arm, his thumb making gentle circles that helped ease away some of the tension locking my body down tight. The touching was coming a little early—normally I had to be a lot closer to a breakdown before that happened—the guy *was* straight, after all. But I wasn't about to complain, even if I knew I got a lot more out of the casual touches than I should.

"What happened?" Luke's voice was soft, gravelly like always, and I closed my eyes and tried to think about the way the sound rumbled in the back of my mind, made something in my chest feel lighter. But as much as I tried, I couldn't keep the monsters inside my head from tearing me away from the present like they always did. For a Seer it was really amazing how much I lived in the past, but I never had been very normal, even amongst my own kind.

"You know how many Latent people there are in this world?" Luke didn't answer, so I took a swig of the chocolate milk and turned to face him. Apprehension was knotting up his features, but there was a little flicker of defeat in his eyes at the same time, and I bored into that shard of him until he finally answered.

"Not exactly, no."

I nodded, staring out at the black TV screen. "I didn't either." I glanced over at him. "The Council keeps track of them all—I went digging around once and figured out the exact number." The milk was starting to lose its chill, so I chugged the last bit, watching as what was left of the syrup drifted back down the walls of the glass to pool at the base. "Three hundred and forty-three. That's it. Seven billion people on this planet, and only a few *hundred* of them can't have their futures Seen." I squeezed the glass a little tighter, and Luke's hand on my arm firmed at the same time. "And right there, on the bottom of the list, is me—Cole Turner, with a little star next to my name. The footnote? *'Latent Seer. Second recorded instance in history'.*"

My teeth scraped against each other as my jaw ticked. I could feel Luke's hand moving on my arm again, but I ignored the way that gentle fucking voice of his said my name, said "Cole…" in that way that he always tried to pull me back to reality with. I set the glass back down and turned fully on the couch to look at him head on.

"There are whole discussions about me in the files. They didn't let me see them when I was younger, but I made them show me now. It's mostly Seers writing them, arguing back and forth about the pros and cons — emphasis on the pros. How perfect it must be to be *me*." I scowled. "Imagine, a Seer who's spared the Sight's curse! *Cole Turner* doesn't have to know the exact moment he's going to die. *Cole Turner's* life doesn't have to be a ticking countdown. How did *Cole-Fucking-Turner* manage to get so lucky —" The words caught in my throat, and I swallowed down the emotions that were trying to rise up. Luke shuffled closer, wrapping his arm around my shoulders and holding me close to his comforting warmth. "They don't — They don't get it, Luke, they don't *know*…"

The Dreamwalker ran his hand over my arm, helping to spark some heat in the skin that I was just starting to realize was bitingly cold. I shut my eyes and let out a breath. "If it was just me, just *my* future that I was blind to, I could deal with this. But the Sight has to account for all eventualities. If their future is too closely tied to mine —" My breath hitched, and I had to stop, squeezing the ache that was forming in my temples.

Luke's voice rang out in low registers. "Cole, I know your dad's birthday's coming up, but —"

I shook my head forcefully. *No.* No, that was the last thing I needed to be thinking about when I was already feeling like a wreck. "Luke, I... I don't wanna talk about them right now. Okay?"

"Okay." His smile was so easy, so natural, and it made me feel a little warmer for it. He pulled his hand off my far shoulder and set it on the one closer to him, squeezing gently. "What do you want to talk about?"

I laughed softly, shaking my head. "You should get some sleep, you've gotta be exhausted. You've already had to listen to me rant enough."

His face steeled, his expression becoming serious. "You know I'll listen whenever you need me to."

I smirked. "I know. I just don't know *why*."

Luke's brow furrowed, and he looked at me like I'd gone insane. "Because you're my friend, and I care about you." The *duh* attached to the end of that was silent, but obviously there. Not for the first time, I wondered how I'd ended up with someone in my life like him — and, more precisely, how I hadn't managed to make him run away screaming yet.

I settled for smiling again, rubbing at an ache in my neck. "Thank you."

The Dreamwalker's arms spread and he swept me up in a tight hug, giving me the chance to bury my face into the crook of his shoulder. I breathed in deep, letting the smell of cologne and pot and that rich tone underneath that was pure *Luke* seethe across my senses. I knew I shouldn't push my chances, should just be happy enough that he was so touchy-feely, but somehow each moment I had with the Dreamwalker just made me want more, tempted me to swing a little closer to the point of no return that could wreck this friendship. Luke was never going to like me like that, but knowing that didn't stop me from enjoying what moments I could.

But that particular moment seemed to be extending for a little...*longer* than I would have expected. Luke was still holding onto me, his hand still moving across my back slowly, tracing tiny patterns into the fabric of my shirt with his fingers. But a second later, as if he could hear my thoughts, Luke abruptly slid backward, pulling his arms to his sides and looking down at his hands like he'd never seen them before. My brow furrowed, but before I could push him for details, he looked up at me fervently. Something seemed to flicker around in the green there for a second, but by the time I'd noticed it, it was already gone as Luke ran a hand through his hair, looking at some nondescript point above my shoulder.

"Cole, did you...um—" He licked his lips. "Did you...drink the Night I gave you?"

I blinked for a second, confused, before it actually clicked what he was even talking about. I'd practically forgotten about the little silver bottle. "Yeah." I tried to add more, but Luke almost immediately cut me off, his eyes boring into me.

"How *much* of it did you drink?"

I cocked an eyebrow, even more lost than before. "All of it?" Luke let out a slow breath, flashing an "I was afraid of that" look if ever I'd seen one before scrubbing at his face. He was moving minutely away from me, tiny shuffles backward that I probably wouldn't have even noticed if he hadn't already been acting so weirdly. "What was the deal with that stuff anyway? If it was supposed to help my Sight, then you got ripped off. You should set that Max guy straight."

The Dreamwalker ran a hand through his hair, looking more preoccupied than I'd seen in years. I chalked it up to being distracted by thoughts about what to tell the Shifter. "Yeah, I'll... I'll have to talk to him." He glanced over to me, catching my eyes for less than a second before turning to look back down at his lap. "*Soon.*"

If I hadn't been so tired, I might have been more inclined to figure out why Luke was being so *weird* all of a sudden, but three a.m. was finally deciding to make itself known, and my day hadn't exactly been relaxing. I yawned and looked up at Luke with the biggest puppy dog eyes I could manage. "Is it okay if I spend the night here? I really don't wanna have to drive this late."

The Dreamwalker's eyes went wide like that was some kind of a surprise, and I almost thought he was going to say no, which definitely would have been a first. But after a half second more, the panic seemed to pass, and he smiled, however shakily. "Sure, yeah. No problem." He took a deep breath before standing and pointing awkwardly toward the bathroom. "Lemme...uh...get you some blankets and shit."

Luke disappeared around the corner of the apartment like someone was following him with a gun. I didn't know what to make of that, but I also couldn't deny the fact that my eyes felt like fucking lead. Tomorrow morning, when I'd had a shower and was actually awake, I'd push him for more answers. Maybe get a better idea of how some shit from an Incubus was supposed to help a Latent Seer in the first place.

My eyes drifted closed for a second, and I forgot I was supposed to be waiting for the Dreamwalker to come back with my stuff, letting the swirling images of laser lights, flashes of skin and Luke's smiles rock me gently down into oblivion.

Chapter Two

My back slammed into the door of my apartment with a bang, but I was too busy remembering how to breathe to mind the noise. Luke pulled his mouth off mine for a half second so he could pull my shirt off, and I took advantage of the tiny pause to gulp down the cold air that we were rapidly heating up in the hallway. My hands slipped under Luke's shirt, and the fever-hot skin there shivered under my touch as his abs squeezed tight, showing off a far more developed six-pack than I'd expected. Some part of my mind fleetingly wondered when that had happened, but before I could worry about it for long his mouth crashed into mine again.

Luke dropped my shirt onto the ground and pressed me back again, and the cold wood of the door reminded me that we were still out in the hall. I took a hand off him—which earned me a frustrated groan against my lips—and groped behind me for the door handle, the tips of my fingers stealing across it just as his thigh pressed its way tightly in between my own. The motion ramped up the pressure on my dick, straining as it was against the denim confines that I was a little too busy and a lot too in public to release just yet, and in the moment of white-hot blackout it caused, my hand jammed down on the door handle blindly.

The catch released and I plummeted backward, death-gripping Luke's shirt for support in a move that just ended up dragging him down on top of me as I slammed unabashed onto the floor of my apartment. I was on the third floor, so I was sure my second-floor neighbor would have some choice words for me in the morning, but sandwiched between my cheap carpeting and the hot body pressing down on me, I couldn't find it in myself to give a shit. Even through the fall our lips hadn't stopped moving against one another's, and I wasn't in a mood to stop now. I kicked out blindly and managed to catch the door with my foot, knocking it closed. My shirt was still in the hall, but that could wait—right now, it was only fair that I not be the only one who was half-naked.

I tugged up on Luke's long-sleeved shirt, trying to get him to lift his arms so I could get the damn thing off, but he was too busy laving kisses across my jaw to be bothered. He'd always kept that body of his covered too often. I gave up for a second, using my now-free hands to pull Luke's lips up to my own so that I could kiss him properly. His lips parted automatically, and I pushed into his heated mouth with my tongue for a brief collision somewhere between our teeth. He pressed back in reply, trying to plaster me to the floor again, but I took over, fisting his shirt just below the collar and pushing him backward as I let go of his mouth until he was in a sitting position straddling my hips. The distance seemed to clear some of the heat swirling in those green eyes of his, and I took advantage while it lasted to lean up just enough to pull the shirt up over his head, this time without resistance.

But something…something wasn't quite right.

Don't get me wrong, Luke looked amazing — more than amazing, really. Perfect. Sculpted pecs, ripped abs, built arms that were solid, but not steroid-swollen past the norm. But something about the picture wasn't synching up with the face above them that I was so used to… I had seen Luke shirtless before, and he looked good, but nothing like this. I must've made some kind of face, and I know for sure that my hands paused after they threw his shirt to the side, because Luke looked down at me in confusion… Or maybe…

"Something wrong?"

The muscles I was staring at, transfixed, seemed to grow slightly more developed the longer I looked at them, the biceps a little bigger, the line between his abs a little deeper.

"I…"

Luke flexed, causing his pecs to bounce tauntingly as the crooked smirk he was forever flashing me spread across his face. Somewhere under Luke's hips my cock throbbed painfully, squeezing the dripping head agonizingly tight against the hard metal zipper, and my mouth went dry.

"N-no. *Fuck* no…" I grabbed Luke by his shaggy hair, dragging that smirk down so that I could give it back a little bit of the sweet misery he was giving me.

Luke settled back down on top of me, his knee coming down between my legs so close to my groin that I jumped, which just made him smile as he parted my lips with his possessive tongue. My dick throbbed again, and this time he gripped the waistband of my jeans, pressing the heel of his palm down onto my crotch. I bit down on his lip to keep myself from moaning, squeezing it so tightly between my teeth I thought I might draw blood. A sweep of his warm tongue across my lips brought me back down to earth and I released him, bringing his forehead down to touch mine so that I could take a breath in the pause.

Skilled fingers flicked open the button to my pants as Luke brushed his lips chastely across mine. It felt so right as he tugged down the zipper and shuffled my pants farther down my thighs—felt like we had done this a hundred times before. But this wasn't our hundredth time…it wasn't even our tenth, or third or second. Somehow, for all the signs otherwise, I knew it was the first time, and I couldn't manage to shake the feeling that it was going to be the last.

Every time I started to think about it for too long—started to focus on *any* one thing for too long, actually—I would lose myself in some move Luke made against my body and, even though I could recognize that, I was powerless to stop it. This time was no different.

Thoughtless oblivion surged over my mind as Luke gently dipped his hand under the elastic of my boxers, rolling his hips slowly against mine as he did. His palm flattened and dove lower. I hissed out a breath as his warm hand found my cock, wrapping around it at the base and squeezing possessively. The angle was a little awkward, so Luke slid his hips farther up my body and laid back down on top of me, capturing my mouth along the way. With his arm no longer bent so uncomfortably he started to slowly stroke up and down, rocking his hips against mine to the rhythm. Electric heat lanced up me every time the tips of his fingers scraped along the head, and I tried to move underneath him, get him to speed up, but Luke was laying over too much of my body to move like I needed.

His hand stole over my hip, squeezing for a second as he pulled me into the position he was looking for. I let him move me easily, trying to relax—it was always an effort for me when I was taking rather than giving. Inhale, exhale... I would go for either without much argument, but there was always that can't-breathe-oh-shit-here-it-comes moment of panic before the guy entered me that I just couldn't shake. But with Luke, the role just made sense, felt right. The guy was my best friend, my rock, the one who always kept my head above the water when shit got rough. The feeling of his arms holding me, his body around and above and in me while his mouth whispered sweet everythings and his lips nuzzled against my neck, my hair... It was the ultimate peak of the physical-mental comfort he always gave me so selflessly.

I heard the sound of Luke's jeans unclasping and his zipper being tugged down. Something bright and loud was blaring in the back of my mind, trying to make me stop and focus, but the details of the scene unfolding there in the middle of my apartment floor were burning out everything else, leaving just the motions and feelings in their wake. I leaned my body upward, propped up by my forearms as I stared up at him across my clenched abs. Luke's muscles tightened again, swelling so minutely I shouldn't have been able to pick up on it. He flicked his head to the left to knock the messy brown hair back up out of his eyes, making the shades of chestnut and chocolate glint beautifully in the light. The world seemed to be moving in slow motion, and I struggled through the molasses-speed drag to remember what I'd been to trying to think of before Luke had started to take off his pants…

Luke grabbed my hips gently, and somehow I knew that even though there had been no preparation, no condom or lube, it was all going to be okay — it always had been before with him…even if this was the first time. *Fuck.* The thoughts weren't adding up. Hell, a *lot* of this wasn't adding up, but then Luke was pushing into me, and in the stabbing heat that burst to life between my legs, my brain was too busy cracking in half to bother figuring out what I was talking about.

It was pleasure — shards of white-hot candy and kisses and velvet arcing up through my body as Luke rocked his hips forward closer to mine, driving his cock farther into me. The gentle heat was tipped with just enough pain to make it sting, but in the best way, and my head lolled backward onto the floor as the Dreamwalker fell into stride, picking up the pace as he found his rhythm. My fingers dug into his bared arms. Luke's mouth fell onto mine, and the effort of matching the dance of his tongue kept me grounded, kept my body in the apartment as my mind whipped violently against its tether, begging to snap free and make sense of a situation that couldn't be explained.

He thrust again and the image behind my eyes shattered like spun glass as the head of his erection slammed into that spot inside me. Pure voltage surged my veins molten hot in an instant. I cried out, something between Luke's name and a guttural moan, but it didn't matter — the Dreamwalker immediately swallowed the sound as his lips moved against mine, pouring a groaned reply in with the rush of breath with which he was fueling me. Luke kept thrusting, and I focused on getting my tongue as far down his throat as I could, on running my hands over just the right places with just the right pressure. My dick was painfully hard, rubbing against my stomach every time Luke rocked into me, but I left it alone—coming before Luke just seemed selfish.

He was speeding up, tightening up, and I knew it was going to be coming soon—no pun intended. I rocked my pelvis upward, changing up the angle so that the friction would ramp higher. Luke moaned his approval, pulling away from my mouth and holding onto my hips with both hands as he started to peak. I hadn't so much as touched my dick and it still felt so throbbingly tight that I swore I was going to come whether I wanted to or not. Luke's hair had fallen down over his eyes again, casting shadows over the flickering green as they met mine, and he smiled down at me again. I wanted to say something, *anything*, but the words just wouldn't come out. Instead I could only look up at my Dreamwalker as he tilted his head back, letting loose a shuddered groan as he rocked into me once more...twice.

The muscled chest in front of me squeezed tight and his hands dug in hard as Luke came. *"Fuck, Cole!"* tore out of his throat violently, resounding against the apartment walls. In the heat of the aftershock, I screamed his name in reply, realizing at that second that the jizz spraying onto my chest was my own. My arms shook underneath me and gave out, dropping my body to the carpet again, and Luke's body collapsed down onto mine in a wash of familiar heat a second later.

The Dreamwalker's shaky breaths shuddered across my chest, and in the black I was falling into I managed to keep it together long enough to reach up and rest my hand on his scraggly hair, carding my fingers through it gently. I felt Luke swallow and start to lean his head up, moving his mouth like he was going to say something, so I dragged my eyes open to look at him.

* * * *

Blinding light washed over my vision, pouring into my bedroom from my window. I jerked wildly, suddenly aware of the lack of weight on me, and after staring up at the ceiling frozen in place for a few seconds, ran my hands over my temples as I realized what had happened.

Fuck.

It wasn't my first dream of Luke. Not at all. It wasn't even one of the more intense ones... This one had stopped after the first round of sex, among other things. But damn if they weren't starting to get to me, and they were happening more often, too.

It wasn't enough that I had to have sex dreams about my straight best friend. I was me, and God knows how lucky *I* was, so of course, he would also have to be a Dreamwalker. Which meant these dreams weren't just messed up, they were dangerous. Thinking about a Dreamwalker too much while asleep could summon them to the dream—wouldn't *that* be a fun one to explain?—and by his nature, if Luke was ever to enter them there was a good chance he'd pick up on the latent memories floating around in the mental soup anyway.

I let out a sigh as I swung my legs out of the bed.

Wait.

I wasn't *in* a bed—and, for that matter, I wasn't in my apartment either. I was on a couch. Luke's couch. In Luke's apartment. With Luke a few dozen feet away while I'd just had a fucking *sex dream* about him!

I scrambled to my feet wildly, almost knocking a lamp over in my fumble. My eyes jumped from the couch to the door of Luke's bedroom again and again as I tried to remember how to breathe. Sure, the smaller-than-normal physical distance didn't make it any more likely he would have known about the dream, but that did make it a shit-load more awkward, and I shook my hands mindlessly like I could somehow throw off the conspicuous memories.

Need to leave. Like, now.

My day was supposed to be spent hanging out with Luke—but if I had to look him in the eye in that moment, I was sure he'd somehow see the thoughts and wants that I'd kept buried for so long staring back at him plain as day, and if that happened—If I lost him, too…

I grabbed a Post-it from the counter and scribbled out something about Will needing me to do a Sighting for him and set it on the couch where I'd been sleeping. After I'd had a little while to pretend the dream had never happened, I'd drive back over and jump back into the delicate dance that just hanging out with my best friend was becoming.

* * * *

The milk splashed onto my Rice Krispies, and to my aching head it sounded a lot less like *Snap, Crackle, Pop* and a lot more like *Snap, Crackle, Fuck You.* Considering the cereal and milk I had just eaten were about the only things left in my apartment, I decided I probably needed to swing by the grocery store. Usually Jake took care of that, so I needed to pick up the slack before he got back from his trip and lectured me.

I scarfed down the Krispies and headed for the door, scruffing up my hair a little on the way out. I'd used up some more magic that morning to more or less fix the monster bruise on my head, so I didn't have to worry about where my hair landed on my forehead. I scooped a hoodie up from the floor by the door and tugged it on, making a mental note to clean up before my resident germophobe got back too.

* * * *

"Sell them tomorrow at one forty-five. Put it all into the other stock—" I checked left and right before proceeding through the four-way stop. "Trust me, after tomorrow, you don't need a diverse portfolio for another week—none of the other favorites will be climbing at a close enough rate to bother. I'll keep you posted once it gets closer. Okay… You too. See ya, Will."

I swung my car into the parking spot in front of the grocery store. I checked my phone one last time to see if Luke had responded with a confirmation of our plans for later, and when I saw that he had, I slipped it back into my pocket on the way through the door.

The first department was Produce, and seeing as I was morally opposed to the thought of eating anything leafy, green, or unprocessed, I'd normally charge triumphantly to the frozen food haven six or seven aisles over. All of Jake's fruits and veggies had gone bad in the time he'd been gone, though, and being the thoughtful roomie that I was, I decided to grab some of the basics for him—not that I had any idea how to tell when any of the shit was ripe… Some things were supposed to be firm, others soft. Some were supposed to thump, or sound hollow, or feel heavy. I couldn't keep track of it all, but I figured that was what they paid the produce kids to know.

I spotted one stocking bananas, and he seemed nice enough. I angled toward him and scooped up a bunch off the cart as I huffed out a breath of agitation. The sound caught his attention, and he turned to me with an eyebrow cocked. He opened his mouth to say something but paused, relaxing into a genuine smile and leaning against the display. I guess he had expected his manager or something.

"Anything I can help you with?"

I smiled back, laughing a little as I held up the bananas. "I'm kinda clueless when it comes to..." I paused, then signaled the entire department with my hands. "Any of this." The produce guy laughed, setting down the bunch he was holding and crossing his arms. "I gotta get some stuff for my roommate before he gets back and I don't know how to tell when the shit's good." I cringed when I realized I'd cursed, but Produce Guy just laughed again, so he couldn't have minded too much.

"When's your roommate going to be back?"

I shrugged. "Two days?"

He smiled and reached his hand out. Not knowing what else he could mean, I handed him the bananas. "These probably aren't what you want then. He eats them yellow, right?"

When I tried to remember a time when I'd been interested enough to notice what kind of bananas Jake had been eating, I understandably hit a blank. The thought of making eye contact with *anyone* eating a banana just made the Immature Cole inside giggle, so I doubt if I would've ever been able to answer that question anyway.

"No clue." I shrugged. "We're not exactly close, I never noticed."

Produce Guy's eyebrow cocked at that, but he trudged on. "Well, most people prefer them that way. If you buy these ones, they'll probably be brown by the time he gets back. A bunch with a little green on them would be better for you, like..." He rooted around for a second, then handed one to me with a grin. "This one!"

I laughed and took them, then asked him about a few more items. With each of them he explained exactly what I'd need, and always with a smile or a chuckle. It was...*nice*. Especially after the fiasco from the night before. Just having someone be civil, much less this helpful, was a relief.

Produce Guy held out a watermelon, the last thing I needed. "Knock on it." I raised my eyebrow, and he laughed at my hesitation. "You won't hurt its feelings, promise. They're used to it." He added with a conspiratorial wink.

I did as he asked and looked up. "Sounds hollow."

He smiled. "That's what you're looking for." I took it from his hands and dumped it into the kid seat of the cart with some of the other produce. "Just think, now you can impress your roommate with all the random crap you know," he laughed.

I smiled back, but I shook my head. "Eh, don't know about the impressing part. Jake's not really *impressed* by anything I do."

"Seems like there's a lot to be impressed with to me."

My brow furrowed and I looked over at Produce Guy, but he didn't seem fazed in the least with the weirdly personal thing to have come out of his mouth. I thought about calling him on it, but hey, it was a compliment, and he seemed like a nice guy. I really didn't have anything to complain about, so I let my natural response take over — that being, blushing like a fucking kid. I looked down at my shoes like a geek and grinned stupidly.

"Well...thanks. It's nice to know someone thinks so."

Produce Guy's lips curled upward, and he opened his mouth to say something but was cut off by a call over the loudspeaker.

"Owen in Produce to the back room, Owen to the back room, please."

Produce Guy scowled up at the ceiling, and for the first time I noticed the name tag hanging off his shirt said *Owen* on it. He looked at me with a frown. "That's me. I gotta go before someone gets pissed..."

I gestured noncommittally toward the rest of the store. "Yeah, I gotta finish grabbing everything too." I let out a breath and prayed I hadn't taken our conversation the wrong way. "Maybe I'll see you again soon?"

Owen smiled. "I'd like that." He gave me a wave as he headed toward the door to the back room, and I gave him one back, pushing my cart in the direction of the main food aisles.

Fuck yeah!

Yes, I wanted to be with Luke — but I was enough of a realist to know that that wasn't going to happen, and I needed to try for things I actually had a chance of getting. I gave myself a pat on the back, grinning like an idiot as I meandered down the first aisle I went past. Apparently the night before *hadn't* been the kiss of death to my dating potential. Sure, it was nothing in stone, but I still felt damn good about myself.

Speaking of which, there must have been something to that saying about when you're happy, people pick up on it, because I swear the rest of the store had nothing but smiles for me. I was a big enough person to admit that I was pretty average in all respects — Foresight aside. I wasn't the kind of guy that people felt the need to stare at. The stars must've just aligned for me that day — perfect outfit, hair, demeanor, something.

Case in point, I swung by the coffee shop they had in the store to grab a little caffeine buzz, and since there wasn't a line, I headed straight up to the counter. The barista's eyes widened — literally *widened in surprise* — when I walked up, and she smiled suggestively at me, leaning across the counter. A hand trailed up into her blonde hair, and she tousled it as she purred, "What can I get started for you?"

I laughed a little in confusion. I'd never had someone be quite so...*blatant* before. It seemed like that was reserved for the nines and tens, not we sixes-maybe-sevens-on-a-good-day.

"Um... Double shot espresso?"

The coffee girl bit down lightly on her acrylic nail, bouncing her eyebrow as she did. "You got it." She spun around to start it.

"Don't you need me to pay for it first?"

She glanced back over her shoulder, as she worked. "On the house. I'll promo it out."

Normally I wouldn't be one to turn down free anything, but it seemed like she was getting the wrong idea, and I didn't want to lead her on. Nothing personal, but the girl had a few fundamental problems I wouldn't have been able to get past...like the two big ones that had been staring me down from the deep V of her uniform shirt.

"Thanks, but you...you don't have to do that, I mean—"

"Shhhhhh..." She slid the drink across the counter to me, winking as she did. "It's my pleasure."

There didn't seem to be much point in arguing, so I just grinned and thanked her instead. I turned to head back to my cart, and two different people sitting at the little tables there stood excitedly, talking over each other with phrases to the effect of "This seat's open!" I half-laughed again in confusion and declined both with a thank you, pointing toward my cart. The girl slumped dejectedly, but the guy at the table closer to me was a little more persistent, asking if I was sure I couldn't sit for just a few minutes. I refused again, and I swear I saw him... But... He wouldn't have, you know, *adjusted* himself right there, in front of everyone?

Fuck, I must've looked *good* that day. *Shit...* An hour out of bed and I was already doing better for myself than I had been for the past *month*.

I grabbed my last few things and checked out, going through the self-check while the attendant there kept smirking and making eyes at me. I grabbed the receipt and used the motion as an excuse to smell myself— was it a new cologne or something? I mean, really... I was trying to stay skeptical, but the more people smiled at me, the less and less this felt like some kind of prank. I reached out with my magic, but the only other person with power in the place was a Were-shifter toward the back of the store, and they didn't have the kind of command over magic it would take to make all these people act this way.

I headed out to the parking lot. Maybe I really *was* hot... It was a little weird that it had taken twenty-three years for people to realize it, but hey, there was a lot of shit in my life that was even weirder. If it got me free coffee and conversations with cute boys in the Produce department, I wasn't about to complain about a little attention. It was actually a nice change, truth be told.

A bagger glanced over from the back of a huge line of carts he was pushing. His face was red despite how cold it was that close to Halloween, probably from the strain of pushing the things from one side of the lot to the next all day. Just to test it, I flashed him the best million watt smile I could dredge up, one so bright it bordered on looking utterly fake.

The kid's jaw dropped—actually *dropped*, right then and there—but before I could take the shot of ego-booster I rightfully deserved after that, a loud *crash* resounded across the parking lot.

Distracted by me, the bagger had been too occupied to notice as he had pushed the line of carts right out into the path of an SUV on its way out. I hurried to open the door to my car and toss the bags into the passenger seat with a muttered "Shit!," but the oddest part was the way the kid just kept staring at me—even as a *Real Housewives* wannabe stepped out of the driver's side to publicly castrate him for his fuck-up. I was in my seat and heading out to the main street by the time she reached him, and sent out a "Sorry!" to the guardian-whatevers that might have saved the poor kid at that point. I decided I didn't wanna look at his future, just in case. But in a stroke of good news, I had at least proven my point.

Apparently, I was officially a hottie—at least for the day. At a grocery store. And you know what? That was more than enough for me.

* * * *

I hurried up to the apartment, passing Two-A maneuvering a couch toward his doorway as I went. At first glance the thing definitely didn't look like it'd fit, but more power to him. Maybe I'd help him if he was still working on it when I left again to meet Luke—but right then I had cold shit that needed a fridge, pronto.

I climbed one last set of stairs up to the third floor, and balanced an armload of bags against my side so I could shove my key into the lock of Three-C, the spot I called home. As soon as I got in the door I dumped half the bags on the floor, hoping idly that they didn't have anything breakable in them. I unloaded the stuff into the fridge and cabinets and came to a stop in my bedroom, staring at myself in the mirror.

Still looked the same as ever. I couldn't see any difference, other than the half smile that I think was officially plastered on my face thanks to all the attention I was having doted on me. But honestly, I knew for sure there was no change between that day and the night before, and I hadn't even been able to keep Derek's attention then, much less that of strangers. Whatever it was, it was subtler, but for the life of me I couldn't think what.

I checked my watch and decided to head for Luke's a little early—it wasn't like he'd mind. I headed for the door, reminding myself again to get some cleaning in eventually, and closed and locked it behind me.

* * * *

I took the stairs two at a time on my way down, rushing from my place on the third floor down to the second. Moderately-Cute-Two-A was still outside his apartment, trying to push the new couch in through the door. The sofa was tilted at a ridiculous angle and was only halfway through the doorway, while Two-A shoved on the thing with all he had. He was kind of scrawny, so it wasn't working very well. After a moment of hesitation, I walked up behind him, hoping I didn't freak him out in the process.

"Did you, uh…want some help?"

Damn. Kid still jumped halfway to the ceiling—he had always seemed a little skittish. Two-A spun to face me, but when our eyes met, the anxious look I'd been expecting didn't last long. As soon as he realized who I was, he actually mellowed completely—more relaxed and comfortable than I had ever seen him before, come to think of it.

"What kinda 'help' did you have in mind?" He smirked at me, leaning his arm against the couch.

Wait… *What?*

Was that…? No, no way. Maybe I'm just misunderstanding… Maybe the guy took some public speaking classes or something. It wasn't really my place to judge, so I tried to roll with it, even though the look in Two-A's eyes was mildly familiar, but not at all what I would've expected from *him*.

I laughed lightly, trying to keep it natural. "I, uh, kinda meant the couch." He just kept staring at me, and *Christ, did he really just bite his* lip? Don't get me wrong, the guy seemed nice enough, and he kinda cute in that comic-book-reading sort of way, but…

Well, honestly, I really hadn't been able to think of a good enough 'but' to that. Apparently my newly developed charms had bigger stomping grounds than strictly the local grocery store.

His smile spread, and with the hand he'd been leaning on he reached up to smooth out his rumpled shirt, lingering just a moment longer than normal over where I imagined his nipple would be. "Sounds like a good place to start..." He turned to face the couch and gave an exaggerated push, sticking his ass out blatantly toward me before he flashed me an innocent look over his shoulder. "I can't get it to *budge*."

Fuck it.

I slid up behind him, reaching my arms around his until I was touching the couch with my chest pressed firmly against his back. "Let's see what I can do..." I whispered into his ear with a smile. There was something really wrong about everything that was happening, but right about then I didn't care.

I shoved against the lead edge of the couch, letting my biceps swell slightly at the strain as they framed Two-A's face. I wasn't 'roided out or anything, but apparently it was enough, since he bent his arms so I would be pressing him more solidly against the couch. All flirting aside, the damn thing *was* heavy, so I pushed a little harder. I almost pulled back immediately at the half-moan Two-A let out at the motion.

His eyes were closed and his breathing was sounding unnecessarily heavy as he riled backward against me. I was trying to take being sex-on-legs in stride, but damn it, I was still *me*, so I pulled back until we weren't touching any more than was needed. To cover myself I slammed my shoulder into the couch, knocking it completely through the doorway and onto the apartment floor with a bang.

Two-A had almost fallen over when the couch he'd been leaning against had suddenly shot out from under him, but then he turned back to face me with a smile on his face. "*Damn,* you're strong..."

I smiled back at him innocently, rubbing my biceps with my other hand like it was a shy habit, not the planned move that it really was. I wasn't hot or ripped enough to get away with being cocky, so I tended to shoot for modest. Get more dicks with honey than vinegar, and all that.

Two-A walked toward me slowly, a self-assured, sensual way of moving that wasn't adding up with the cheap polo and badly fitting slacks he was wearing—or with anything I had ever known about him till then, either. His hand came to rest on my arm, and he squeezed it so tightly and possessively that I almost jumped backward before I caught myself again.

"What else can this body of yours do?"

I opened my mouth to reply—not that I had any clue what was going to come out—when I was cut off.

"Nick, did you get the couch— Well, *hello* there..."

I really did jump backward, then. I probably took half the apartment in one stride, plastered as I was against the door.

A woman had walked out of what I assumed was the bedroom, wearing just a man's button-down and—please, God—panties, not that I could see them. Brunette, mussed hair trailed down to the bottom of her ribs, and her pouty lips shimmering a dull pink below bright blue eyes. Call me crazy, but normally I would have thought being seen in her current state by a complete stranger would have left a girl somewhat embarrassed.

Not in this case.

After a half-second pause, she melted into the same confidence that Two-A was showing, walking toward us with the same effortless sexuality. "Where'd you find this hottie, Nick?"

"W-who are you?"

It took me a second to realize the words had come out of my mouth, but I had to admit, even as I edged toward the doorway, I did seriously want to know the answer.

The girl smiled, her delicate fingers chancing over the single button on her shirt keeping it closed. "Lexi — I'm Nick's girlfriend."

"Girl...*what?*"

Oh... Oooohh... Shit. Fuck. Shitfuck.

I need to get out of here, like now.

My mouth started to go on auto-pilot as I stumbled sideways, trying to find the doorway. "Look, I, um... I appreciate the — I mean it's flattering that you'd want to, but I'm not, you know, and — it's just —" I was a few '*such as*'s away from being a panicking pageant queen, but the way the two of them were slowly coming toward me like crazy cult members was leaving my articulation something to be desired.

My groping hand touched empty air and I spun and bolted, ignoring the "Wait, where're you going?" from behind me. I was landing with a slam in the lobby before I even had time to try to process what had just happened, having shot down the flight of stairs at light speed.

Okay, so I was just propositioned by a couple... That was definitely a first. I didn't know whether to shudder or laugh. It was certainly a twisted new addition to an otherwise damn good day... I couldn't help but think I'd probably have to use the fire escape to get in and out from then on just due to sheer awkwardness.

I headed for the door, trying to think normal thoughts. Maybe if I pretended it hadn't happened, it... I sighed and scrubbed at my face. *Aw, fuck it.* At least I had *another* story to tell Luke that night.

* * * *

When I had climbed into my car to head to Luke's, the check engine light had glared hatefully back at me in angry red letters. Apparently the rattling I had tried to drown out with music had finally come to a head, so I walked to the bus stop at the corner instead — there'd be time to deal with the car later. I didn't want anything to spoil my good day, not yet.

On the way, the same smiles from random people greeted me, and I tried to get the sick enjoyment out of it that I knew I should while it lasted. The bus was pulling up to the spot just as I got close, so I jogged to get there without being left behind, chancing a glance at the far side of the street while I did. What I saw almost made me fall flat on my face.

A guy had set up a hotdog stand, which by itself was nothing worth noting — the problem was what he was *doing* with his stock.

Eyes deadlocked with his, I watched in shock as the owner opened as wide as he could and shoved an entire hotdog into his mouth in the most disturbingly sexual way possible, pause to deep throat included. It was a miracle of God that I only tripped instead of eating concrete as I desperately tried to tear my eyes away from the spectacle.

For the second time that day, I didn't know if I should shudder or laugh — at least this time I was inclined to go with the latter. It was probably some college kid getting his rocks off on freaking people out, but...*shit.* I shook my head and walked the last few steps to the bus stop.

It was midday on a Tuesday, so it wasn't very packed. I already had my creeper-defense in place, courtesy of my phone's music collection and a set of cheap headphones, so I stepped onboard and headed for the bench directly across from the door—I didn't really like having to push past people when I was trying to get off. The only other rider was a guy sitting on the bench across from mine, and as I took my seat he shot me a pretty heated smile. No red flags were going up, so I smiled back to be polite before looking down at my phone.

I pressed the Shuffle All button and let a wash of Top 40 assault my ears, an endless tirade of Gaga, Katy, Rihanna and every other pop princess and heartthrob to hit the charts in the last few months. I closed my eyes and tried to pretend that the thrumming of the bus was part of the music. I periodically opened my eyes to see how close to my stop we were getting. The next song in the line-up came on, and I cranked the volume. I knew I was swaying to the beat, but it was a practically empty bus of random people—I didn't especially care what they thought of me.

'I'm not Snow White, but I'm lost inside this forest. I'm not Red Riding Hood, but I think the wolves have got me...'

My lips mouthed the words silently as they blared in my ears, and when I opened my eyes again, the guy across from me was still smiling. At the risk of making it sound creepy, the look he was giving me was a lot like the one Two-A and his girlfriend had been shooting me some ten minutes prior. I didn't see a girlfriend in the vicinity though, so my outlook for this encounter was a little more hopeful. I smiled back again and looked at my phone, but my eyes shot to the left when I felt something brush my arm.

What the fuck?

I barely had time to realize it was the guy's hand and that he had moved to sit next to me before soft lips were pressing firmly against my jawline. It all happened so fast the only thing I could think to do was slide away, but after less than a foot of movement my back pressed against the division between the main body of the bus and the raised seating in the rear section, effectively pinning me. One of the guy's hands came up to turn my chin to face him while the other trailed toward my hair.

I knocked his hand away from me and slammed my foot into his chest, pushing him leg-length away from me. The freak just smiled wider, and I was about to kick straight up into his jaw when he pressed a finger over his lips and pointed his other thumb back toward the front of the bus, where the driver sat. It took me a few seconds and a few deep breaths to realize what he meant.

Huh...interesting.

I wasn't normally one for exhibitionism, but I'd try just about anything once. To the guy's credit, as soon as I'd pushed he'd stopped...and he was *damn* good-looking. I pulled my shoe off his chest and slowly set it on the floor, and he kept his hands up in a sign of goodwill the whole time.

If this weird stage I was in didn't last, I doubted I'd ever get a chance like this again... A little bus-ride-fun couldn't hurt anybody, right? The worst that'd happen was we'd get kicked off, and I'd been kicked out of better for doing worse.

I slid a half-step closer to him, and when he kept his hands up I leaned in tentatively. My lips came within two inches of his...then one. I paused, then pushed forward fast while I still had the nerve, fusing our mouths together.

His hands came down to rest on the side of my face and my shoulder as we moved against each other. I fisted a hand into his curly hair and slid back into the corner of the seat as I pulled him with me, trying dismally to be quiet. It wasn't exactly perfect. Our mouths were moving with different intentions, his slow and personal, mine fast—so I couldn't quite get my lips to synch up in the short stretch I knew we had. To buy time I used my leverage to pull my leg up onto the seat and against my chest, pulling the guy down onto it as I slid my leg between his to up the friction.

Bingo.

His eyes snapped shut for a half-second. The shuddered sigh that he let out gave me a chance to slip my tongue into his mouth. Nothing too heavy—a quick glide over smooth teeth then an even faster dive in to taste the cinnamon of the gum he had been chewing. He pulled up against my leg, flushing me with heat. I shut my eyes and tilted my head back, enjoying the feel of his warm kisses laving down my throat.

Hands crept up under my shirt and fanned out over my heated skin, and another moved back into my hair. Soft lips pressed against my stomach and I arched into them, forcing the ones on my neck to bend to follow me.

Wait.

Hands on my...? Two and two...?

"What the fuck?"

I jerked backward, slamming my head against the metal divider with a resounding clang and a lightning shot of pain in my skull. I kicked out with my leg, slamming up into the hot guy's balls even as I shoved at whoever the fuck else was touching me, knocking them onto their ass on the floor of the bus.

I pulled my limbs into myself defensively as Hot Guy tried to hold his nuts with one hand and the bus railing with the other, gasping for breath. The guy on the ground looked up at me in confusion, and I suddenly noticed what he was wearing.

Blaine was embroidered on his uniform black polo, right under the logo for the bus company we were riding on. My mouth opened in shock, and I frantically glanced up at the front of the bus to see...nothing. No one was sitting at the driver's seat.

"What's the problem, man? I'm clean, swear!" Blaine climbed back toward me, and all I could do was stare at him dumbfounded.

"Who the hell is driving the bus?"

He rolled his eyes as he went to put his hand back on my leg. "I put it on cruise control..."

I kicked him away, struggling to get to my feet as the bus started to shake and the sound of blaring horns filtered in from outside. "This isn't a fucking *plane*, you *psycho*, that only controls the spee—!"

I got to the short walking strip between the seating area and the driver's section just in time to see the front of the bus slam head on into a fire hydrant with a clang of twisting metal. The force of the hit knocked me to the floor, and the last thing I remember seeing was Blaine's eyes going wide before another, louder crash drowned out my thoughts and sent me spinning into black.

* * * *

"Explain it to me one more time...slowly." The police officer leaned forward slightly toward me, taking off his sunglasses. "In *detail*."

I squeezed my temples to try to work out the headache threatening to roar to life in the space between my eyes. He was a cop, and he was trying to help, but I was about to blow up if he didn't just *listen*.

"I *told* you, the guy went *crazy*. He put the bus on cruise control and decided that was good enough, then tried to grope me." I pointed toward Blaine, sitting on the curb now—soaked by the broken hydrant, where an EMT was tending to him. When he saw I was looking at him, he grinned and tried to get up, but the EMT made him sit back down. I turned back to the officer. "*Arrest him.*"

The officer bit down on the end of his aviators and turned sideways so he could lean against the cop car I was sitting on the hood of, bringing his body closer to mine. "Guy's got a pretty bad scrape on his head."

My brow furrowed and I stared at the officer like he'd gone insane, because right about then, it seemed like he had.

"Then patch the freak up, *then* arrest him!"

"Let's just go over the story one more time, from the beginning."

I sighed in frustration and leaned back to put my face in my hands, and caught sight of the officer shifting how he was standing, almost like... *No, that wouldn't make sense.*

"What were you doing before he came up to you?"

I bent forward again, trying not to look as suspicious as I was pretty sure I did as I cast a furtive glance at Hot Guy, who was explaining his side of the story to another officer.

"Sitting."

The cop smirked slightly, leaning off the car to stand in front of me, setting both of his hands on either side of my knees with an eyebrow raised. "Just…sitting?"

I focused in on the notepad the officer in the distance was writing on and reached for my threads. My eyes closed as the rushing currents of the time stream rocked through my veins, and a painfully detailed description of every sweep of tongue and squeeze of hand that had occurred on the bus exploded in my mind's eye, scrolling past my vision like a perfected outline as the officer's pen rushed along the page in fast forward. I snapped my eyes open to kill the Sight and breathed out a sigh, resisting the urge to show how tense and tight my muscles felt as a result. I didn't sense any magical beings in the area, but it was safer to just prevent any suspicion outright.

"And… Kissing."

The cop's hands flattened on the hood, sliding his body a little closer to mine. "Kissing?" he intoned suspiciously.

I huffed out a shot of air and scratched my head, refusing to make eye contact. "With…you know…" I pointed toward the other guy. "Him."

Out of the corner of my eye I saw the cop turn to take a look at him, then turn back to me. "And while you were kissing, the bus driver came back and tried to join in?"

"Well, yeah." I took a breath and looked up into his eyes, and slid back slightly when I realized for the first time just how close he was. His brown eyes weren't looking at me with judgment, but damn, they were *right there*. He smiled a little, and I noticed the way we were positioned left my only way of getting some space to be backward over the hood.

"Well, between the two of you, can you really *blame* the guy?"

Wai...

Oh, fuck.

It was happening again... It couldn't have just been me blossoming or whatever the fuck I'd tried to convince myself. But I didn't have much time to give it more thought, because this time around the guy had a gun. And the power to arrest me. And handcuffs. *Shit. Shitshit*shit.

Breathe...

A little flirting wasn't dangerous, even if he was a cop. Inappropriate? Hell yes. But I'd been dealing with it all morning. It just came with the territory of being a newly instated hottie, right? *Just play it cool.*

"I...u-um—"

A little cooler than that.

I cleared my throat and pushed myself forward so my feet were resting on the ground solidly, expecting the cop to back up in turn. He didn't. That put our faces so close that I was basically crossing my eyes to look at him, but I told myself I wouldn't freak.

"Look, Officer..." I glanced down at his uniform and name badge, "Brand. I—"

The officer moved back slightly, just enough so he could stand up straight to his full six-foot-five, six-foot-six height. He smiled down smugly from the six or so inches above me. "Aaron."

I shuffled sideways, expecting him to just naturally move his arm so I could pass. Again, he didn't. My blood was started to pump a little faster through my veins for it, but I still tried to keep myself in control. "Yeah... I think I-I should just...you know..."

Aaron suddenly shifted, bringing his thigh up tight between mine, pinning me close to the fender. He laughed lightly and bent down to whisper into my ear, leaving me with a clear shot of nothing but uniform shirt.

"Tell me, Cole… Whaddya think about handcuffs?" He shifted a little, pressing his thigh up higher into my legs, threatening to lift me up if he went much farther. I heard a clinking of metal, and realized the guy was probably reaching for them as we spoke. "I mean, they're part of the job description for me, but…how do you feel about them in, say, your *personal life?*" Aaron's voice whispered against my ear, and, at the last words, I felt his mouth come down around my lobe, grazing it with his teeth.

My mind was burning nuclear white, but for the life of me I couldn't bring the shattered parts of my thoughts together long enough to form some kind of plan. I looked around Aaron as best I could, trying to see something, *anything* that could help.

"Blaine!"

Huh. Interesting choice, vocal cords.

The bus driver looked up at me excitedly from his position twenty or so feet away, and he tried to stand again before the EMT pushed him back down. Aaron's tongue slipped into my ear, and I coughed as I tried to form more words before I could get them out.

"I, uh… I think I scraped up my hand pretty bad! Think you cou…could—" I put my hands against Aaron's shoulders for support as his molten hot mouth moved lower, working down the line Hot Guy had been playing with just a while earlier. "Take a look?"

You'd have thought I'd just told a kid Christmas was coming early. The lovesick creeper jumped to his feet excitedly, shouting out "Sure!" and all but running toward me. The EMT looked at him in confusion, then to me—probably because I had just asked a whacked out bus driver for medical help instead of him—but my plan worked. As soon as we made eye contact, a suave smirk spread across the tech's face, and he walked my way confidently, shouldering Blaine out of the way.

"Sounds like you need an *expert* opinion..."

Wait... Oh God... Of course.

I could infatuate people with a look. My very presence inspired groping, kissing, touching. Everyone I spoke to wanted to have my babies, and everyone I smiled at was a touch away from blowing. Those weren't the powers of a Seer.

They were the powers of an Incubus.

"This is Night... This is what makes an Incubus tick."

Sweet Jesus...

How had I not put it together before? I wasn't suddenly *hot*, I was suddenly pumping out Incubus...sex *stuff!* I hadn't thought anything more of the Night because I'd figured it must have not worked, but oh no—it was working perfectly fine. Maybe a little slow building, but working perfectly fine nonetheless. Until now, it hadn't made any sense to associate it with what had happened—sure it was from an Incubus, but they could do a wide array of magic, and Luke had said it would give me control. Meanwhile, the events of the day had made me feel *less* in control than I ever had in my life.

The EMT came up close, knocking me out of my bullet train thoughts and back to the present, but just as I started to get my hopes up, he walked right past Aaron to where my "injured" hand was extended out from behind him and crouched down in front of it.

Shit! I needed a knight in shining armor, not another *creep!* The EMT started to press chaste kisses across my knuckles, and, not to be outdone, Blaine grabbed my other hand and started to slobber smooches on it.

Great. I'd looked for an out and ended up creating an orgy. *Fuck. This.*

If I made it out of this intact, I was going to throttle Luke until he was dead, then I'd bring him back so I could find out how to make this stop, then kill him again. With guns. And bombs. And sharp things.

Back in the twisted world of reality, I braced myself against the fender of the police car. Fantasies aside, I had a situation to take care of and no one to help me, so it was time to take my life in my own hands. Whatever was making these guys obsessed with me was making them completely ignore each other, and I needed to change that.

I yanked my right hand away from Blaine, ignoring the hurt look that spread across his face at the motion. With a roll of my hips I managed to sit myself on Aaron's leg instead of riding it like some weird, ball-separating tree branch, which gave me just enough room to lean back and grab Aaron's face with my free hand, pulling him off my neck and shoving his head aside so I could lean down to the EMT.

I bit my lip, trying to copy the smut-face Two-A had leveled me with. "That feels *so good!*" I gushed, trying to be as flirty as my current, terrified state would allow. It felt painfully fake, but apparently it was good enough for him, because the EMT grinned up at me and dropped my hand, reaching for my face.

With a growl, he was suddenly shoved backward as Aaron spun around, finally giving me a breath of space. The cop stalked toward the tech, reaching for the Taser at his side.

"He's *mine…*"

Blaine shoved the officer in the side as hard as he could, knocking him off balance. "Who says *you* can have him? *I* saw him first!"

The EMT scowled at them both. "He wants *me*."

Aaron shoved him again, almost knocking him over this time. "*I'm* the one he was touching!"

Blaine rolled his eyes. "Holding him against a car doesn't *count*..."

Agreed. Point to the bus driver. But I was a little too busy running my ass off to keep score for the rest of the fight. A quick duck under the still spewing hydrant's fountain and I was off, racing down the sidewalk back to my apartment before one of them decided they were the winner and deserved their prize.

* * * *

Admittedly, I should have just gone straight to Luke's and not home first, but my mind was running on autopilot. All I was hearing was *flight*, not *fight*, and the natural destination was home turf. No way in fuck was I getting on a bus again until this was fixed, so I rushed past the stop and headed for the parking lot, trying to ignore the looks that seemed even more fixated than they'd been in the hours prior.

I slid into the driver's seat of my car, ignoring the way my still-damp clothes squished as I settled in. I jammed in the key and cranked it despite the horrible grinding sounds the engine gave off at the motion. The check engine light was as bright as ever, but I ignored it, tossing the car into reverse and heading out.

Luke's apartment was about eight minutes away. I cranked the radio to drown out the awful sounds drifting through the firewall, and kept my eyes on the road. If the pedestrians could pick up on the whatever-this-shit-was even through the car, I didn't want to know. I just drove, making sure I stayed in the speed limit—the last thing I wanted was big, bad Officer Aaron pulling me over. I had a feeling I'd see those cuffs up close if that happened.

I swung into the lot and parked in the spaces near the adjacent building. They were all open, probably because people didn't want to be too close to the construction going on just in case. Didn't much matter to me—my car probably wouldn't last one more crank anyway. I threw the thing in park and headed into the apartment building.

Chapter Three

Luke's complex had an elevator, classy fuck that he was, so I hopped inside and slammed the Close button so I wouldn't have to face any wannabe suitors till I hit the fourth floor. Luke's place was toward the back of the hall, but my path was blissfully clear of any opposition.

When I reached the door of four-ten, I slammed my fist against the wood three times, and when it didn't open immediately, I hit it three more times even harder.

"Luke, it's me, open the damn door!"

A muffled "It's open!" rang out from somewhere in the apartment, so I grabbed the handle and let myself in.

Luke's apartment wasn't huge by any means, but what it lacked in size it made up for in comfort. The entire space was composed of warm reds, oranges and browns, pops of color that stood out on accent walls against the dark wood furnishings. There was a *warmth* to the place that had nothing to do with the thermostat. Though he never volunteered the information, Luke had designed the entire place himself from the ground up—the only thing he had had to work with when he moved in were white walls, empty rooms and some cheap carpeting. The guy had an amazing talent for design, but like most of us with power, college had never really panned out—we couldn't ignore the gifts we had, so before long they just became our careers by default. In Luke's case, he had at least managed to keep it mostly aligned with his interests. As a consultant to the Dreamwalker Council, he specialized in defensive dream design, letting his architectural talents keep the minds of some of the magical world's more important figures safe from invasion while they slept.

I pulled off my damp hoodie and threw it over the arm of the couch. "Luke, what the fuck was in that shit you gave me last night?" I called out to the bedroom, but there wasn't an answer, so I continued as I headed in that direction. "There's more you're not telling me—you were being weird, people are going nuts now and I—*Shit!*" I stumbled on something and almost face planted, grabbing the back of a chair just before I ate carpet.

I looked back to see what tool of Satan had tried to trip me, and rolled my eyes when I realized it was one of Luke's bongs. I stooped and picked it up, and as I stood again and went to set it on the coffee table, I jumped a half-foot into the air when I saw the Dreamwalker standing right in front of me.

Luke was about the same height as me, maybe an inch or so taller. Laziness more so than fashion choice dictated his constant five o'clock shadow and shaggy brown hair, which cut across his forehead naturally in the way so many angsty teens worked hours to mimic, and he had the characteristic green eyes of

Dreamwalkers. He was thin, a point made more obvious by the slightly oversized long-sleeved shirts he almost always wore, and the easy smirk he was forever giving me was there as usual.

"Finally getting the attention you deserve?" Luke's gravelly voice was coming out in soft, low registers, which wasn't synching up with the obvious aggravation I was leveling at him. He reached up and brushed aside the hair that had fallen down over my eyebrows, stepping closer as his eyes started to close — almost like he was going to...

"Very funny." I shoved him in the chest, pushing past him and heading into his kitchen. The least the dick owed me for all this grief was a drink. I just hoped he had something strong. "That Incubus shit you gave me has all the humans in town humping like rabbits, with me as the main target! Why the fuc — Hey!"

Strong arms wrapped around my chest as I went to open the fridge door, pulling me backward. "Luke, wha—" Before I could push back I was spun around and pressed tight against the refrigerator, Luke's warm body holding me in place against the cold steel. His lips closed around my ear and I shuddered, forgetting for a second that I was supposed to be pushing him off me.

"Shhhh, buddy... Shh..."

"Lu—" My words were cut off as he dragged his lips from my neck and angled for my mouth. I couldn't squirm left or right because his arms on either side of me were holding me in place, and with my back against the fridge and his face already so close to mine, I couldn't twist my head out of the way in time.

I hadn't even considered that the Night would work on him too — it had just been natural to assume it would only affect *normal* people. Now I had to face the fact that everyone, magic or otherwise, wanted a piece of me — my straight best friend included.

Fuck — he was going to kiss me. Luke was really about to *kiss* me, and what scared me most was that right then, with no time to think and nowhere to move — for one tiny second, I almost let him.

The next instant I flattened my palms against the stainless steel door behind me, closed my eyes and promptly let myself land flat on my ass.

My back slid down the fridge easily — maybe a little *too* easily, considering my knees caved before I'd been expecting it — and I slammed my tailbone into the tile so hard I thought I'd fucked up my spine for good. When my legs splayed out underneath me I naturally grabbed onto something — *anything* — for support. Problem was, what was handy were Luke's legs. I death gripped the Dreamwalker's thighs.

Shit.

I was officially eye-level with my best friend's package. My best friend's long, *hard* package, currently straining the zipper of his wrecked jeans, and I had maybe a half-second before he realized he was making out with his refrigerator door instead of me.

Okay. I can work with this... Probably. Hopefully.

"Col...?"

I let go of Luke's legs and used my hands to shove against the fridge and slide out from under him, between his legs. I shot to my feet as he turned around, swinging his leg well over my head so it wouldn't hit.

Luke was laughing, showing off those white teeth of his as he shook his head at me. "Where're you going?"

My head was on fire, and even though what I needed most was to just sit and think this all through, I couldn't even get a train of thought on the track, much less rolling. My only plan was to keep as much space in between the two of us as I could until I found my brain's on switch.

"This isn't happening…"

I needed answers, a calm explanation of exactly what the shit was doing and how. But now the only person who knew anything about it was strung out on sex, and I didn't know how to get any sane help out of him.

Luke came around the side of the island and reached for me, and reflexively I shoved him as hard as I could, banking on surprising him. It worked—the Dreamwalker stumbled backward, taking his hands off me just in time to catch himself before he could smash his back into the counter on the other side of the kitchen.

"C'mon, man, what's wrong?" Luke *sounded* confused, but he was looking at me with so much heat that there didn't seem much room to be conflicted. I grabbed my head in both hands, trying to hold down the *JesusChristRunNow* panic response stabbing me in the chest.

"*All* of this! Luke, you're fucking *straight!*" I tried to breathe, desperate to slow the beat gunning around in my chest. "What. Was that shit. You gave me?"

Luke walked toward me slowly, like I was a scared animal or something. Not too far from the truth, really, but I still put the nearest chair between the two of us anyway. He squinted and ran a hand through his hair.

"What shit?"

That made me stop for a second. "Whaddya mean, *what shit?* The Night you gave me. Incubus…whatever it was?"

The hand carding through his hair halted for a second, and his brow furrowed. A moment later, the look of thought had melted into the easy grin he usually wore. "Riii-iight…the Inc jizz…" He chuckled the last words out in such an innocent way that it took me a second to actually comprehend what they were — and what that meant.

Fuck. No.

I grabbed my stomach with one hand as I felt my gag reflex seize tight in my throat. "You — *what?* You had me drink… In-Incubus *cum?*"

Luke sidled closer, leaning his weight heavily against the other side of the chair I had maneuvered between us. "Concentrated," he added with a nod.

My stomach was too sick and my head too confused to even think of a response, much less try to get the words to come out of my dropped jaw. All I could do was let go of the chair and slump backward onto the couch behind me. I opened and closed my mouth a few times silently while Luke plopped down next to me.

"I— You…" I shook my head, trying to pull it back down to earth, ground myself in real life. I didn't even know where to start, so I let my mouth take over for my brain. "What— What do you mean, *concentrated?*"

A soft little sound to my left, almost like a purr, filtered in through the white noise swirling around up in my head. A half-second later, the rest of my senses decided they'd had enough time off and cranked it up to a ten as well. With a snap, I suddenly realized that Luke wasn't just sitting next to me — his head was currently jammed between my neck and my shoulder, inhaling deeply as he nuzzled against my overheating skin. One of those hands I was so used to seeing wrapped around a joint was suddenly on my body, sliding against the place where my shirt had ridden up just enough to show flesh.

Oh Jesus... The feeling of those hands on my body was the definition of temptation.

I pushed him backward, trying to find the space to breathe, but Luke pushed right back, eyes squeezed tight. I grabbed his head, my hands framing his face, and I shook him. "Luke — Luke, look at me. Look at me!"

Those lids shot open immediately, and for a second I almost wished they hadn't.

Luke's hand on my shirt pulled upward, exposing more skin to the open air. "I'm *trying* to..."

Emotions that I didn't want to consider were arcing around in those seas of green, oceans that looked like they would swallow me without a second thought. I snapped my eyes away from them, focusing in on some indiscriminate spot above them.

"What did you mean, concentrated?"

Just like that, Luke's eyes closed again, and he let out a low groan, sliding his hand gently across my stomach in a move that *really* needed to stop, before something...*happened...*

"Aww, Cole, I can't...can't..." His free hand gestured noncommittally around his head, not any kind of sign language I recognized — and *fuck*, his other hand was still sliding against my skin just as slow, just as soft, dancing up toward my ribs in a way that was making it *really* hard to breathe, and even harder to...

"Think?" The word stumbled out over my lips in a rush of air.

Luke's eyes snapped open again, hooking into me with renewed vigor. "Yeah! That…" He lowered his mouth down onto my neck again, scraping his lips against me even as he pulled my shirt's hem higher and my collar lower.

I pushed against him, this time locking my arms so he couldn't get close no matter how much he pushed back into my hands—and he sure as hell pushed back. I prayed the physical distance might make him focus a little more.

"Luke—Luke, look—" With a sigh, I levered myself backward so his groping hands couldn't reach me as easily. "I *need* you to think. I need you to explain, explain what's going on…"

"*Cole*…" he whined, resolving to slide his hands over my arms since they were the only thing in reach. And damn it, it shouldn't have been sexual, but I was having hell's own time convincing my already straining body of that. "Just, just lemme—" He pushed harder, trying to scrape his fingertips across my stomach again. "It'll help…help me…focus."

Wait.

I stopped squirming—hardly even dared to breathe for the next few seconds. I locked onto those eyes in front of me, waited until they finally rose to match my gaze before I let slip the words whose potential left me more terrified than anything else had that night.

"What do you mean, 'help you focus'?"

Luke paused for a moment, finally letting his hands drop to his sides, even as my arms stayed locked against him. Slowly, that crooked little smirk I was so used to spread across his face.

Oh, *fuck*…

* * * *

"Can't we just... I don't know...touch?"

I was plastered against the far side of the couch, and even though my arms weren't up holding Luke away anymore, I couldn't help but be as far from him as possible while staying, however precariously, on the piece of furniture. For his part, apparently the promise of touching had helped Luke to calm down a little, since for the moment he was giving me my space— mostly. I had my legs pulled up to my chest and I was facing him on the couch, arms wrapped protectively around my knees. Luke's thumb rubbed gently against the tiny section of skin that was visible between the now-hiked-up hem of my pants and my shoe, making sure I couldn't forget what his hands felt like on me. He smiled softly, and his words of reminder sent...*something* rushing through my body. Ice or lightning, I couldn't tell.

"Incubi are fueled by sex, man. Not cuddling."

I groaned and dropped my head down onto my knees. "Oh, *fuck* me..." The instant the words were out of my mouth, I realized that I'd said them out loud—and with Luke less than three feet away from me, that shit wasn't going to work. I threw my hands out, only just catching Luke by the shoulders before he could plaster me to the arm of the couch. "Not like that!"

The Dreamwalker slumped backward, a pout on his face. "'S not nice to tease, you know."

"I'm not having sex with you, Luke." I tried to keep my voice as level as possible, given the circumstances. I may not have been able to put much force behind the words, but I could at least be proud of the fact that I didn't stumble over them.

Luke didn't seem very impressed. He lolled his head to the side to look over at me, and even though I knew I should've stopped him, all I could do was watch as he reached over for my hand slowly, sliding his own fingers underneath mine so that he could gently stroke his thumb across the top. "Ten minutes ago, you weren't willing to do *anything*."

My other hand was squeezed so tightly that it was starting to ache. I took a deep breath, but refused to look away first. I couldn't explain what was happening to me, but I'd be damned if I was just going to hand over control that easily. "Some things *aren't* negotiable."

Luke smiled softly, and looked down to where our hands were joined. "Shame..." He started to move like he was going to look up at me again, and right then I knew I wasn't going to win another staring contest. I pulled my hand away from him to distract myself, but the Dreamwalker seemed to take that as an invitation, following it backward until he was sliding on top of me, swinging his leg over mine so that he was straddling me in one fluid motion. I wanted to ask how a normally bumbling pothead managed to learn how to move that smoothly, or just where he'd learned a move like that, period—or why he seemed plenty able to focus so long as it was sex we were talking about, not Night, or what I had done wrong to deserve having the straight best friend I constantly wanted suddenly want to fuck my brains out, but only because of a mind-bending drug. For his part, Luke seemed perfectly content to just lean against me, head beside mine as his hands roamed under my shirt, one arm wrapping around my back to hold my body tight against his. The question that finally worked itself out of my mouth wasn't the one I'd expected to ask.

"I thought you said Incubi don't get off on cuddling?"

Luke didn't answer. He chuckled softly into my shoulder instead, happy for the moment to just keep his hands moving on me. That was the part where the side of me that kept yelling that Luke was my only friend and that if he remembered any of this after the effects wore off, I'd have officially ruined the one good relationship in my life—that part of me was supposed to chime in, push Luke away and insist that he just fucking tell me what I needed to know so I could go. Unfortunately, that part was speaking a little more quietly than my dick... You know, that thing between my legs that was *screaming* inside my pants to just be *touched* already? I couldn't decide what hurt worse, the head trying to wrap itself around all this, or the one that Luke was torturing with every rock of his hips.

So yeah, maybe I'm letting this go a little further than I should. Sue me.

Luke still wasn't answering, and the lips scraping against the spots where he was pulling my shirt away from my body were keeping me a little too occupied to think up another question. I turned my head away, trying to find something in the apartment to focus on so I could stop thinking about the fingertips that were gracing the edge of my boxers' elastic. The move just gave the Dreamwalker better access to the skin he seemed obsessed with tasting, but it also finally gave me something to lock in on—a lonely joint sitting on the coffee table to my right.

I reached out and dragged it closer, then pulled open the drawer of the table to try to find one of the thousands of lighters he had strewn around the apartment. I couldn't see and I couldn't feel the shape of one, so I tried to lean farther over the arm to get a better view. Luke's lips faltered on my neck as he groaned in complaint, so I yanked down at the collar of my shirt with my free hand, giving him plenty of new places to cover with his chaste kisses. A happy little purr bubbled out of his throat as he moved his way down to my collarbone, and in what I can only assume was some kind of a thank you, I felt him redouble his efforts to get into my pants.

That was *not* happening. Fate may have had a damn sick sense of humor, and I may have had less than perfect morals, but I also had my boundaries—exploiting my straight friend while he was under some sex spell was one of them, no matter how bad I may have wanted him.

I caught hold of a lighter, yanked it out of the drawer and held it clicked over the joint until I was sure it was lit. The lighter fell out of my fingers as I scooped up the rolled tube and pressed it between my lips, taking as long a drag as my lungs would let me. I hadn't done it much—pot was Luke's vice, mine tended to be Jack, or Svedka, or Captain Morgan—but it was enough to keep me from coughing it all back out as I slid against the couch to try to keep my crotch out of the Dreamwalker's reach.

Luke was not at all happy about that. His hand squirmed in between us, matching my slide so that if something didn't break fast we were gonna end up on the floor. I rushed another hit and pulled Luke's head away from my body, extending the joint to him until those green eyes glinted up at me mischievously and I was sure he'd take it.

"Trying to lower my inhibitions?"

It wasn't fair that in the middle of the Night-induced...whatever this was...the craziness taking over Luke still got to keep that soft, scrappy little voice of his. I rolled my eyes as he rocked backward to breathe in a drag of the weed. "I'm hoping at this point it'll give some back."

Luke grinned before putting the joint back up to his lips. I took advantage of the pause to finally redirect him.

"You seem pretty focused, now. Ready to tell me about the Night?"

The Dreamwalker tapped the end of the joint against the table, before dropping it there and turning back to me. With a sudden rush of air, my vision became a fog of smoke as Luke huffed out his last hit all over my face. I couldn't help but cough, which just made him smile even more.

"Whaddya wanna know?"

Everything. "Why everyone wants to have sex with me. What that shit really was. How long it's gonna last, why you even fucking *gave* it to me in the first place…"

"Shhh…" Luke's finger clumsily pressed against my lips. "Just chill… I'll explain. Just…sit back…" Luke pushed lightly on my shoulder, encouraging me to lean back against the couch, and I tried not to make it obvious how much it felt like a trap. He leaned in toward me, and I put a hand between us to keep some distance — an idea that was kind of ironic, seeing as the guy was sitting on top of my hard-on.

"You said it was concentrated Incubus…" My mouth opened and closed a few times, but I couldn't make myself say it. "You know?"

Luke wrapped his warm hand around my wrist, gently pulling it out of the way so he could press closer against me, his lips dropping kisses along my neck again. "Cum." Kiss. "Max got it by blowing an Incubus—" Kiss. "He cast a spell to keep it from—"

I was waiting for the soft press of his lips again, but when I opened my eyes to check, I saw that he had pulled back just enough to show the look of confusion on his face while he made another completely unhelpful hand gesture.

"You know…going all…Pop Rock-ish in his mouth." He moved back down, nuzzling into my hair while he rolled his hips gently into my waist. "He spat it out and did something to amp it up, make it more potent."

That actually made sense, now that I had a little more to go on—after having sex with an Incubus, people tended to be a lot luckier at getting laid for a few hours. I'd always just assumed a little of their sex magic stuck around with you for a while, but apparently it had to do with the cum itself. I was about to open my mouth to ask another question when I felt the Dreamwalker's hands reaching for the clasp of my jeans again.

I pushed his hand away, squirming to try to get out of his reach. "Luke, no, we're not… I don't…"

His brow furrowed as he leaned back to look up at me with pained eyes. "Cole…" One hand rested softly on my chest, heating me up through the thin fabric of my shirt. "I *need* you…" He shuddered slightly, and for the first time I noticed that his hands were shaking. "You don't know what it's like, being this close and not just…n-not…"

Oh, you have no idea…

He closed his eyes and turned his head down, and for the first time, seeing how hard he was fighting with it, I wondered what it must have been like to be on the other side of this shit. The thought of anyone wanting me so badly it *hurt* – that was just...disturbing. I struggled to think of what I could say.

"Luke, I'm – I'm sorry, but I *can't*... You're my best friend, I can't – "

"Kiss me."

Those green eyes snapped open, boring into me desperately. I'd never once seen emotions like that play across his face, and they were fucking scaring me.

"I – What?"

"Just kiss me. If I can't have... If we won't do...*that*...then at least let me have this." Luke's hand on my chest had twisted up into a fist clutching my shirt tight. He was looking down at me with a kind of need that I couldn't even conceive of, much less understand. He saw me start to open my mouth to spout some kind of denial to him again, but he beat me to the punch with a knowing stare. "You've done it before."

Fuck.

I didn't even want to think about that. I *hadn't* thought about that for years – had myself half convinced it had all been just a drunk dream. "That was..." I struggled for a word that wouldn't end up implicating me somehow. "Different. I was confused, and you... We..." It had been two years earlier, and I'd been drinking, deciding, as usual, that a handle of Smirnoff was preferable to talking. Luke had shown up at my apartment and when he'd seen the state I was in, he'd stayed with me like he always did, weathering the storm with little touches and soothing words I probably didn't deserve.

Somehow, that had translated to my lips pressing against his. It hadn't lasted more than two, three seconds, but it had seemed to happen so slowly, getting so close to that face I'd been looking at for five years and just...letting it come naturally. Luke hadn't said a word, just stared at me the same way he had before I'd done it. In a way that could only happen when I was drunk, I'd just smiled at him, rested my head on his shoulder and...fallen asleep. Just fucking *fell asleep*, like there wasn't a care in the world.

I was feeling anything *but* tired this time—scared was a better word. Terrified, actually. But Luke didn't let up, banking on my shock to keep me from arguing. "Shh...just...think about how you felt that night." His hands pulled up to frame my face, one of them sweeping my hair up over my eyebrows again. "Think about how you felt that second before your lips—"

Oh fuck, stop, stop, stop, don't—

I didn't have time to argue, didn't have time to *breathe*, just slammed my eyes shut in the tiny second as the Dreamwalker's face came within millimeters of mine. Soft, warm lips pressed against my own for one infinite moment, and I didn't even dare to think of what that meant as they pulled back just enough to breathe out a few more words. "Brushed against mine."

Luke's mouth opened against mine with a delicious pressure, and before I could think any better of it, I opened in return, letting him take control as the alarms in the back of my head spun up to full alert.

The Dreamwalker's hands fanned across my chest, finding my biceps and squeezing them tightly as he worked my mouth open. I let myself have one second of freedom—gave myself one tiny rush to kiss him back with as much vigor as he was giving me—then I pulled away. Luke tried to follow, so I pushed, forcing him to sit back on the couch beside me instead of riding my lap. I could hardly believe I had the strength to talk, much less say something coherent, but I was making a habit of surprising myself.

"T-that's enough. Now talk."

His reply came without so much as a pause.

"Maybe I'm bi."

Silence stretched from one second to two, then three, and I couldn't tell what was going to snap first, the tension in the quiet floating between us or the lonely thread holding my mind in some semblance of order.

"W — Wha — ?"

Apparently the latter.

"You said talk — you didn't say what to talk about." He shrugged like it was the simplest thing in the world. Before I could answer, he was sidling up against me again, hand on my crotch, mouth on my shoulder. "Did you ever think about that? Maybe I'm bi, and I just never told you…"

It was just too much, all at once, all the ideas and possibilities I really couldn't afford to be thinking about right then… I knew I should be pushing him off me. Should have been fighting harder — but that would require coherent thought, something I was lacking, so for one brief second more, I took in his words and just let him move against me. Let myself feel every motion and emotion as his lips graced my skin and his hand squeezed my cock lovingly. All for one perfect second.

Then I let my mind and my mouth take over again.

"Maybe the Night will make you say anything so I'll let you fuck me."

Luke didn't seem fazed in the least by my words. If anything, it just made him move along my body more forcefully, letting a small, smug grin creep over his lips as he did.

"I let you kiss me that night. What does that say?"

Something about those words—or maybe it was that self-assured way he said them—with no time to think it over, a part of me just *snapped* inside.

The anger that washed over me, the sheer fury—it was on fire and boiling over, a screen of red resentment. Luke was still smirking and I just wanted him to *stop*, stop smiling and just *shut up*, because damn it, I'd wanted him for *seven fucking years*, and when I finally had the chance to make him mine, it was all just because of some fucked-up Incubus magic. It was beyond unfair, the worst kind of temptation, and now he was going to try to tell me that he might actually be bi? As if I could have had him at any time if I would've just asked? It was a lie, I was sure of it, and damn if it didn't make me *lose* it. In the next moment my fist was twisting tightly into that shaggy hair of his, gripping hard and yanking him back up my body so I could crush my lips against his. It wasn't exactly romantic, could probably be called vicious, but I dragged my lips against his for a second more, anything to shock him into just a moment of silence.

I let go of his hair and slammed my hands into his chest, knocking him off me and nearly off the couch as well. I glared down at the Dreamwalker, splayed against the far armrest looking more than a little tousled and confused.

"Stop talking about that and start talking about *Night*."

Luke cocked an eyebrow with the barest trace of a smile. Apparently being a little rough helped clear his head. I made a note to remember that.

"Ask away."

I stood and started pacing around the living room, circling close but still keeping some distance. Now that I seemed to finally have his attention, I was having trouble coming up with questions – so I started at the beginning.

"So the Night made me into some kind of...sex magnet. Fine." I closed in, placing my hands on the armrest across from Luke. "Then *why* would you give me something like that? You said it was supposed to give me control." I shook my head, twisting a hand up into my hair in frustration. "I don't know how it looks to you, but I don't feel very 'in control' right about now!"

"It *would* have given you control, if you hadn't taken *all* of it." He looked up at me with almost childlike innocence and excitement, which was a little disturbing paired up with his next words. "You could have fucked anyone you wanted to! Control over your sex life is a big part of having control of your life."

He said it so matter-of-factly, like it was the most logical thought process in the world. And if I didn't know he'd decided to give it to me *before* the Night made him go sex-crazy, I could have understood his reasoning. But since he'd obviously given me the cause before the effect had kicked in, I was having more trouble putting it together.

"Luke, I wanted to be able to *See* my future – not turn it into one big orgy!"

He rolled his eyes, and the fact that he was sidling closer to my side of the couch didn't go unnoticed. "Well, you weren't supposed to drink the whole thing..."

I backed up, putting more furniture in between us. "All right, fine. *I* fucked up. So why has this been getting worse as the day went on? This morning it was just flirting, but then a few hours later, I'm getting groped by some cop in the middle of an intersection!"

Luke stood to follow me, and the needles prickling at the back of my neck had nothing on the hornets' nest in my stomach. I kept circling the living room, making sure I never got too close to a wall—and especially not a corner.

"The Night in your system is reacting to the sexual energy around you. The more you fuel it, the stronger it gets, and the stronger your sex aura gets, too." He smirked. "Which makes people want you more, which fuels the Night. Pretty dope, right?"

I came to a halt. The full strength of what Luke had said was starting to trickle down into my consciousness, and honestly, I didn't know what that might mean—I just knew I didn't like the sound of it. My legs felt weak, and I slumped back onto that damn couch, letting the air huff out of my lungs while Luke wandered back over to plop down next to me. All I could do was shake my head.

"What kind of drug is this?"

Luke's fingers brushed over mine gently. "The best kind." I felt the cushions shift as the Dreamwalker leaned in closer to me, pressing his lips softly against my temple while I stared forward blankly. "The kind that works."

I sat there, floating somewhere between thinking and dreaming, noticing only idly as Luke moved against me, kissing, touching, tasting. It was as if it was happening to someone else, someone who might have actually had time to care, unlike me. My mind was too busy trying to make sense of something that I was starting to think couldn't be sensible.

"*I want you…*"

Somehow, those words, more than anything else, managed to creep their way into my awareness. I'd been praying to hear them for long enough, after all.

Oh yeah. Real life.

My eyes drifted closed, and I let out a sigh. I reached out blindly, catching hold of Luke's shirt and balling my fist into it. Then I used my leverage to push him away, standing to my feet at the same time and turning to him.

"And I want answers. That's the only reason I agreed to do...*this.* You're my best friend, Luke! What we've already done is...seriously messed up. I don't even know how we're going to go back to normal after this is all over. But thanks to the fucking *Night*, sex is now a prereq for you to think straight..."

Luke shifted uncomfortably, and the motion caught my eye, made me turn to face him. "Weeeell, not exactly a *prereq*... More like," a chill started to run down my spine, even as heat rushed to my cheeks. The Dreamwalker had the decency to almost look embarrassed as the next words slipped from his mouth, "an added bonus."

"*What?*"

In an instant I was on my feet, heading for the door, not caring what fucking excuse Luke might come up with. It wasn't until he actually grabbed my hand and tugged backward that I came to a stop and faced him, that much more furious when he didn't even have the consideration to look scared at the seething rage I was leveling him with.

"Well, you wouldn't have said yes if I would've just *asked...*"

I couldn't even begin to explain how pissed I was — except to maybe compare it with how *confused* the whole fucked-up situation had left me. Either way, I wrenched my hand away from the Dreamwalker's, throwing tact to the wind and letting my mouth take over.

"*Fuck* this, Luke. And fuck you!"

A dreamy, faraway look immediately glazed over his eyes, and for a second I swore I saw drool at the corner of his mouth.

"God, I wish you would…"

Jesus Christ…

I grabbed my head and growled in frustration as I stepped out of the door and slammed it shut behind me.

* * * *

I was halfway across the parking lot before I took a breath that wasn't huffed past gritted teeth. And it wasn't until I was fumbling to jam the key into the lock of my car's door that I paused to finally take a *truly* deep breath.

This isn't Luke's fault.

He wasn't in control of his actions. So I wasn't really mad at *him* then, I was mad at the *situation…* Even if the situation came about thanks to Luke. But he had only been trying to help in the first place… I took a break from my little rationalizing session to finally unlock the door and climb inside, settling down into the driver's seat with a sigh.

I just needed some time and space to breathe, and Luke needed to sleep it off. Tomorrow, when the Night had worn off some, I'd talk to him again, and ask—

Fuck.

For all of that, I hadn't even asked him how to *stop* this shit. I mean, presumably, if this stuff was fueling itself, I could just hide out in my apartment until it wore off since there wouldn't be any energy to keep it going. But knowing magic, it was probably going to be more complicated than that.

And in the meantime, I was a newly instated hottie with nowhere to go—and the only person who could probably help needed a cold shower.

Hmm.

Never let it be said that I don't have an...*inventive* imagination. Because damn if that little thought didn't get the wheels in my mind turning—and unless the tracks changed fast...

I smiled. *If you can't have the one you* really *want...*

Well, let's just say, the town was about to get to know its in-house Seer a little more *intimately...*

Chapter Four

Even the most blindingly, *naturally* attractive person in the entire world wouldn't have *everyone* trying to have sex with them. The hottest woman in the world, for example, would have most men wanting to screw her, and even some women — but what about every *straight* woman, and every *gay* man? She could have almost anyone she wanted, but that's the key word — almost.

Me? I was throwing that right out of the window.

See, magic was an amazing thing. So amazing that it could, at least temporarily, override a person's *normal* sexual orientation and make them fuck someone they might not normally consider attractive. Someone like yours truly.

So yes, a sweet, virginal submissive like the ones I liked to read about in my huge collection of vehemently hidden erotica e-books, if stuck in my situation, would probably have shied away from the contact, been utterly terrified at the prospect of being the focus of so much attention, much less so much sexual desire. He would have hidden, tried to get the condition reversed and along the way almost undoubtedly fallen for some big, sexy Dom who had wanted him even before the Incubus sex stuff had kicked in, and they would be assumed to live happily ever after, with plenty of scorching sex along the way too, of course.

Problem was, I *wasn't* a sweet, virginal submissive. And damned if it was wrong, but I had the kind of gift no one *ever* got, and I was going to live it up if it killed me… Which was a somewhat lengthy way of explaining how I ended up handcuffed on the bed of one Aaron Brand.

* * * *

It was the morning after the Luke debacle. Not only had my car managed to drag itself home, but that obnoxious little light had actually turned off halfway through the trip, too. I got some sleep, woke up fresh and bright-eyed and promptly headed out onto the highways and byways of Kelvin.

I drove nice and slowly around the blind turn on the approach to the town proper, the spot where cops were still apparently sure they could bust someone, even though the entire populace knew they'd been hiding there for years now. True to form, a police cruiser was camped out behind an outcropping of trees, and the officer in the seat, looking decidedly bored, was none other than…

Bingo.

I slammed the pedal to the floor, whipping the hamsters in my little four-liter engine into a frenzy. The light-speed-inducing roar of the engine was a lot more bark than it was bite, as my acceleration left more than a few things to be desired, but the sound alone was more than enough to catch the eye of the officer in question. I heard the sound of a siren growling to life, and I was sure to gun it through a few more twists and turns before I finally pulled over — you know, to make it a little more *interesting*.

* * * *

Slam!

I was pushed hard into the fender of the Crown Vic, rolled up against the cold steel by the pelvis grinding into my ass. Calloused hands wrapped around my wrists, pulling them back firmly, though with a surprisingly gentle grip. The metallic clinking I recognized from yesterday again rang in my ears, though this time with a torrent of blood that it sent rocketing to my crotch. I writhed into the fender, craving the pressure it put on my dick.

"Criminal speeding? Evading arrest?" The metal ring looped around one wrist slowly, immediately followed by the gratifying cl-cl-cl-cl-clack as it snapped down tight. I felt Aaron's weight shift as he leaned forward, grinding my cock down onto the steel deliciously as he pressed into me even tighter. "And that's not to mention the way you just ran off yesterday… I still had a few questions left…" He growled out the last sentence, following it up with a quick bite to my ear and a long, torturous kiss to ease away the sting.

My breath shuddered out on a moan, and I barely kept enough composure to lean back into the cop's body, tilting my head to address him more clearly. "What kind of questions?"

The other cuff slid across my skin gently, teasingly as he chuckled into my neck. "Well, you never did

answer me about the handcuffs—" The other half of
the loop locked firmly into place as Aaron rolled his
hips against me, so close I could easily feel the hot
length of his straining dick pressing desperately
against me through his uniform slacks. Our difference
in height made it grind against my spine just above
the waist of my low-slung jeans, pinning the chain of
the handcuffs between us so that I couldn't move my
hands more than a few inches, not nearly as much as I
would need to wrench down that fucking zipper and
give that cock of his the worship it deserved. "Guess
we'll find out now, won't we?" he purred.

Aaron wrapped his hands around my shoulders,
pulling me backward off the fender and putting a little
space between us—just enough for me to grope
backward, getting a handful of rock-solid steel that
had nothing to do with cars or cuffs, before he could
pull a step farther back. Tease... But I couldn't help
but grin as electric heat shot through my cock again,
especially when I felt him shudder behind me at the
tiny moment of contact. I turned back just enough to
catch his gaze, looking up at him through my lashes
like he was the messiah of sex. Innocent, and oh so
wrong. And the perfect choice, apparently—Aaron's
chest swelled confidently as I parted my lips for a
moment while I took in the sight of him before I
spoke.

"Is this the part where you take me to the station?" I
did my best to look mock-scared, letting the Night fill
in the gaps in my acting ability.

Aaron smirked down at me through his aviators as
he turned me back around to face the car, walking me
slowly but firmly toward the front passenger side
door. "Funny thing about that... See, I was about to
end my shift when you drove by." He came around

my side, opening the door and placing a hand on the back of my neck to help keep my head from hitting the roof, not that I didn't notice the intimate way his thumb stroked along my skin while he did. "Now, it seems a shame to work on my off-time." I settled back into the front seat, hiding any discomfort at having my hands stuck behind me by instead looking up at Officer Aaron with the biggest doe eyes I could manage — something I thankfully had more experience in than you might have thought. I leaned forward to keep up the image of hanging on his every word. Aaron made the barest of smiles as he bent far enough to tuck his head just under the roof. "In the morning, I can take you in for booking." One of those big hands of his pressed into my chest gently, easing me back into the seat again, spreading warmth across my already overheating skin as his fingers fanned out. His other hand pulled off his sunglasses, giving me another look at those twin worlds of bronze and chocolate. "Unless, of course, we can find some…use for you in the meantime." His hand pulled away from me to close the door, and I suddenly felt cold without his contact.

A second later he had crossed to the driver's side and was sliding into his own seat, a fluid motion that could be construed as something of an art considering his height. I watched, somewhere between pretending and truly staring entranced as he reached forward, gripped the key and cranked the ignition, causing the engine to roar to life. The rumble of the motor captivated me more than I could remember it ever having done in the past, the tiny shudders of the frame reverberating their rhythm through me. I turned to look at Aaron, tightening the muscles in my groin to scrape the head of my cock against the inside of my jeans just a little harder.

I opened my mouth to speak, but the moan that stumbled out of my lips wasn't exactly what I had in mind. It sure as hell caught Aaron's attention, though, causing him to turn his head so fast I thought we might fly off the road.

"Don't worry, Officer—I'm sure there must be something I can do for such a big, strong man of the law..."

Aaron turned his eyes back to the road for a quick glance before he looked back at me, unashamedly squeezing his shaft with a shudder while his eyes poured over my arching body again.

"After all... Uhhh..." The line between acting and reality was blurring a little as I rolled my hips again, ramping up the pressure on my dick as I imagined just what tight bunches of muscle and long, delicious planes of skin were hiding under that uniform. My eyes practically rolled back, for Christ's sake! I dragged myself down to Earth for a few moments more to finish what I'd started. "I'm a firm believer in civil service..."

Molten flames smoldered in the space between our gazes as Aaron held eye contact for just a few seconds more, then glanced back at road.

"Shit!"

The brakes screeched painfully as we slammed to a halt, just barely staying out of the intersection as the light ahead of us snapped to red. I jolted forward, not having put on a seatbelt, but used the momentum of my bounce off the dashboard to land exactly where I'd been wanting to go for what felt like hours—the space between Aaron's legs, face first.

I felt a hand slide into my hair softly, carding through it. I shook my head slightly as if shaking off the impact — a move that may or may not have actually been a maneuver to slide my face against Aaron's straining nuts and the rock-hard base of his dick.

I pulled my face up off Aaron's crotch — harder than you might think when your hands are behind your back and you're pivoted sideways across the front seats of a car — angling my eyes up, intending to look up into the officer's.

Those fingers still stroked softly through my hair, rubbing gentle circles while their owner looked down at me with possessive heat. "Careful...don't want you getting hurt."

I was too busy losing the ability to breathe to reply. Somehow, along the path up to Aaron's eyes, I had been understandably distracted by the fucking colossus not six inches in front of me. Apparently Mr Officer wasn't a fan of tenting, because he'd pulled his erection up to lay flat against his abs, held close by his waistband. Fine by me, considering that made it that much more obvious that the head of the thing practically hit his fucking sternum — which on someone six-foot-six wasn't exactly close. It was obviously extending up over the top of his boxers, and I watched as the velvet-wrapped steel rocked with another pulse of blood, pressing it against his shirt where a rapidly growing spot of salty wetness was forming.

The air shuddered out of my lungs as my dick throbbed so strongly I swore it would just explode. My breathe fanned over Aaron's shirt, and I know he felt it through the thin fabric when he groaned loud and low above me, his cock jumping again. Aaron leaned back, and I watched with bated breath as it dragged the hem of his shirt dangerously close to untucking from the waistband of his slacks. The bottom snap was pulled tight against his straining hard-on — tighter still. Aaron rolled his hips downward, increasing the pressure just that little. Bit. More...

Pop!

The snap unclasped, opening a window between the two halves of his button-down at the base of his abs.

Fuck.

Me.

God.

Maybe it was just all the build-up. Maybe it was the Night. Maybe it was because I needed a lay bad, and was horny as fuck.

Whatever the reason, my jaw literally dropped when I caught sight of the throbbing head of Aaron's cock straining behind my little window into pure sexual nirvana, framed on either side by the curtains of standard issue officer uniform.

The air locked in my chest, making my breath hitch. My mouth was still open, though if it was shock or expectation, I couldn't tell — just like I couldn't tell if the closing distance between my lips and that leaking, beautiful shaft was due to my own need or the hand still holding the back of my head, still moving through my hair softly. The voice drifting down from above me, one I was normally used to describing as growling, or deep, sounded almost breathy as it gasped out a question.

"What was that about—" Aaron glanced up at the stoplight with a gulp of air, sporting a look that seemed to say it would soon be green. "Civil service?" His eyes turned back down to mine, and the heat of desire had melted down into something I would more easily call…need. Desperate need. Like Luke's, but so much stronger at the same time.

Lucky for Mr Aaron, it wasn't in my nature to be completely cruel.

I looked up at him one more time, gazing up innocently at the object of my mostly-acted devotion. "I'd say this qualifies." Aaron's eyes lit up warmly as he watched my own drift closed, angling for that opening with my eager mouth wide.

I felt the familiar rumble of the engine kick in underneath me as the light finally turned. I slowed my approach, waiting where I could feel the waves of heat just barely grazing my lips until I was relatively sure we'd made it through the intersection. Then, more or less safe, I rushed forward and made him mine.

I may not have been cruel, but I wasn't gonna give it all to Aaron at once, either. I parted my lips just slightly, keeping my tongue back as I pressed my mouth to his hard length. I slid along the portion I could reach in the small space, increasing the pressure every so often as I graced along his feverish skin. Aaron gasped, and I felt his hand slip in my hair, coming to rest haltingly on my neck where he could keep a better grip.

When I reached the lead edge of his boxers, I inhaled deeply, nuzzling down into the musk of his crotch as best I could. The angles were getting difficult, suspended as I was across the console, and I could feel Aaron starting to falter at the wheel. The last thing I needed was to be involved in another accident, so I decided to cut the teasing for now and give him exactly what he wanted.

I opened my mouth and blew out a whisper of cold air against his cock before finally laving my tongue up the skin I'd been craving to taste for what seemed like days.

Sweat and need and sex exploded across my taste buds, a cocktail of smut that I swear I could have lived off. Salty pre-cum had been pouring down his cock for long enough to leave nearly the whole length slick before I even got a hold of it, and I lapped at it like candy, making Aaron quake underneath me. I pushed closer, leaning myself dangerously far over the center line so that I could swirl my tongue around to the spot where the throbbing head was pressed against his tight abs. The sheer taste of Aaron poured into my mouth as I pulled his cock away from his stomach and into my mouth as we hit a bump in the road, dropping my head down over his. I hollowed my cheeks, ramping up the pressure on his dick before swirling the head one more time and pulling back, letting it slap back against his abs.

I moved to go in for more, opening my mouth to take him in again, when the hand on my neck pulled upwards, dragging me away from my target and forcing me to look back up into those eyes I was getting so used to. I finally noticed that the familiar sound of the engine had ended.

"We're here."

* * * *

A gentle push from Aaron was all it took to knock me off balance, landing backward on the huge bed that practically consumed his bedroom, my still-cuffed hands trapped underneath me. The cop sidled up on top of me as I shuffled back toward the headboard to make some room. It was a kind of mirror of my own moves just a few days before with Zac—shoulders rolling, back arching, predatory, possessive flames burning behind his eyes as Aaron eased his body down on top of mine. Our lips met for the first time, but there was no smooth and slow introduction, no getting to know one another's pace. Aaron dominated the kiss, taking control in more ways than just the freedom of my hands. Fast and strong, five o'clock shadows scraping, and that tongue of his—I guess I shouldn't have expected anything less. It dove into my mouth, tangling against mine in a battle that was heating up fast and definitely leaning in his favor. It was only after its sudden retreat that I realized he'd pushed something into my mouth with it—something that tasted...*metallic.*

I slid the thing forward until I could catch it between my front teeth, then pushed it with my tongue till it was almost out of my mouth so I could try to look down my nose at it.

A key?

I looked up to stare at the now-shirtless Aaron, cocking my eyebrow at the way he was smirking down at me, his warm hands gliding over my thighs. "Freeing the suspect, huh?" I got out as best I could through my clenched teeth.

Aaron's smile widened as his hands went higher, straying dangerously, *teasingly* closer to my screaming erection. "Provided you put those hands to good use..."

I leaned up and tugged at the cuffs, trying to get my hand around in front of my body, something decidedly out of my range of motion. I glared up at Aaron, who was chuckling to himself at my predicament. "Little help?"

"I'm enjoying the view a little too much."

Ass.

Fine. I knew how to improvise. Glaring up at that smirk of his defiantly, I shuffled backward until I could use the headboard to help slide myself up into a kneeling position on the bed. I arched my back so I could more easily roll my head back and to the left, a balancing act complicated even more when I tugged my cuffed hands as far forward on that same side as I could. Just as I started to lose equilibrium I managed to open my hands and turn them palms up. The key slipped from my mouth and bounced off my shoulder, falling down until it landed softly in my waiting grasp just as I lost balance and collapsed backward onto the sheets. I was already opening my mouth to snap off some sarcastic line at Aaron, when I suddenly realized he wasn't kneeling in front of me anymore.

He was actually right above me. Or was for a half-second, before the fucking six-foot-six cop tackled me full on.

The weight of Aaron's body settling down on top of me pushed the air out of my lungs, a point that wasn't made any easier by the way his lips sealed down tight over mine. I was starting to have trouble remembering why that was a bad thing, though.

Aaron's hands slipped up under my shirt, points of heat that slid over cold skin and left trails of warmth in their wake. Something like a purr bubbled out of his mouth, murmuring across my bruised lips, and I longed for the umpteenth time for the freedom of my hands, not that I didn't love a little bondage.

"You're cheating." I managed to shudder out.

Aaron chuckled against me, pulling his lips from mine so that he could move down to my neck. "Well, I didn't say I'd make it *easy* for you…"

The handcuffs and my knuckles dug harshly into my back, trapped tight under my body by the crushing weight of the officer experimenting with just how hard he had to suck at my skin to start a hickey. The key twisted in my fingers, and for a second I thought I might lose it—and that just wasn't happening. *Time for a little multi-tasking.*

I rolled my hips upwards, pressing tight into Aaron's body. He growled in approval and pushed down with equal force, grinding our pelvises together, but I locked up my muscles to keep from losing any ground. In the tiny space under my body I now had, I groped around blindly for the lock on my left cuff, and when my thumb scraped over it I twisted the key into the opening until I felt it click. I turned the key and felt the cuff spin loose.

My lips spread into a smile as Aaron's pressed against them, and a few seconds later, my freed hand wound up in his hair to pull him even closer.

Aaron's mouth only left mine for the barest of seconds as he grabbed my shirt, tugging it up over my head faster than I ever could have. He tossed it backward, grinding his hips down onto mine so that there was no way I could've gotten away—not that I had any intention of trying. When I moved up to reach his lips again, he placed both palms on my chest and pressed me back down into the bed, his huge hands eating up serious real estate as they moved over my exposed skin. My head lolled backward, eyes drifting closed as I felt the magic start to rise inside me. I barely managed to rein it in before something broke, softening it just enough on the way out to instead send power rushing into the ceiling fan and lights. The blades flew into a flurry of motion, kicking the air in the room into a breeze even as the light bulbs flared brightly before going out. Without any magic in his own body to balance mine out, if Aaron wasn't careful more spells were going to start slipping out of me.

I felt him hesitate for a half-second at the sudden change, and I used the distraction to throw my hands forward, locking the cuff down tight on the cop's right wrist, same as mine.

Aaron's eyes flew open, and I couldn't help the grin that spilled onto my face. An expression he returned after a few seconds more, adding to it a growl of approval as he swept his left hand under my body and seamlessly used the motion to flip me onto my stomach.

My left arm got stuck underneath my body even as my right was extended backward, cuffed to Aaron's. He put that hand on my back, holding me in place as he reached over to the nightstand, fumbling with the drawer. I reached down with my free hand, finally unbuttoning my pants and wrenching down the zipper. I'd just made it to trying to one-hand-shuffle my jeans down my legs when Aaron was back, setting down what looked like some kind of bottle of lotion before he rushed to help me get my pants off. I didn't have time to question the odd choice in lube, because in the next second his right arm wrapped around my chest, hoisting me into the air while the cuffs kept my own arm pinned against his. The cop's left hand grabbed the waistband of my jeans and yanked downward jerkily until they finally came off. It wasn't exactly fluid, but he more than made up for it when his hand came back up to squeeze my ass possessively. I moaned openly, and he lowered me back down to the bed, pulling our cuffed arms back out from under me to give him more room to move.

I heard the cap of the bottle snap open, and in the next second I felt those big fingers of his filling and stretching me with a white heat that had me shuddering out a groan into the sheets.

A loud buzz abruptly rocked through the room, drifting up lazily from somewhere on the floor. I twisted my head over my shoulder to see what was trying to disturb us, and from the pocket of my jeans I could just make out the top of my phone. The screen had lit up, and I realized after a second of racking my brain and writhing under Aaron's machinations that it was a reminder I'd put into my phone, a notification to meet up with Luke that I'd made almost a week ago.

For some reason, the thought of the Dreamwalker made something in my stomach tighten. I ignored it, losing myself more fully in the way I could feel the cop lining up our bodies, even though the action was making something in the back of my head rumble. I chalked it up to the annoyance of the phone, and without looking back I let loose a spell of silence to wrap around it, creating a sphere of air devoid of any sound.

I couldn't help the gasp of pain that slipped out as Aaron suddenly thrust into me. It had been a long time since I'd bottomed, and the six-foot-six officer was definitely the biggest I'd ever had to deal with... Needles of pain were rocketing up into my abdomen, but at the same time spiking pleasure made my cock throb underneath me. It was a delicate balance, and I danced across the line as Aaron rammed himself in me all the way to the base.

White points of light burst in front of my eyes. I knew I was gonna have bruises the next day where his free hand was digging in tight on my hip, but the warmth of the fulfilled Night was humming in my muscles like molten whiskey, and the sights and sounds of the scene were burning across my senses with desperate urgency. Aaron's breath on my back, the way he squeezed his hand a little tighter every time he pushed himself in deeper, the moans he wasn't bothering to stifle—they were all a magic of their own, something so much more primal and potent than the spells I could weave. I set my free hand against the headboard and used the leverage to shove myself back harder onto Aaron's length.

I tugged at the handcuff, pulling his arm down under me so that I could grab his right hand with my own, winding my fingers between his so I could direct him to my aching dick. He got the hint, working me hard and fast. I was already close, but I tried to steady my breathing to keep from blowing too soon—Aaron was almost there, but he wasn't quite as far gone as me.

Ramping heat shot up my body like sniper rounds, piercing my mind with every thrust. My skin felt like it was seething with static, but that just made me want more, made the Night inside me rattle its cage and seem to get even stronger with every moan or touch.

Aaron was tightening up, and that made him squeeze my straining cock with that big calloused hand of his even more. I cried out his name, getting dangerously close to the quaking black at the edges of my vision as I started to lose myself in his warm embrace.

Grenades seemed to burst behind my eyes, and I cried out as I collapsed onto the bed, darkness coiling in my mind to the throbbing beat fading out at my crotch. Aaron growled out a moan above me, wrapping our cuffed arms around my chest as he came deep inside me. He fell forward heavily, and I barely had enough mental capacity left to roll to the side so he ended up next to me instead of crushing me into the mattress. I shut my eyes, letting the black there soothe me as the shuddering strength of my orgasm finally drifted away.

Minutes passed, but I was more than content to just lay there catching my breath, floating in the gentle waters of my afterglow for a while longer until I finally decided I needed to move before I risked passing out completely.

I poked Aaron gently in the side, gauging just how knocked out he was. A few more pokes, each stronger than the last, had me pretty well convinced the guy was practically in a coma.

Perfect.

I slid the key from my clenched right hand into my left and spun the cuff so I could get at the lock. With a clack it unlatched, and I promptly rolled over onto Aaron's chest to grab his left wrist and spin the cuff down onto it.

I take it back. That image was perfect.

It was funny how peaceful the officer looked lying there, his hands locked together by his own set of cuffs. Those big brown eyes were closed while he floated in unconsciousness, his close cropped hair mussed. All those tight, naked muscles begged for attention, but I'd already taken more than my fair share of pleasure from them. I slid back from between his legs and stepped off the bed. My hand clasped the key tighter while I rooted around for my clothes, potential futures swirling around in my head, each more devious than the last.

I could string the key up from the twelve-foot ceiling of his living room. That was a great image—Aaron, naked, struggling to set up a ladder and reach the key all while handcuffed. Or I could hide it in the pocket of one of the shit-load of pants he had thrown around the house. Or I could just take it with me, throw in a little blackmail—this game could be even more fun with the roles reversed. I couldn't help the grin that spread across my face as I tugged my shirt down over my head, chancing a glance over at Aaron's sleeping form.

Shit.

The guy looked so innocent... I mean, yeah, he'd just plowed me into the sheets not ten minutes earlier, but asleep he looked so cute, lying there with his hair all ruffled and those big hands of his stuck together with those little cuffs...

Unbidden, images of the future if I took the key rocked across my mind's eye. He'd be late for work, have to explain himself as best he could, which wasn't very well... His superiors would be upset, he'd be hit with a serious reprimand. His bosses hadn't run into me yet, they couldn't understand just what a sex magnet I was.

I turned away from him, looking out across the floor of the darkened room until my eyes strayed onto my jeans. The top of my phone was still sticking out of the pocket, and the notification light blinked a dim green every few seconds like a lighthouse of reality in the sea of sweat and sex I was standing in. My eyes strayed over the cop's body again before settling on the space between my feet.

Fuck.

I stepped slowly over to the bed, sliding the key into the locks of each cuff and slipping them off Aaron's wrists, setting the pair and the key gently on the nightstand when I was done. I turned and walked for the door, shoving my phone deeper into the pocket as I scooped my pants up off the floor.

* * * *

Luke. Zac. Luke. Aaron. Did I mention Luke?

Skin, and smiles, and cuffs, and — *God I feel like I cheated on someone and I'm not even in a relationship* — and just *shit* clouding my mind. I needed to clear my head. And what better way to do that when you're a sexual savant than to go fuck your brains out?

Made sense to me at the time. Or, more truthfully, it made sense to the part of my mind I'd long ago hard-wired to distract myself so I could ignore real problems to try to stay sane.

I hadn't stopped with Aaron — he'd just been the first on the list. Owen, that produce guy, had been the next in line. His roommates hadn't exactly been afraid to jump in either, but no matter how many of them I toyed with, no matter how long I took to work them up and drag them ever closer to climax, I still felt just as disappointed when it was all over. My stock reply was that I clearly just needed more sex.

Owen was going to the university, so his house was relatively near campus. And as it just so happened, I had to drive right past it on my way home, when I went five miles out of my way, wove down three side streets and made a U-turn. In an even greater coincidence, thanks to the roommates, I also just happened to know that the fraternity Owen was a part of was having a party that night. A party where dozens of juiced, buzzed jocks would be milling around with Solo Cups looking for something fun to do.

Personally, I thought I fit the bill.

I swung my car into a spot in the parking lot nearest to the frat house. After everything I'd been through earlier that day, my shirt was a wrinkled mess, and I probably had cum smeared all over my pants, but since I didn't intend on wearing either of them for very long I wasn't going to sweat it. The lights on that side of campus weren't as common as I might have liked, but since any attacker would have probably just turned into some pile of sexual goo at the sight of me, I decided I shouldn't be too worried.

It was that slightly unfounded thought process that resulted in me splitting the difference between two buildings as a shortcut, despite the fact that it was pitch black and the only thing I had to defend myself was a half-hard dick and a half-dead cellphone. I wasn't even a full step out into the light of the courtyard beyond the buildings before a hand was clenching tight over my throat and dragging me off my feet and back into the alley. I didn't have time to *breathe*, much less scream, as the back of my head was slammed against the brick wall of the building, my body held one-handed a foot off the ground.

"You have my aura. *Why?*"

The voice growling into my ear was low, quiet, but utterly furious, and there was a fire in the words that literally ran my blood hot. I gurgled unintelligibly, a reply caught up in the fist trying to crush my windpipe.

I felt the face of my attacker lean in close, and in the darkness I could just make out eyes that swam with an impossible shade of bronzed copper peeking out from under choppy black hair. Once I had the mind to notice the aura rolling off him, I could tell from the churning heat it sparked in me that he was an Incubus.

"I can't hear you, *Seer*." He spat the title with a disdain I'd only encountered a few times in the past.

"*Answer me.*" The words were laced with power, magic that flowed smoothly from his mouth and down my throat, forcing the airway to expand under his hand without him needing to adjust his death-grip.

An Incubus with control of free magic that precise was...unnerving. And definitely not good for me.

"I—I..." I coughed uncontrollably, only managing to reign it in by the thought of the Incubus growing bored and ending the spell that kept air, however little, moving into my lungs. "I'm sorry, I didn't— didn't know the Night—"

A terse growl cut me off as the Incubus shifted his hold on me, lowering me just a bit so he could pull back to look me in the eye. At eye level, I was still almost a foot off the ground. "*Night...*" The word twisted across his lips, and he looked away a moment as though it left a bad taste in his mouth to say it. Not a half-second later, though, his eyes had flown back to bore into mine as he squeezed with renewed vigor. "Who gave it to you?"

My oxygen-starved mind tried to race, but the tar that was flooding my brain slowed it to a crawl. It was all I could do to bring up the words Luke had said to me that night that felt weeks distant.

"A Were— Were-shifter." I coughed out something between a gag and a gasp for air. "Max!"

The Incubus' eyes narrowed for a moment before I saw those full lips of his flicker into the barest of smiles. "York... I'll take care of him soon enough." I let out another gurgling sound as the edges of my vision started to go black. As if just noticing for the first time that I couldn't breathe, the Incubus rolled his eyes and released my neck nonchalantly. I collapsed into a heap at his feet, clutching the stinging skin that I knew must now be covered in bruises.

"Looks like you're in luck, this time." The Incubus took a step backward as if he was going to leave, then apparently thought better of it, moving back in close and crouching down. I tried to quell my violent hacking and gasping breaths long enough to make eye contact with him.

"But know this, Seer. Use my power even one more time, and the Council will have to scrape what's left of you off the *sidewalk* to have a proper funeral." A wash of heat rocked my body, draining me of what little strength I had left. I pitched forward, landing on my hands and knees. *"Understood?"*

I couldn't find the breath to speak, and my vocal cords were probably beyond repair for the moment anyway. I settled for nodding, haltingly.

It seemed to be enough for the Incubus, who, without another word or glance my way, stood and disappeared into the shadows behind us. I let my eyes drift closed, and my limp body teetered forward until my forehead was resting against the cold cement.

Oh. Shit.

* * * *

Warning! Battery below 5%. Connect to a charger.

"Fuck you... Come on, come on..."

Apparently my thought that my phone was only half dead was a little off. I flew through my contacts and opened up Luke's, slamming my thumb down frantically on the Call button. I pressed it to my ear and heard it ring once.

"Please don't die, please don't die, please don't die..."

Beep! *Buzzzzz...*

The vibrator trickled off plaintively as the screen went black. I only just stopped myself from chucking the thing into the ground, no matter how much it had cost.

Great. Just great. I'd just gotten a death threat from what I could only assume was the Incubus that Max guy had fucked over to make the Night, and before I could even tell the only person who might be able to explain why the guy was so pissed — and how to make this shit wear off, like *now* — my worthless, piece of shit, never-shoulda-spent-a-dime-on-it phone had died.

I'd made my way back to the parking lot by that point. Of fucking course I didn't have a car charger for my phone, but that was fine, it wouldn't take long to reach Luke's place anyway. I threw the car in gear and headed down the road, trying to shake off the adrenaline needles coursing through my veins like knives.

* * * *

Somewhere between the university and the turn for Luke's, I inexplicably managed to talk myself down from driving straight to the Dreamwalker's place. It was the middle of the night, Luke was asleep and I should be too, at this point. As long as I didn't seduce anyone in my sleep, the Night aura wouldn't flare and theoretically the Big Bad Incubus would leave me alone. There was nothing to keep me from driving over the next morning, like a sane person.

Funny, how every time I really tried to think something out and be rational about it, it ended up biting me in the ass.

I managed to force my shit-box of a car to limp home, and thanks to the fact that it was almost two in the morning, I didn't run into anyone on the way up to my apartment. No lewd interactions with Two-A or any of my other neighbors, nothing. I practically fell through the door, nerves still leaving my body shaky from my scrape with the Incubus. My rationalization that I should just go home and sleep was probably some kind of self-defense system to keep me from losing it completely—the urge to just block out the problem, slip into the dark unconsciousness waiting between my sheets—it was too hard to resist, especially when I was so *tired*... My body ached with the strain of too many awkward sex positions and the exhaustion left in the wake of adrenaline surges. I barely had the forethought to plug in my dead phone before I was falling forward onto my bed, still fully clothed again.

As I plummeted into the realm of dreams, it never even occurred to me that this overbearing desire to sleep might have a more...*magical* source than biology.

A more sinister source.

Chapter Five

'*Infect me with your love and fill me with your poison…*'

The music roared louder as the latest remixed song pumped out of the speakers, and this time it came with a rush of club-goers all but launching themselves off the bar to get to the dance floor. I was swept up in the motion, pushed by the mass of bodies rushing to be the first one to grind their partner in the laser-lit center of the room. An instant later the solid wall of drunken dancers locked the bar out of view, and I was trapped in the middle of a dark, thrusting mass of heat and bass.

'*Take me, t-t-take me…*'

Bleached-blonde hair whipped me in the face as some girl spun on her heel in the too-tight space of the dance floor. A shoulder ground into my back and I stumbled forward, tripping over a bottle and falling into the tiny space between some jock — I remembered him vaguely, but I couldn't think of where from — and his slut of a girlfriend. The music chose that exact moment to roar into a series of *whirs* and *whomps*, and rather than expressing any concern at me falling literally right into the middle of their little moment, the couple apparently decided that they might as well include me.

'Wanna be your victim…'

Slender hips slammed into my ass from behind in time with the dropping of the bass and the ripped jock who was also at least four fucking inches taller than me did the same on my front, gyrating his hips against my pelvis so that I was relatively sure my lower body was going to be crushed between the two of them.

'Ready for abduction…'

Glow-in-the-dark pink nails gripped the hem of my shirt, slipping up under it and trailing soft hands over the fever-hot skin of my torso. Across my side, over my ribs, coming to rest on my pecs where she tweaked my nipple in a move that made me gasp. The other hand carded into my hair, pulling my head to the right just enough so she could kiss up the left side of my neck.

'Boy, you're an alien!'

The jock's huge, rough hands pressed against my abs, sliding over my skin where his girlfriend had exposed it. Behind me, I felt her pull higher on my shirt, as if trying to get me to raise my arms and take it off, but I pushed against the two of them, panicking. The strobe light rotated over to our part of the floor, turning the scene into a still-shot rapid fire chain of images as the jock pressed closer, tugging the collar of my shirt away from my neck so that he could lick the skin approaching my shoulder on the opposite side of his partner in crime.

'Your touch so foreign…'

I tried to remember how I had ended up in Seethe… Last thing I could think of clearly was crashing on my bed, which triggered the memory of the Incubus. And *Luke...* I was supposed to talk to Luke...

I needed out of this. *Now.*

I shoved my hands against the jock's chest, but rather than backing up he just groaned against my neck before covering my hand with his own notably larger one. He shoved downwards, pressing both of our hands into his pants. If I had thought Aaron gave off heat, that was nothing compared to the furnace this kid had in his jeans.

I pulled away, trying to get my hand back, but the jock squeezed, forcing my fingers to wrap around his cock even as his did the same.

'It's supernatural!'

I was an instant away from screaming Luke's name, which really didn't make any sense, since Luke never went clubbing and wouldn't be there... But it didn't matter, since the next thing I knew a drunk guy doing what he must have thought was a dance of some sort slipped on the bottle I had fallen over myself. It shattered under his foot and he pitched forward, slamming into the jock. They stumbled into the crowd of dancers together, ripping my hand out of his grasp at the same time. Without giving his girlfriend any chance to try to continue in his absence, I jumped forward into the next opening in the crowd I could find, praying that the crazy fucks wouldn't be able to find me again.

'Ex-tra-terrestrial!'

Laser lights punched through the dancers around me, sweeping over my body and blinding me in half-second bursts of color as they shot across my eyes. *Fuck*, the place was ridiculous! My ears were ringing, my body was drenched in sweat that wasn't even mine, I could feel livid bruises starting to appear on my skin and if one more person —

As if to fill in the blank, a girl spun around, slamming into me. I heard something snap, and realized in the half-second pause as she fell into my arms that it was the heel of her six-inch stiletto breaking off. I hoisted her to her feet, then immediately dropped her in surprise.

Lexi — Two-A's girlfriend. What in hell was she — ?

No... Wait!

I spun around, noting idly that the glow sticks that were now twirling above the dance floor must have been some weird new decoration I'd missed last time, and I tried to make out the jock from before. Unless I was really losing it, I could have sworn that was a guy who lived on the floor above me. I'd seen him taking groceries up before.

I turned back to face Lexi, half expecting to see Nick beside her, but she was already back in the crowd of dancers, her heel somehow perfectly fine. Sure enough, though, she was dancing with Nick, and next to them was the couple from Two-B, their neighbors. And wasn't that crazy redhead behind them the lady who lived on the top floor? But that just didn't make sense — she had to be almost fifty, what was she doing in a place like this? Was there some kind of fucked-up party for the whole building? I couldn't remember anything about that, and how had Lexi's heel fixed, and *why* were half of these people suddenly *naked?*

Seethe had gotten crazy in the past, but I'd sure as hell never seen that many people just...take everything off. And the weird part was, as soon as I looked away from where they'd dropped their clothes and tried to look back, I couldn't make them out anymore. I had the strangest urge to go up to Nick and Lexi and ask if they knew what was going on—that, or slide up in between them, take that long, *hard* dick of Nick's into my mouth and run my hand over Lexi's—

No!

I shook my head, trying to clear it of the foreign images that were trying to burn their way into the backs of my eyelids. When I opened my eyes again, I stumbled backward in shock, almost tripping over the people behind me.

The glow sticks swirling lazily above us had broken open, and the luminous trails of orange, yellow, blue and pink fell like syrup from the ceiling. They poured down onto the rapidly-undressing bodies dancing all around me, painting patterns of glow-in-the-dark symbols that I could only just recognize on their bodies as they gyrated without a care. They were symbols of power, images for magic that was complex and ancient. Magic that I could now feel pumping through the dancers like a cloud, coursing through the walls, the floor, even the sound waves, like electrical lifeblood. When I finally honed in on the source of all that magic, I had to close my eyes again to keep from throwing up in fear.

Standing up on the stage of the club, like some arcane DJ, was the Incubus from before. The Incubus whose aura Max had concentrated, amped and unknowingly given to me. The Incubus whose mark I could see clearly painted on the bodies of my dancing neighbors, in the powerful magic that held us all prisoner in this twisted sex fantasy of his creation.

Gavin.

The name came unbidden, and with that realization my eyes opened as well. The only thing that kept me from screaming was the sudden lack of air in my lungs as Gavin stood smiling right in front of me.

I reached for the threads of power within me—I didn't know what kind of spell I would cast, but I had to do something, anything—but I felt only emptiness inside. The Incubus chuckled lightly at that, and a sudden flush of heat from his eyes had me spinning around and backing into his body, my hips grinding back into his in a dance move that I had no power to stop. Only then did I notice that the song had changed as well.

'I can see you stalking like a predator, I've been here before...'

"Not so fast, Cole..." The way Gavin purred the words against my ear somehow made me cold and hot at the same time, rushing heat through my groin and face but leaving my fingers bitingly cold. "Seers can only use magic in the waking world." I gritted my teeth, trying to fight the invisible forces that were coursing through my muscles, making me bend and twist against the Incubus's body. The same forces spun me around again, made my hands slide over Gavin's tanned, feverish skin wherever it was exposed.

'Temptation calls like Adam to the apple, but I will not be caught...'

He chuckled again, pulling me closer. The people nearest us were now completely naked, fucking standing up, on the floor, anywhere they could find room. Gavin turned his body into mine, blocking everyone else from my limited view.

'Cause I can read those velvet eyes, and all I see is lies...'

"Do you need a refresher on what it is to be a Seer, Turner?" At that I finally managed to make some tiny move of resistance, a sporadic jerk of the head that was at a discord with my otherwise fluid, if unwilling, dancing. The Incubus smiled against my neck at that, surging me with more heat to still any more wayward movements. "Yes, I know your full name—Cole Elias Turner. The only Latent Seer in centuries. Born September thirteenth, parents lost on that same date when you were seventeen and nineteen..."

I railed against the power burning through the air around me, but the magic was too strong, reinforced by the marks painting themselves along my neighbors' bodies, growing too powerful for me to stop alone even if I *could* access my magic. The fact that it was a dream made it no less real, and no less terrifying.

'No more poison! Killing my emotion, I will not be frozen, dancing is my remedy, remedy...'

Gavin's hands moved over me, nothing too personal, but the very fact that I couldn't move of my own will made every contact infuriating. "Yes, I know more things about you than even that little Walker friend of yours knows—Cowen." The magic in my veins walked me backward, out of the Incubus's arms to stand a few feet in front of him, still dancing. "I've become quite...*intrigued* by you, Cole, ever since my fingers first wrapped around your throat."

'I'll stop, stop praying, 'cause I'm not, not playing. I'm not frozen, dancing is my remedy, remedy...'

I spun on my heel, a move I pulled off much more successfully than half the girls I'd seen in the club throughout this dream—girls who were now moaning their ecstasy from the floor around me. As I did, my fingers trailed up toward the hem of my shirt, pulling it up just slightly in a move that made the fire in Gavin's bronze eyes burn brighter. I felt something warm hit the side of my neck as I spun my head around my shoulders, only realizing a second later that it was from the glow sticks above. The magic was reinforcing the binding spell surrounding us all, but I also felt something primal in it flicker in response to the currently-dormant power within my own heart. It wasn't much, but I prayed it might be enough, if I could just stall as long as it needed.

'Move while you're watching me, dance with the enemy, I've got a remedy...'

"You said..." Even talking took an extreme effort on my part, my lips only just free of the magic forcing my body to move for Gavin's viewing pleasure. "I needed a refresher in being a Seer?" I pulled my shirt up over my head, tossing it aside and letting electric blue fluorescence pour down over my pecs to trace intricate patterns over my abs. In real life, I would have been terrified of instant cancer, but in the dream, the stuff was harmless—it was its creator I needed to worry about. "Interesting words, from an Incubus."

'Move while you're watching me, dance with the enemy, here is my remedy...'

Gavin's hand trailed down into his skintight leather pants, clearly moving down to squeeze his package appreciatively at my show. He smiled at my words. "Do you know the history of Seers, Cole? Do you know what they were before the Councils came to be?"

I spun around again, showing the Incubus my back as I shook my hips and settled down toward a crouching position, feeling the blue spill down and form marks of power again while I seamlessly rolled back up till I was standing straight. The magic thrummed in my core again, and I closed my eyes, praying it would work—all I needed were a few more marks...

"I was under the impression that they were *Seers*…" I tossed over my shoulder petulantly, rolling my shoulders backward farther than I thought I had the center of balance to do. *Gotta love magic.*

'Spin me faster like a kaleidoscope, all I've got's the floor…'

The Incubus waved his hand, and I spun in time with it, swirling across the dance floor until I was pressed tight against his body, my hands gliding along his legs in moves that made my fingers go numb with the resistance I was pouring into them. "Before the Councils got together and decided they could speak for *all* the races," he purred against my ear as I shimmied back up from my tour of his waistband, "the strongest took what they wanted. The prizes they deserved."

I was biting my lip so hard I could taste coppery blood spilling onto my tongue, but I still tried to ignore the words trickling into my ears, the history my kind had tried to erase from the past—a distraction I couldn't afford when I had to try to get away from Gavin, back into the flow of the glow sticks and the magic they would draw.

"*You*…" The word was whispered with painful grace, and for the first time I gave the force in my body full reign, since even dancing against my will was better than the truth.

The Incubus was smiling again, and only magic could have kept my eyes open now. "Or, more precisely, your predecessors." A hand gripped my chin, holding me in place and forcing me to look up, even as my body danced against his. "Seers were the *pets* of their betters. Playthings, good only for snippets of the future." Boiling hot eyes trailed down my body, looking with a familiarity that made my stomach turn.

"Well—and whatever pleasures their *tight* bodies could bring..." Gavin's finger swirled on my chest, twirling the symbols of power around one another.

'Yeah, you can try but I've found the antidote, music is the cure...'

For the first time, I truly ignored the man in front of me, and focused in on the music pumping down from the speakers above. So far, it had been bizarrely in keeping with all the events of the dream—was this some kind of clue? 'Music is the cure'?

Gavin's hands moved on me, heading lower, but I pushed that physical sensation aside. *Could it be that simple?* The magic was in the glow sticks, yes, but it was in the music too—I could feel it, coursing through the airwaves. And because of that, in its own way, the magic was inside me, rattling around in my head, bouncing off the marks tracing across my body. It was imprecise, but it was there. If I had any luck in the world, it would be enough.

'So you can try to paralyze, but I know best this time...'

I focused all of the energy moving over and through me into one, bright light in the center of my mind. I didn't have control over my own magic in dreams, true, but maybe I could take control of Gavin's. For one, pure moment, I imagined the spell running through my body breaking, leaving me free and ready to run.

'No more poison! Killing my emotion, I will not be frozen...'

I let the light loose, sending it tearing through the music and the marks and straight into Gavin. There was a flash of blue light, a loud *"Fuck!"* and all at once the lights in the club suddenly snapped to black.

Without waiting to see what else might happen, I turned on my heel and ran as fast as I could, ignoring the fluorescence spilling off my bare chest as I screamed out the only thing my throat would voice — "*Luke!*"

* * * *

In the dark, I had no real idea where I was going. I relied on the shaky hope that Gavin had managed to copy the blueprint of Seethe to the letter, because, theoretically, I was in the hallway leading out to the parking lot. Before long, I would hit the door and could really run for it. If I could get far enough away, then the Incubus's power over me might fade enough to let me wake up.

I spun around what should have been the last corner, only to find — nothing.

Sheer black emptiness burned where a door should have existed. I stepped back from it, slowly moving into the more familiar darkness again — it was a dead end. I'd managed to walk myself into a dark corridor with no escape, just like the first time Gavin had found me. I doubted he'd be as accommodating this time.

"*You can't hide from me!*"

Yeah. Didn't think so. The furious roar was *far* too close for comfort, and I knew that, at any second, I was going to know what it felt like to have an Incubus's hand around my throat again.

God, I wish Luke was here... I'd always hated dreams. I felt powerless, which I *was*, and only knowing I had a Walker with me, especially my best friend, made it better.

To my left, I suddenly heard something that sounded vaguely like a transporter from some sci-fi show, and when I turned to look, the black wall had suddenly become a doorway, leading to a hall that kicked the sluggish memories of my mind back into place.

Kelvin High School.

My high school. Where I'd spent four years of my life, wandering down halls just like this, meandering from class to class, usually with Luke. I don't know if it was reflex or self-preservation, but I found myself stepping forward to walk down that hallway again.

"You rang?"

The voice rose up from behind me, and I almost lost my lunch when I thought for a second Gavin might have found me. Then I realized that the voice was nothing like the silken knives of the Incubus.

Gravelly. Gentle. Low and soft.

Luke.

Without a second thought, I spun around and ran forward, practically jumping into his arms as I felt relief crash down over me like I hadn't experienced in years. For one tiny second, there was no Gavin, no Night, no *nothing* except Luke in my arms and just knowing that everything was going to be okay. I felt the Dreamwalker's hands moving on my back, but they didn't go for my ass, or reach around for my crotch. He just held me close, squeezed me tighter like he had on those nights when the guilt and the dark were just too much to keep inside anymore. I felt unshed tears burn behind my lids, but I pushed them down, willed them to go away. I wasn't going to fuck it up by crying.

But as it turns out, it didn't take tears to ruin a moment. A pissed-off Incubus could do the trick just as well.

I felt the oppressive power of his aura sweep into the hallway, and I immediately pulled away from Luke, only what little scrap of pride I had left keeping me at his side rather than cowering behind him.

Gavin was scowling at us from across the hall, his brow furrowed in frustration.

"*Luke...*" he spat, an odd sort of mocking of the way I'd yelled his name earlier. "This doesn't concern you, Walker."

Luke's hand found mine and he squeezed briefly before placing his hand on my arm and gently pushing me behind him. He stepped forward, closing the space between himself and Gavin. "This isn't your dream, Incubus. So I'd say *this* doesn't concern *you*." The words had power behind them, subtle magic that I couldn't understand completely without being a Walker myself. Gavin seemed noticeably unsettled by them, though, which I took solace in. If things started to go wrong, I wouldn't be able to help Luke in any way, without access to my own magic.

"Even *your* kind," Gavin intoned with obvious disdain, "is stronger than *his*. Surely you aren't going to play his *lapdog*, Cowen."

Luke scowled back at him. "There are different kinds of strength. And I wouldn't expect a *worthless, mindless*, sex-driven *automaton*," the words were ones of power again, and Gavin visibly recoiled with each one, flinching back and losing little shreds of his confidence, "to understand the difference between being a *lapdog*, and being a *friend*."

Luke was stalking forward, white lightning coiling over his fingers as the Incubus tried, unsuccessfully, to look intimidating while backing toward the black doorway leading back to the club. Luke flicked his head at the darkness nonchalantly, and the passage collapsed in on itself, sealing Gavin in the hallway with us.

"You're not welcome. I suggest you *leave*."

Luke swung back and hurled the seething brightness at the Incubus. I had to shield my eyes from the glare, but when it hit I heard a boom followed by a sound like sand pouring out onto the floor. When my vision cleared enough to make out the sight in front of me, I couldn't hold back my gasp.

Gavin was slowly pulling himself up to a full standing position, but something was very wrong. His entire right arm was completely gone, leaving ragged tears on the side of his chest, where it looked like the dark solidity that held his dream-form together was trying to stitch itself closed.

Luke didn't give it the chance.

More white electricity boiled a trail across my eyes as it slammed into Gavin's left leg, obliterating it and leaving only dissolving darkness in its place. The Incubus looked truly shocked, though I don't know if it was at the extent of the damage or just the attack in general. Either way, he collapsed to the ground, falling forward. Luke moved still closer as Gavin looked up at him incredulously, apparently shocked out of even anger by the assault. He hoisted himself up just high enough with his one arm to look up at Luke's eyes.

"You can't—"

The magic coiled in Luke's fingers flashed brightly, and his spell of silence took hold in Gavin's throat. Without breaking eye contact, his hands moved above the Incubus's body, letting the white energy pool into a solid plate hovering above his crumbling form.

"Yes, I can."

With a gesture of finality, Luke threw his hands back down to his sides.

The brightness hurled downwards, crushing what was left of Gavin's dream-form into nothingness as black sand exploded outwards and the hallway shuddered underneath us. I blinked a few times to clear the white after-image from my sight, and when it had passed, I saw nothing standing where Gavin had once been.

"Is he...gone?"

The Dreamwalker turned around. Luke was smiling, walking back toward me even as I saw his eyes flare brightly and the hallway around us started to shift. The harsh fluorescents above cooled and coalesced into a single, round sphere of pale light—the moon. The walls faded away, the farthest one shifting backward and transforming into rocky cliffs in the distance, even as the floor shifted under me, becoming soft sand that crunched up around my shoes. By sound and the soft, salty breeze rising up from behind me, I knew an ocean had materialized.

A beach. I was at the beach, with Luke—something that had only happened once before, but in conditions exactly, perfectly identical, to these. The place where I'd told Luke the first real piece of the horrible guilt that lay burning inside me, when he'd taken me there to help keep my mind off the one year anniversary of my dad's death.

"I only forced him out of the dream. I can't really affect his physical body, though he'll have one hell of a headache." Luke was still walking toward me, but with the craziness of the dancing and running and fighting done, I felt so drained I couldn't even stand. I collapsed onto my ass in the sand, only just staying upright enough to look Luke in the eyes as he approached.

The Dreamwalker kneeled in front of me, looking up into my eyes from under the messy brown hair that had fallen down past his eyebrows again. "Did he hurt you? I wasn't too late, was I?"

I laughed, and it sounded almost as odd as it felt, like it was an emotion I hadn't experienced recently enough to remember how to express it properly. "You were right on time. I didn't think you'd actually know to come."

"I told you, I'll always be there when you need me."

It was true, he had said that, and more than once. But even so, the words were spoken with an assurance I wished I had myself. I couldn't look into those eyes, so bright and open in front of me, even if I could see the heat of the Night lurking somewhere in the back. Maybe in dreams the effect was less pronounced, or maybe the adrenaline of the fight had cleared his head for a while. Either way, I was happy for it, and knowing it gave me the confidence to reach forward, pulling Luke into another tight hug.

"Thank you." I struggled to think of what to say after that, but my mouth kept opening and closing like it had more to tell. I managed to rein it in to add, "For being there." But there was more to it than that, no matter how much my mind fought the words.

I finally pulled back, giving Luke some breathing room, but he stayed close anyway, his eyes straying over the remnants of the glow sticks on my chest. The magic in them had broken, but the signs still shimmered in the blue. His fingers reached forward tentatively, and I shuffled forward to bring his warm hand into contact with my cold skin, a silent plea for him to chase away the memory of Gavin's hands there. Luke obeyed.

Slightly calloused fingers trailed over the symbols, tracing them from their start at my neck down my chest and over my stomach. He frowned, and I looked up at his eyes with desperation, needing to know what was wrong, so that I could fix it. Anything to keep his hand on me, his warmth, so I didn't have to think about the Incubus.

Luke kept his hand on me as if he understood what I needed, but he still shook his head, sadness melting down into anger. "These are spells of binding. Control." He looked up, his gaze boring into mine, but I couldn't look away. "*Force*." He leaned forward ever so slightly, flattening his palm against my chest so that his gentle heat seeped down into the heart beating plaintively beneath his hand. "He didn't hurt you?" he repeated, urgently.

Words were slow to come, so I tried shaking my head, but that didn't seem to be enough for Luke, who stayed frozen until I finally got out, "No. I broke the binding before he could do anything other than touch a little. And...watch."

Luke kept his eyes on mine for what felt like an hour more before finally nodding. I barely caught the motion, lost as I was in those bottomless fields of green, but when he shifted back and finally pulled his hand off my chest, that got my attention. I thought he was going to pull away completely, but his hand just slid down to hold my own.

"Are you ready to wake up?"

The thought of the real world—where the Incubus was waiting, and where I had to find a way to get the shit out of my body before he killed me, and where I had to live with the pain and the guilt of being the only Seer in a century who couldn't save the people he loved from their futures—was something I didn't think I could handle quite yet. I tried to say so, tried to even shake my head, but my body wasn't listening.

As if a completely different spell of compulsion, this one coming from inside myself, was pouring life into my muscles, I felt myself shifting onto my knees, sliding closer to Luke. His eyes stayed locked on mine, and I trailed a hand into his hair, tilting his head down just that tiny bit until our lips could brush against one another's.

It seemed to be the answer Luke was looking for.

The Dreamwalker slid forward, settling his body down onto mine smoothly. My legs straightened out and spread, giving him room to slide his hips down on top of mine. His lips moved against mine gently, slowly, nothing like the desperate, gasping kisses I'd been enduring all day from Aaron and Owen. This was intimate. Personal.

Loving.

I knew that realization should have scared me. Hell, if it was any place other than that beach, and that dream, I'm sure it would have. But I'd already shared so much with Luke there, and it *was* just a dream, and God knew I'd had enough dreams of Luke in the past. A little more couldn't hurt anybody.

I opened my mouth to let him in, and my Dreamwalker's hand came to rest so gently on the side of my face, nudging me just enough to make the angle perfect as we kissed. Here in a dream, unhampered by the free radicals of reality, I could finally feel the emotions overflowing through the magic as his other hand traced lazy circles on the marks of power still painted on my chest.

Love. Lust. Want. Need. Desperate, desperate need, and passion, and heat, and —

Night.

All of it, caused by Night. I couldn't feel the power of the Incubus magic, but I knew it had to be there, down at the bottom, directing all those beautiful emotions like a master tugging at the puppet strings. I pulled back before I had to feel it, before the one wonderful thing in my life right now had to be spoiled too. I hated to do it, but I had to pull back physically as well, tearing myself from the kiss and pushing myself to my feet before the black could creep over my walls and stain one of the only good memories I'd made over the last few days.

"I'm sorry, Luke, I... I can't."

He was on his knees in the sand, looking up at me in confusion. "Why can't you?"

"I—" I had so many reasons in my head, so why wouldn't they come out of my mouth? They all made sense. I could organize them in a clean little list in my mind, in order of importance, every reason why it was deeply wrong to take advantage of my friend when he had no control over his own actions. It might as well have been a binding spell on him, forcing him to do things he didn't want to—I wouldn't be like Gavin. I wouldn't do what had been done to me. But I was so caught up in my head that I barely noticed when an item that wasn't even on the list came out of my mouth. "Because, you...you're...*you*."

"Am I not what you want?"

I tried to reply, tried to rush out that that wasn't what I meant, but Luke didn't look hurt in the least— instead, he looked practically *excited* at the prospect. I couldn't figure out why, until he stood in front of me, slowly advancing forward.

"Because here, I can be *exactly* what you want."

I found myself stepping backward slowly, losing ground but too nervous to speed up my pace at all.

Luke's eyes were flaring brightly, with excitement as much as magic, and I started to see subtle changes in him, materializing faster than my eyes were meant to track. "Derek's hair was black. Do you like that better than brown?" His hair grew darker, a swirl of inky blackness that trickled down the strands and pooled there. I didn't even have time to respond before he steamed on.

"And I know you like a guy who's *ripped.*" It was like my dream from earlier, but something was different—his shirt disappeared just like I was expecting, and his abs became cut and his pecs and biceps swelled, but I didn't feel my dick stir like it had that first time. Something felt...wrong. On a very basic level, and I couldn't pinpoint it even as the Dreamwalker caught up with my slow retreat. "Are my muscles big enough for you yet, Cole?" He flexed his arms nonchalantly, and the swelling of the muscles there set something in me on edge. I kept trying to walk backward, but I could feel a wall coming up behind me, not that there should have been one on the beach, and sure enough I was plastered against it a second later.

"And maybe you like them taller—you seem to go for tall guys, usually." Luke's height slowly crept upward, past the half-inch he naturally had on me and even past what I could remember Aaron's being. He still didn't pause long enough for me to reply, as if I could've found some words to give him. As it was, he was probably almost seven feet tall by the time he spoke again. "What if I was this tall for you, Cole? Tall enough that when I press you against something—" He took a half-step forward, his muscular chest nudging me tight against the wall, hemmed in by his warmth.. "You could barely look up enough to meet my eyes." Luke tilted his head down, shrinking himself just enough that he could get close to my ear to whisper huskily. "Is that the kind of man you want, Cole?"

For a second, I almost thought it was. Closing my eyes, just listening to that voice playing across my mind with the kind of intimacy I'd only ever been able to dream of, not experience... But then his hand came to rest on my crotch, and it just felt...wrong. Too big, too rough. It didn't add up with the Luke I knew, with the voice whispering against my neck between kisses. I didn't want the new body, I just wanted that voice, and the man that went with it. I wanted the passion, and the love, and the sentiment that was flowing out of the person in front of me, not the shape it was pretending to be for this brief moment.

I didn't want some big jock. I didn't want muscles, or black hair, or someone tall, or someone who was *anything* other than the scrappy little pothead that Luke was.

I wanted Luke.

I wanted *Luke.*

Then reality came down on me. Which, considering the fact that I was trapped in a dreamscape with a psycho Incubus and my Dreamwalking best friend who was in control and constantly shifting his form — it made the whole experience of *reality* feel a little...*surreal.*

I really wanted Luke. Wanted him forever, not just for a few days while the Night flickered around in my system. I couldn't hide behind the sentiments of, 'Oh, wouldn't it all just be so much more convenient if he were gay, too?' or '*Maybe* I like Luke like that. For now. But only because it's been a long time since I got laid...'

I was in love with my straight best friend. This was real, and it wasn't going away.

And that was very, very bad.

I don't know how I managed it, but somehow, a tiny squeak of an "I'm sorry" managed to cross my lips just before I threw myself as adamantly as I could out of the world of dreams and back into my body.

Back into cold, harsh reality.

* * * *

I slammed to earth with a wave of nausea and disorientation that was unique to hurling yourself out of one form of consciousness and into another. I gasped plaintively, dragging air into my lungs like I had almost drowned. In a way, it felt like I had. My sheets were too close, covered too much of my body. Everywhere something touched my skin it felt like the binding spell had returned, was wrapping itself around me all over again, compelling movement, forcing me to —

I clawed at the blankets, shoving them off until I sat alone in the center of my barren bed, knees pulled up to my chest and shaking.

My eyes scanned across the room, trying to make out the tiny details swimming around in the black. It was dark. Too dark, and I couldn't shake the bone-numbing fear that it would never be bright again. The light switch was on the other side of the room, and I would have to wade through the pressing waves of shadow to get there. In my current state, I didn't think I could survive that. I pulled my legs in closer.

Then the thoughts started to trickle back into my mind, like tar bubbling out of cracks in asphalt, unbidden.

When the Incubus was trying to kill me, or seduce me, or I was in the middle of fucking someone, or, hell, even when I was trying to fend off Luke, at least I had been too busy to stop and think about how I'd gotten in this mess—too busy to remember that I should've been able to *See* all of it coming before it did. But there, alone in the dark, there was nothing to help distract me from the pitch-black maelstrom that it was to be Latent.

A real Seer would have cast wards to keep his mind safe while he slept, so the Incubus-laden future could never come to pass. A real Seer wouldn't have walked into Gavin's trap at the campus. A real Seer would never have *taken* the Night in the first place.

A real Seer wouldn't have let his parents die.

I trailed my hands in my hair, tried to twist my fists until the pain would be the only reason for the tears welling up in my eyes. I was starting to hyperventilate, and I covered my ears to block out the roaring of my own blood, but nothing was working. I was losing control again.

September thirteenth. *September thirteenth...* A good birthday, or at least it had been. For thirteen years it was perfect, then for a few more it was somehow even better. Then they started to get darker, and nothing I did could make them better. Seventeen passed, and a part of my heart was destroyed as cleanly as Gavin's arm had been. Nineteen, and another part was lost like his leg. There wasn't much left, and unless I was a hell of a lot luckier than I thought, I was about to lose that part too. The part that Luke's name had branded itself onto, stronger than any marks of magic.

A horrible highway pile-up had taken my dad. Two years later to the day, my mom was killed in a botched car-jacking. Luke had been with me for each of them, tried to keep me grounded, reminded me more times than I could count that it wasn't my fault, that they wouldn't have blamed me, that I couldn't *help* being Sightless to the people I cared about. But no matter how many times he said the words, there was a dark place inside me that would never be placated, that would always know that, in some intangible way, I was responsible. I buried it under drinking, and clubbing, and video games, and any other thing that could distract me from the horrendous guilt, but it would never be enough to really kill the pain, and one day, something would happen to Luke and—

Blinding pain exploded in my hand, and it took me a few seconds to realize I had turned to the wall above my bed and crushed my fist into it with as much force as I could gather. For an instant, the agony knocked my thoughts off track, forcing a blank expanse of white into my mind so that all I could think of was the pain. I cried out in sheer, blessed relief as I was freed of my own torturous thoughts, and I felt a voice rise up through the white.

No.

No, I wouldn't lose Luke. It didn't matter if I never had him the way I truly wanted again, just so long as he stayed with me. There was no time for misery, or guilt, or pain, just action. I had to get the Night out of my system *now*, before I could do any more damage to our friendship.

The words and the plans were so compelling that I tried to swing my legs out of the bed at that moment, ignoring the darkness and the shadows. But the exhaustion from a lack of true sleep coupled together with the workouts of the day before, and I found that without the terror to keep my adrenaline pumping, I could barely keep my head up.

Tomorrow.

It wouldn't do me any good to be exhausted — I could only guess at what it would require to work away the Night. Powerful magic would probably be called for, and without sleep that was far out of my grasp.

I let my head fall backward, this time in biological need rather than magical coercion. In the morning, I would go see Luke and find out exactly how to make it stop. As it was, I barely kept my eyes open long enough to cast the most basic of sleep wards, protecting my mind from invasion. Gavin would be too spent to trouble me anyway, but it never hurt to be safe.

Hmm...safe... That made me think of Luke, of that moment when he took me in his arms and I could just sink into the warm, close strength of his embrace...

A second later, I slipped back into the realm of unconsciousness.

* * * *

Lips were on mine again. Kissing me, but not the slow and gentle way that Luke's had. These were fast and passionate, just like everyone else's before. It felt good, but like there was something that I needed that was being missed. I tried opening my mouth in return, wondering if that would help me find it.

The lips moved faster, and I heard a moan of approval shudder out over the air. Hands were moving on me, too, but my body was responding sluggishly, like it wasn't sure if this was really worth getting excited about. My cock started to stir, and energy started to flow through my limbs, but it was still slow to come.

My eyes started to flicker open briefly and my hands gripped the hips of the person on top of me. It was dark, but I could tell it was only due to the curtains covering the window somewhere off to my right. Shards of light occasionally flickered out from between them as the air currents rolling off the fan above us stirred them into movement. I opened my eyes a little further, trying to take in the details swimming in the darkness.

I was in my room, which was odd for a dream. Normally, I wasn't somewhere so...mundane. The shadowed figure on top of me pulled backward, staying low over my body and heading for where my boxers clearly showed above the waistband of the jeans I'd wrestled down low on my hips in my sleep. And that was weird, too — the precision to detail was just bizarre, not at all like a natural dream...

The breath caught in my chest. I jerked backward violently, pushing myself back toward the headboard, but the figure on top of me just used that to his advantage, grabbing the elastic of my boxers' waistband as I moved so that all at once my addled, but still hard erection sprung out. The guy practically threw himself down on it, taking my entire length all the way to the base in the most seamless transition to deep-throating I'd ever seen. In the white-hot moment of feeling his arousal rumbling up around the head of my dick, I grabbed at his hair in a panic, yanking his head up enough that I could look into his eyes.

"Oh, *fuck!*"

Jake Hice stared back at me plaintively, brown eyes burning warmly as he tried to push against my hand enough to take me down farther into his throat again. My roommate — the one who I'd thought was still on vacation—my *straight* roommate was trying to practically swallow me whole.

I didn't even think. There wasn't any time, weren't any thoughts that could possibly make sense of this. I wasn't dreaming, this was the reality I had been dreading so much, and obviously the Night was still working its own twisted form of magic.

I yanked backward, dragging Jake off me and inadvertently throwing him off the bed with the same motion. My hands were shaking again, but I ignored it, stumbling to my feet as I tried to get numb fingers to tug at my zipper, put the button back in place on my jeans. I think Jake said something, but I didn't hear him. I was already halfway out of the apartment, scrambling to get a hold of my keys and not trip over myself on the way to the door.

Jake came up behind me while I struggled to remember how to turn a doorknob, still talking, not knowing I might as well have been deaf to him, or anyone else for that matter. There was a void in my head and my chest, something blank and white that I couldn't seem to work around. The only thing I could think of was Luke, that I needed to get to him, that he could make this better. The latch opened with a click, and I threw myself out into the hall, slamming the door shut in Jake's face.

I practically fell down the stairs, stumbling to a halt on the second floor—Two-A was there, opening his own door with an armload of groceries, which he promptly dropped when he saw me. A smile spread across his face, and I saw his mouth moving to form words, but the roar in my ears was too loud again, and I heard nothing even as I saw him reach for the topmost button of his shirt. I bolted again, this time tripping and literally falling down the stairs.

A few somersaults later that somehow managed not to break anything, I was dragging myself to my feet in the lobby, half walking, half crawling my way to the door out to the street beyond.

I ran for the parking lot, already silently praying that my car would start just one more time, the keys jingling in my hand. Only the sight of the bus pulling up to the stop just a few dozen feet to my right made me pause. What if the car didn't start? Then I'd have to wait until another bus showed up, and who knew how long that would take? I was seized by an overpowering sense of urgency, a belief that if I didn't reach Luke, and soon, all hell would break loose. I hesitated for just a second more, taking an awkward half-step in each direction that just made my head hurt with the sudden jerkiness of the indecision. Then I was shoving my keys into my pocket, making a break for the bus stop at top speed before it could pull away.

I literally jumped through the doors, only just crashing onto the floor of the bus before it could pull away. The driver seemed completely unfazed by the fact that there was someone sprawled on the floor of his bus, checking his body for bruises that were surely going to be appearing any second. If anything, he ignored it, turning the volume on the music a little higher so that it would crackle out of the speakers even louder.

With a groan, I rolled onto my knees, relatively sure nothing was broken. But as soon as I did, I felt something sickeningly powerful seeping through the air. For a second of gut-wrenching panic I thought Gavin was there, on the bus, trapping me again, but with a moment to pause and think it through, I realized that the power was pouring out of *me*. The strength in the air I felt was the magic being reflected by the minds it was trickling into — the minds and libidos of the other people on the bus with me.

Fuck.

I hadn't really considered that.

Fuckfuckfuck.

People were moving, starting to stand, coming toward me. Unbuttoning shirts, loosening ties, unsnapping bras. It was all happening so fast, but it was like I was watching it in slow motion, watching a mass of sex-crazed maniacs bear down on me with terrifying grace.

I spun around to face the front of the bus, but somehow the bus driver was still trapped up in his own world enough that the Night at least hadn't started to affect him. That was about my only hope at this point, as I felt the first set of hands coming to rest on my shoulders, pulling me backward, tugging at my jacket and my shirt and my pants —

Magic seethed in my mind, desperate power that didn't have any specific spell to focus it. The energy exploded outwards from me before I could rein it in, flinging people back toward their seats and shattering every window on the length of the bus. The engine suddenly roared, and over the screams of the passengers I heard a smashing sound as the bus flung itself forward, undoubtedly slamming into some car that we had been more than a safe distance from just seconds before I had poured my power into the vehicle. We ground to a halt in the middle of the street, but there was no time for regrets. Already the other people on the bus were recovering from their surprise, returning to the only thing on their desperate minds — me.

Erik Clarke

I dragged myself to my feet, gripping the emergency valve release to let the doors swing open. It was easy, with the protective glass already shattered. I spun it, venting the hydraulics holding the door closed, and fell out onto the street, not even pausing to assess any injuries before I was crawling back to my feet and running as fast as I could.

The bus hadn't gotten very far before the accident, and I knew there must've been almost three miles left to get to Luke's, but I didn't have the capacity to consider the distance. All I could do was run, run as fast as I ever had in my life.

As I flew past people, they turned and started to follow me. Some of them even tried to run after me, but I was just too fast, driven by something in between terror and need. My shoes pounded the cement and I barely had enough coordination and independent thought left to pull off my jacket, torn by groping hands, not bothering to see where it fell.

Magic flowed through me, invigorating muscles and forcing the oxygen into my lungs and down to my legs. But even as it sustained me and my breakneck speed, the magic drained in its own ways, and I knew as soon as I grew too tired to hold the spells in place that the effects of this suicide run were going to come back tenfold worse. But there was no time to doubt myself, no extra air to spend on thinking. It was taking everything I had to outpace the crazed people behind me, and dodge the ones in front of me as they came under my allure.

I sprinted through an intersection, not caring as car horns blared behind me. There was no time for them. I pushed myself harder, willing the magic to give me more speed. My vision was starting to tunnel, the edges turning a ragged black, and I only just jumped high enough to clear a dog that bolted out in front of me. When I landed, my ankle rolled, and I slammed to the pavement, practically somersaulting until I could claw my way back to my feet. The spells shot down to my wound, repairing it just in time as my shoes began to beat out another tune on the concrete. I ran for what felt like hours, minutes that stretched endlessly as I vaulted from block to block.

I was starting to lose control of the magic, worn thin by overuse. Air wasn't moving into my lungs properly—I couldn't get enough oxygen, but I didn't know how to fix it, didn't have time to care. The bile was rising in the back of my throat, my spit thick and viscous from dehydration. Acid was burning in my chest and my legs, but I still ran. I was just two blocks from Luke's place, and the crowd behind me was gaining ground.

With one block left, the wards broke completely. The full brunt of my pain slammed into my adrenaline-strained muscles—no one was supposed to run this hard. I wasn't an Olympic sprinter, for God's sake—I wasn't built for this sort of thing! My ankle spiked with pain, and I fell again just as I entered the parking lot for Luke's building. I couldn't stop the vomit from exploding out of my searing throat, couldn't stop the way my hands shook as I grabbed a light pole to drag myself back to my feet.

The fastest of the runners behind me caught up to me then. Magic was still out of my grasp, so I had to improvise. I spun around the pole just as he reached out to grab me, leaving my leg out in his path. When he tripped he hit my leg so hard he almost dragged me down with him, but I used the momentum to limp to the door of the building, even jogging beyond my strength at this point. As soon as I got in the complex I stumbled into the elevator, pressing the glowing number four and leaning my entire body against the Close Door button.

Just as the fastest group of my very own Cole-addicts burst through the door of the apartment complex, the elevator doors snapped shut with finality. It was all I could do not to fall to the floor with the wave of relief that sound brought.

* * * *

Luke. Luke can help.

I didn't bother to knock, didn't bother to talk, just threw open the door to the Dreamwalker's apartment with a silent "thank you" to whatever power had let it be unlocked. I coughed in pain, clutching my ravaged throat, but the sound was suddenly swallowed by the pair of lips crushed tight over mine. Lips that moved with the force and passion of Night.

Before I could even think twice, my fist was colliding with the face pressed close to mine—the face of the one person who had kept me going through my crazed sprint.

Luke fell backward, slamming into the wall with a look of pure disbelief on his face while he clutched his jaw. He looked up at me, and I could see the hurt and confusion swirling in those eyes, and the steel strength inside me finally snapped.

I fell to my knees in front of the Dreamwalker, barely noticing the tears streaming down my cheeks. My voice was hoarse, choked off by pain and emotion, but I spoke anyway, unable to suppress the shakes that racked my body.

"Luke...please... I can't—can't..." I shook my head, unable to get anything else out, praying that he would understand. Praying to something that I wasn't sure I believed in that some small part of the man I loved was stronger than this Incubus infection sweeping through everyone I touched.

A warm hand wound its way slowly into my hair, and I couldn't hold back the sob as I realized that even that had been too much to hope for. Until that hand was joined by another one, this time under my chin, tilting my head up until I finally opened my eyes to meet Luke's gaze. That powerful green that had helped keep me steady all these years stared back at me, the flames of the Night nothing more than tiny sparks flickering in the back, sealed down tight.

"Tell me what you need me to do."

Chapter Six

There was something distinctly *un*-Norman Rockwell about the scene unfolding at Luke's table. Probably because the most prominent feature of the scene was the blunt the Dreamwalker was rolling, his trusty lighter just a hand's reach away.

Apparently, getting high as a kite would help Luke resist some of the effects of the Night, something that he was currently maintaining only through serious effort, and what I could only imagine was a considerable focus on my own emotionally wrecked state, though Luke was nice enough not to mention if that second part was true. Because really, I *was* a wreck. Wearing wrinkled, torn, cum-stained clothes I'd fucked and slept in, eyes still red from shed tears, hands and legs still shaking from my run. We must have been a sight to behold.

Luke finally lit up, taking a long drag with practiced grace. He kept his eyes closed, shuddering out a sigh of what seemed like serious relief. I could only imagine what it must've been like to fight the aura I was pumping out unwillingly, but at least the weed seemed to be helping. Luke offered it to me, but I shook my head, too sick to think about smoking.

I watched as he put it back to his lips, letting the cloud spin out into the air as it rolled off his parted lips. To anyone else, he would've seemed like any other pothead. And as long as I was being honest, when I'd first met him, I hadn't been able to expect much more myself. But Luke was a stubborn fuck.

My school life had consisted of a constant stream of sarcasm and cynical quips, anything to keep people away so that I wouldn't have to let them get hurt. The Dreamwalker had never bought the act, and had slowly broken down my walls until I'd finally let him inside, and when he'd seen the darkness there he hadn't even flinched. He'd never treated me like I was anything other than a normal person, and that was so *ab*normal for me that after a while I hadn't been able to find it in myself to push him away.

The features had changed over the years, the voice had deepened a little, but the more I looked at him the more I realized that he really hadn't changed, and I was so incredibly thankful for that. But that just made it that much harder to be sitting there, risking everything he meant to me when I knew my good intentions could blow like a time bomb at any second.

"You're not gonna like it when I tell you."

The Dreamwalker was looking at me very seriously, and it took a few seconds to superimpose the image of the real Luke over the one from the past that had been flickering across my thoughts. When I finally did, I still had to shake my head to clear it.

"What?"

The Dreamwalker looked down at his hands, to where the nearly-burned-away joint was resting between his fingers. "The way to get rid of the Night.

When I tell you what you have to do, you're not gonna like it."

I ran a hand through my hair, the shakes finally starting to ease away. I could feel my magic starting to recuperate too, flickering warmly in my chest in a soft way that made me feel better.

"I didn't expect it to be easy, Luke. But I have to get rid of this shit, *now*." *Before I lose you.* I only just clamped down on that thought, turning it into, "Before I fuck anything else up." Still true…though not quite as specific as my mind would have preferred.

The Dreamwalker took a deep breath, refusing to look at me. Then all at once, he turned to face me, the words rushing out so fast I almost didn't hear what he'd said.

Almost.

"You have to fuck me."

For a moment, it was all I could do to just stare at Luke's mouth, at the lips that had formed the death sentence to my sanity that the Dreamwalker had poured out in five little words.

In the next second my head had cleared plenty well enough to let my jaw drop in horror as I felt every plan, every perfectly assembled dream of the future crumble before my very eyes.

"I have to *what?*"

"Fuck me," Luke intoned again, his eyes never leaving mine. "Or let me fuck you, if you'd rather. Just so long as it's sex." It was said with such a bizarre calm that if I ignored the actual words and just listened for the flow of his voice, it didn't completely feel like my stomach was being gutted out with a dull spoon.

I didn't know what to think. Didn't know *how* to even think, when the one thing that I wanted and feared the most was apparently the only future on the table. I had known it was going to be bad, had prepared myself for pain, or exhaustion, or guilt. But I hadn't prepared myself for soul-crushing terror.

I had to get rid of the Night before I ended up having sex with Luke and destroying our friendship. The only way to get rid of the Night was to have sex with Luke. I had to have sex with Luke to make sure I didn't have to have sex with Luke. Sex. And Luke. And Luke, and sex, and *fuck,* and I didn't realize that I was really a bad enough person for karma to hate me quite this much. My brain felt like a ship in a storm, anchored to my body but tossing and crashing in violent circles around my head while it tried to work out something that had no answers and even fewer good ones.

Someone was kissing my neck. Logically speaking, it had to be Luke, since he was the only other person in the room, but that wasn't quite clicking the way it should. I was relatively sure my mouth was still open while I stared out at nothing, too, but I managed to rein it in enough to form some words.

"Why... Why does— Mpmh!" Suddenly a mouth was on top of mine, trying to silence me with rushed kisses and tangling tongues. The urgency of the situation managed to take hold in my muscles, stirring them to action faster than any of the other times Luke had made the moves on me. I pushed him away, grabbing him at the shoulders to hold him just far enough from my face that I could talk to him.

"Why does it have to be sex with you?"

That was the part that I couldn't quite figure out. Having to have sex with the Incubus whom it came from—that thought made me shudder—or even with Max, who had made it, were logical possibilities in their own twisted way. But with Luke? That didn't exactly compute, and if there was any way to avoid it, no matter how painful, I would—

Luke shrugged noncommittally, pushing against my hands to get closer to me. "Well, it doesn't *technically* have to be me, but I'm the best option…" He said the words in passing, still trying to reach my lips, apparently not realizing that he might as well have just said I had won the contents of Fort Knox.

I almost kissed him right then and there, I was so relieved, but after a pause to think about that it seemed understandably counterintuitive. Instead I kept him at a distance, intent on knowing everything before I got my hopes up too high. Because if faced with a choice between sex with Luke or Gavin, I knew I'd have to pick the Incubus, but the image of him looming over me in that twisted fantasy version of Seethe still made the bile rise to the back of my throat.

"Who are the other options?"

Luke paused in his efforts to look up into my eyes in confusion, as if I'd just asked him what color the sky was.

"Anyone with a dick?"

I'm sorry, what?

Fury like I hadn't felt in years tried to explode into being in my chest, and only my sudden obsession with getting all the facts straight let me keep it locked down tight. I couldn't stop my hands from tightening down on Luke's shoulders like vices, though, as I held him deadly still so I could ask my question before I lost it completely.

"Wait. You mean, I can have sex with *anyone* to make the Night go away?"

Again, he looked at me like I was nuts for asking him something so obvious. "Well, *yeah.*" He shrugged. "Sex with me makes more *sense,* but anyone would work."

I didn't have a chance to consider how that made 'sense'. I didn't even have time to think about the fact that I'd already had copious amounts of sex and that had only made the situation worse. All I could do was sit there while I felt like my head was splitting in half.

"That would have been a nice distinction to make *before* I almost lost my mind, you *fuck head!*" I realized that I was suddenly on my feet, practically screaming at the Dreamwalker, but I couldn't make myself quieter and for his part Luke didn't seem to care much, still staring at me with the beginnings of a smirk on his lips. I wanted to just crush those lips against mine until he really had something to smirk about, but I didn't have time to think about that mental image.

"But... How can the answer be sex? I've already —" My mouth suddenly stopped working at the exact moment that Luke suddenly seemed most interested in what I was saying. His eyebrow rose, and there was a kind of heat in his eyes that didn't look quite the same as the Night. It was something more...possessive. I swallowed. "Already...done it...since I took the stuff."

Luke was quiet for a while, still leveling me with a look that had me sitting with my head down and my hands in my lap, like a misbehaving kid or something. When he finally spoke again, I was able to pull my eyes up just enough to watch where one hand was fiddling with the zipper of the jacket he had tossed on.

"Well, that's probably part of the problem, then. Night is fueled by sexual attraction and drained by the orgasms of anyone under its effects—so the user *and* their partner." Part of my mind wandered to consider how it was odd that Luke could be remarkably coherent when he wanted to be—especially if he thought his words would get him closer to sex. "So basically, if you have a lot of foreplay, you're stockpiling the Incubus power in your veins, making it stronger. When you come, it drains it, but in your case, not enough. Now you've just made it so you'll have to work even harder to work it off the *next* time you have sex, which usually translates to more sexual attraction but still only one orgasm each, so you're still screwed."

The other part of my mind was looking with widening eyes as Luke's hand trailed downwards, moving from jacket zipper to the zipper on his jeans. My mouth started to open, and I think it was to ask him to stop, but no words came out and I still wasn't looking away by the time he started to talk again. "What you need is a good fuck. One that'll have you coming more than once. One with someone who knows *exactly* what you need..." I watched speechlessly as the zipper dragged downwards, metal teeth separating with terrifying slowness, even as the other hand came into view to tug at the button. "In other words, me!"

The last word was said with so much excitement that I finally managed to drag my eyes back up to Luke's, just in time to see him smiling happily. Put like that, his logic actually seemed relatively sound.

Too bad there was no way in hell I could do it.

"You...need a cold shower."

Luke's brow furrowed for a second. "I thought a bed would make more sense, but if you wanna do it in the shower, I could—" The Dreamwalker was climbing to his feet, tugging down at his now-wide-open jeans. I tried to tell him to stop, but I knew that even if he heard me in time he probably wouldn't listen, so I panicked. I rushed forward, trying to stand, but my foot got caught on the leg of the chair and I fell to my knees. My hands didn't seem to get the message, though, and they followed through with the original plan—grabbing the waistband of Luke's jeans and boxers to keep him from pulling them down.

So put simply, I was on my knees in front of the Dreamwalker, looking straight forward at the hard line where his dick was pressing into the denim, my hands on the top of his jeans, my fingers somehow plunged under the elastic of his boxers in an effort to hold them up. Fingers that were now burning up with the heat of this disturbingly intimate part of my best friend's body, tips brushing against soft hair leading down to—

Fuck.

Apparently my position was enough to shock even Luke's Night-riddled brain, because he was looking down at me with as much a face of shock as I was currently giving his crotch. For some reason, my brain decided that meant I should just pretend I *wasn't* currently in prime blow job position, and ask a perfectly normal question instead of scrambling to my feet as fast as I could.

"I thought—thought you said the weed would help?"

There was a subtle shift in Luke's stance as I felt the surprise relax out of him. He started to move against my hands, pressing into me just lightly enough that I didn't run away. "Guess I lied." He grinned slyly, and I looked up at him in trepidation, half convinced that if I moved too quickly in any direction the

Dreamwalker's pants would just fall off completely, or he'd somehow find a way to make this position even more terrifying without even needing to take them off. I was so concentrated on keeping my body perfectly still that I almost missed it as Luke arched his back, biting down lightly on the thumb that had been playing with his lip a second before. "Does that mean I've been a *bad* boy?"

Damn, Night was some cruel shit. The thought of vanilla sex with Luke already made my heart snap. Getting kinky with it was just beyond my capacity for feeling right then.

Heat was rolling off Luke, and I didn't trust my hands to do the job, so I reached out with my magic and forced his zipper back up into place, clasping the button as well. As soon as I was done I snapped my hands back like they'd been burned, stumbling to my feet at the same time.

"Come on." I pushed past him, heading back toward the other half of the apartment. Luke scrambled after me excitedly, and when I slowed in the hallway he raced past me toward the bedroom. I caught his arm just as he did, using his momentum to spin him into the bathroom.

"What're — ?"

I ignored him, stepping past to pull back the shower curtain and twist the handle to send frigid water pounding down onto the porcelain.

"I was serious about that shower." Surely where weed had failed, the old fallback of cold water on a naked body had to work, right? I forced a spell to flow down through my hand, locking the temperature in place.

"We're gonna shower together?" Luke's voice was gushing with barely contained excitement, and I could practically feel him bouncing up and down behind me.

"No, you're gonna—" Hands wrapped around my waist, pulling up at my shirt to get a hold of my belt. "Luke..." I growled out in warning, not even bothering to look backward as I struggled to make the spell set when he was distracting me in the worst way possible. The hands pulled backward hesitantly, then shifted to wrap around my chest solidly as Luke crushed his body to mine in an unwavering hug.

I ignored him, ignored the way my jeans were tightening in response, ignored the blush rising to my cheeks. Satisfied that the spell was solid enough I disentangled myself from Luke's arms and headed for the door. "Shower." I stared Luke down as I said it, trying to push some level of magic into it as well, but I'd never been good with compulsion spells. I felt the power flicker against him, but it didn't really take hold, crackling along his skin instead. It seemed to be enough though, since a second later he was frowning slightly and tearing off his shirt.

I spun around and practically fell into the hallway in my rush to get out before I saw more. I closed the door without looking then slumped back against it, sliding down the wall to the floor.

God, I was fucked... I'd always told myself that I wanted to help Luke, because it seemed like in our friendship he was always helping *me*—I was the one with all the issues. But this definitely wasn't what I'd had in mind, and right then it felt more like I was orchestrating a clusterfuck rather than 'helping' anybody. Not for the first time, I found myself wondering what in hell I had to offer Luke that could explain why he had stayed my friend for so long. Honestly, it wasn't like *he* was the one who was constantly having breakdowns about his parents, or getting so wasted that only magic would help bring him back. I had the patent on those tricks, whenever the thinly-made guards I put up in my head and heart broke down and I had to actually face the problems in my life, instead of pretending everything was fine behind veils of sex and Smirnoff —

"Ow, *fuck!*"

The shout was paired with that sound that only comes from skin slipping on porcelain then slamming down onto it. Without even a thought to the fact that, fallen or not, Luke was going to be naked and probably hard, and that I was about to run *into* the exact scenario I'd been running *from* for days now, I tore open the door and stumbled over to the shower. I pulled back the curtain, a hand already extended to help Luke up and a spell of healing on my lips, only to find...nothing.

Water cascaded down into an empty tub. I barely had a second to wonder how in hell that was possible when a pair of hands slammed into my back, shoving me forward into the flow of the water. My shins hit the edge of the tub and I fell down, too fast to get my hands up and try to slow my fall. I saw magic flare in front of my face, a shield spell cushioning the fall before I could break something.

Frigid water pounded into my clothes, soaking me through in an instant, and I struggled to roll over in the tight space of the tub. My legs were too long, and when I finally managed to turn over onto my back, slipping and squeaking all the way, my hair was drenched and plastered to my face. I flipped it out of the way to clear my eyes, throwing droplets of water up into the air.

Droplets that immediately sizzled into steam as they hit Luke's naked body.

The Dreamwalker was standing over me, his legs spread wide enough to frame my body. Much as I tried — and I swear, I really did try — my eyes couldn't avoid the rock-hard evidence of just what I was doing to him staring down at me. I closed my eyes, because fuck if it wasn't beautiful, if *he* wasn't beautiful, but the image had burned itself into my eyelids.

I had known it wouldn't be anyone else, had felt the familiar marks of his power flowing in the shield spell, but somehow, some tiny part of me had still held onto the chance that this was all some trap designed to kill me, instead of one designed to tear my heart out.

I felt Luke move above me, and only gut-wrenching fear tore my eyes open enough to see exactly what he planned on doing. But unlike the explosive slideshow that had burst to life in my mind — scenes where Luke tore at my clothes, forced me to finally face just how much I wanted him — the Dreamwalker slowly lowered himself to his knees, shuffling forward until he was straddling my waist.

The worst part was his smile. Because it was still so perfect, still so clearly *Luke* that it made it that much harder to chalk it all up to Night. He smirked down at me gently, with an infinite understanding that scared me even more than the fact that he was naked and on top of me. Luke ran a hand through his soaking hair to push it back out of his face, and I finally caught sight of the marks of heat and warmth rushing over his body amid the droplets, marks that combated any effect the cold water might have had. Wherever the water touched the spell directly, it sizzled and burned up into the cloud of steam that wrapped around the

Dreamwalker, making an already surreal situation that much crazier.

I stared up at Luke's eyes, the only thing in this nightmare/fantasy that didn't leave me completely terrified.

"H-hi."

It was quite possibly the weirdest thing I could have said in that situation, but it was the only thing that came to mind.

Luke's smirk immediately broke into a grin as he chuckled softly, running his hand over my arm. "Hi."

I couldn't decide if it was worse to have my eyes open or closed, and at the same time I cursed myself for making the water so damn cold. The drops streaming down from Luke's body onto mine were warm, but the shower pouring down on my chest and head was icy. I was still too scared to move and now I *really* didn't know what to say, so I tried to just lie perfectly still and not breathe.

I knew Luke's eyes were still on me, but I tried to focus on his mouth instead, something neutral that wouldn't make my heart skip too many beats. Just when the silence and the hand on my arm and the *serious* lack of air were all combining to make me implode, Luke finally showed me some mercy by speaking.

"God, you're beautiful, Cole…"

O-oh, Jesus, never mind.

The breath that had been rushing out of me in relief immediately turned around and flew back down my throat, and my eyes opened so wide it was a miracle they weren't immediately flooded by the water pouring down me. My gaze shot up to meet Luke's, hardly able to believe what I'd heard.

Luke was staring at me with something I'd never seen in anyone's eyes before, a kind of mixture between sadness and reverence that I knew I wouldn't be able to mimic even if I'd had the desire to try. And the way he'd said the words, with something almost akin to guilt, it just didn't make sense, and that somehow scared me even more.

He reached forward, running a hand gently over my soaked shirt, trailing down from my chest to my abs. His eyes followed his hand at first, then locked back onto mine with that same look swirling in the green. "People never really tell you that, do they?" The Dreamwalker sounded truly heartbroken, and I felt myself trembling under the intensity of the emotions roiling off him. Magic flared in his eyes and his hand, and I spared the tiniest glance downward to watch as my shirt dissolved into black wisps of steam that effervesced into the clouded air around us, leaving my chest bare under his fingers. "Even now, with the Night, when people are obsessed with you —" His soft hand traced gentle circles on my skin, warming it. I wanted to look away in shame at the way the gesture was making my dick throb under his hips, but I was too captivated to turn away even for that. "It's all about *thrusting* and *coming*, and never about how truly beautiful you are."

I couldn't breathe. I didn't know *how* to when my heart was slamming like a jackhammer in my throat, choking off anything, air *or* words. No, no one had ever said that to me before, and I was glad, because this felt like something in me was going to blow apart. There was too much feeling in a space that small, bouncing around between tub walls and flimsy curtains.

Luke bent forward over me, his hands trailing up to cradle my head. His body shielded me from the cold water, letting it pound harmlessly against his back as clouds of steam swirled around us. Heat washed into the drain under me and rolled down off the Dreamwalker's body from above, sealing me into comforting warmth.

"None of them know you like I do..." He said the words softly as he brushed aside the hair that had fallen down over my eyebrows, a quiet truth that I almost wish I hadn't been able to make out over the pounding of the water. Because it *was* the truth, and that made it hurt that much worse, made it burn in my cheeks as Luke bowed his head over mine to place a soft kiss against my forehead.

I didn't know what to say, so I just let my hand run through Luke's hair, gently stroking his head as he moved down to nestle against my shoulder, leaving a warm trail of kisses over cold skin. Somehow that seemed like it was okay, like that didn't break any unspoken rules of intimacy since I wasn't the one doing the kissing. Surely it couldn't destroy a friendship to show *some* sign of the unwavering closeness I felt to the man pressed against me? It wasn't really evil to take this little bit of artificial love, was it?

Luke was moving down my arm, lifting it so he could get a better angle for his kisses. I stared at the top of his head dimly, watched as my fingers stole through his hair and he laced my skin with warmth. It was only when I felt something tug in my chest that I realized that it was my right arm he was touching— and that my Seer's Mark was burning against my skin, the three lines of past, present and future and the circle for the Sight standing out in livid black on my wrist. Luke drew closer to it, and the future line rippled, jerking on my skin in a way I hadn't known was possible.

Needles stabbed into my skin where the Mark sat, and the threads inside me hummed painfully. Magic was building up inside my veins, but I didn't even know where it was coming from, much less how to stop it. I tried to open my mouth, tried to ask Luke, but my throat wouldn't work. My muscles refused to answer me either, locking tightly in position as the Dreamwalker's lips moved ever closer to the black.

A crack of white lightning burst on top of my right eye, followed by one on my left, like wavering tracer rounds skittering over my retinas. My threads shook harder, twisting and bending as devastatingly powerful magic coursed through them. Luke couldn't have been a half-inch from my Mark, but the world had ground down into slow motion as fields of white started to cloud into being at the edges of my vision — I tried to scream, or even cry, but my body wasn't mine to control anymore, nothing more than a conduit for something that I couldn't place and couldn't avoid.

Luke's mouth settled down onto the arching, bending black, and I realized in that single second with perfect clarity that he was just as powerless to stop this as I was — a realization that was of little use when I felt my threads of power jerk violently once, twice, then something inside me suddenly snapped.

Ice cold power exploded in my veins, rocketing down to my arm and colliding with the answering magic pouring out of Luke's lips, a metaphorical train wreck on a colossal and magical scale. Something that was somehow more than both of us and yet *purely* us intertwined at the point of my Mark's line for the future.

With an inconceivable boom, I felt myself tear free of my body, thrown backward into the foreboding infinity of Sight.

* * * *

Visions came in different forms. In some, the Seer filled the role of a silent, omniscient observer. In others, I took on the viewpoint of a single person. Some had other senses — smells, tastes or feelings, but the most common is sound. It's rare for a vision to be silent, but since nothing else about me was especially common, I wasn't too surprised when this Sight came without sound. But I was confused when, at first, it didn't seem like the vision had any *sight*, either.

Complete darkness enveloped my gaze, an odd change, since usually visions were flooded with white emptiness, rather than black. It took me a few seconds, or minutes, or hours — time doesn't flow quite the same in Sight — to notice that the black was getting lighter, growing browner, more *tan* at the edges, creeping with delicate slowness to the center. I realized after a few moments more that the 'viewscreen' of my Sight was pulling backward from a shot of what seemed to be skin, but that it was moving in a kind of slow motion I'd never experienced during a vision before. The view pulled back just far enough to make out what looked like someone's stomach, the subtle lines of their abs just evident.

All at once, a beam of purple light burned across the view, flying past the person's body even as the Sight panned up it just as slowly as it had pulled back. With the new angle, it became clear that I was looking at a shirtless man in profile, my gaze slowly moving up his body even as more lasers careened around and over him, in shades of purple, orange, and red.

A hand entered my view, but from the angle it must have belonged to a second person, standing right in front of the first. Confident fingers traced paths along the waist and abs, trapped in detail by the slow motion. It was obvious enough that whoever those hands belonged to was more than just a friend to the man who was the focus of the vision. Under the wavering lights of the lasers and the strobes, it was hard to make out defining characteristics, but one thing was clear—the way those hands were moving, both men knew they belonged there, that they had some claim to the skin they were touching.

The view pulled higher up the man's body, coming level with his pecs just in time to suddenly turn ninety degrees to the left and shoot backward a foot before slowing again to a crawl. As I tried to adjust to the sudden shift, the arm of the first man came up into the Sight. Two glow-stick wristbands smoldered eerily in the darkness, pink and orange swimming together in the laser-light-punctuated black. His hand wrapped around the biceps of the second—the man I now realized was on top of him, rather than in front of him. The bottom's fingers squeezed tight for a second, then started to slip, shuddering under the strength of some unknown force within him.

As bizarre a situation as it was, I realized quite suddenly that I actually knew *exactly* what that force was—I'd seen and felt it myself plenty of times. The bottom was getting close.

The view started to speed up, scrolling to the right to make up lost ground, again coming level with the bottom's chest. Then it ground to a halt again as everything in view shuddered into slow motion—a red laser seethed across the Sight, blocking my view for a few seconds before moving out of my gaze, leaving only the bottom, his back now arching so strongly his head must've been completely rolled back to still touch the ground. Even without the sound, I knew he'd just come—and whoever his top was, it looked like he knew *exactly* how to work his lover. That orgasm just looked painfully strong. As if to reinforce my point, it panned back to his hand, now death-gripping his top's biceps so strongly that he left trailing red marks as his arms slipped down in languid afterglow. But in the next second, the view was moving again, flying up his body so quickly that I couldn't make out any details until it ground to a stop over his face.

Or at least, it stopped where his face *should* have been. Just as the Sight slowed enough to have made his face actually visible, a cloud of smoke burst into life, pouring out from where I knew his mouth and nostrils must've been, not that I could see them under the billowing white. At first I thought the guy must've taken a hit or something, but I couldn't remember having seen a cigarette or a joint—and, more importantly, there was something not right about that smoke.

Drifting in the white-gray haze were marks of power, just visible when the view pulled the world into an even slower speed. Symbols of powerful, primal magic—marks of lust, passion, want, need and desire, crackling in the smoke as it drifted out of the man's lungs. I couldn't even begin to imagine how that was possible, or how any of this was even relevant, until the Sight came to what seemed to be a complete stop. Then in the next instant, time rushed forward, clearing the cloud of smoke in a half-second just as the bottom's eyes suddenly snapped open to bore into the view of Sight. *Blue* eyes.

If I hadn't already been disembodied, I think I would have thrown up right then and there.

The face I was staring at was my own.

* * * *

White stabbed forward from the back of my mind, piercing my line of sight with tiny pinpricks of nothingness until I couldn't see anything beyond the void. Then, just as quickly, the ivory needles rushed backward with a roar like pushing through a waterfall.

I gasped painfully, my lungs burning from a lack of air. Almost as soon as I had enough oxygen to manage it I started screaming out an inventive stream of curse words—my head felt like it was cracking in half, throbbing with a pain so intense I could hardly keep my eyes open. Something in my chest ached in a way that had nothing to do with my lungs, and I knew that if the threads of power within me had actually been tangible in some way there would have been livid bruising on my skin where they'd almost broken under the strain of whatever energy had poured into them.

With that observation, my brain finally became accustomed enough to the pain racking my body to let other thoughts blossom in the new open space— thoughts that left me more unsettled than any measure of pain could.

I had had a vision of myself. I'd had a vision of *me* – but no one who was Latent suddenly *became* Seeable, no matter the circumstances. I somehow knew without even trying that I still would see only white if

I tried to view my future, and that even if Luke were to kiss my Mark again, nothing would happen. But it *was* me in that vision, I knew that more powerfully than I'd ever known anything in my life. Yet even that realization didn't make anything simpler, because the first vision a Seer ever had of themselves—the first vision they had *period*…

It was always the vision of their own death.

But that wasn't the first vision I'd ever had, and I seemed to be doing anything *but* dying in it. I couldn't understand how it was even possible for me to have Seen what I'd Seen, much less how it might factor into some kind of loophole around the whole death caveat. I'd been spared from Seeing that when I'd had my first vision at thirteen, when only blank white had burned across my mind, and it seemed like whatever force had managed to combine my powers with Luke's to override my Latency had decided that I should be spared again. But that just raised more questions than answers, and—

"That's gonna be me."

Luke's voice cut through my thoughts, made me suddenly remember exactly where I was—and who was on top of me. Naked.

"What?"

Luke had let go of my arm but was still poised over me, his body maintaining the heat shield that kept the thundering water from chilling me to the bone. I realized as the question came out of my mouth that I still had my hand in his hair as well, and I went to pull it back. Luke reacted with a speed I'd never seen before, catching my retreating hand with his own and pulling it tight against his chest. I could feel the steady beat of his heart, and that helped put me a little more at ease.

"*I'm* going to be the one that makes you feel that way. The one who finally cures you of the Night." Because that's what it had been, I realized — the Night, venting itself out of my body once and for all. But that Luke would be the one to do it... He said it so adamantly, like it was set in stone in a way that nothing about the future ever really was. I was a Seer, after all. If there was one thing I knew about, it was the mechanics of potential timelines. I almost started to explain that to him, anything to keep from thinking about what I'd just had to See, about what that would mean if Luke was right, but my mouth had other ideas.

"No, Luke. No, you won't."

The Dreamwalker just stared at me for a beat, his brow furrowing in confusion. Then in the next second he was letting go of my hand, twisting his own fingers up into his hair as he let out a growl of frustration, shaking his head. If I hadn't been trapped underneath him I probably would have been backing up as far as I could — in all the time I'd known him I'd never seen Luke look anything more than a little annoyed. In contrast, this seemed practically dangerous.

"Why do you keep *saying* that?" His hands came down to his sides in an expression of aggravation, and I couldn't help but flinch. Luke didn't seem to notice, instead leaning forward farther to place a hand solidly on my chest. "You *know* you *want* it to be me!"

I closed my eyes, trying to hide from his gaze and his words, but he wouldn't let me. Luke grabbed my chin, lifting my face and refusing to budge until I opened my eyes.

"Don't you love me?"

Something cracked inside.

I couldn't look into those tortured eyes, flooded with desires and demands that I knew he had to be fighting with everything he had to keep from just stripping me and having his way right now. I couldn't look into that open, unguarded face and lie.

But I couldn't say the whole truth, either.

Somewhere in between the two, my mouth stumbled through as best it could.

"Luke, you're my best friend. And I do love you." I finally couldn't keep my eyes open anymore when I saw something that I didn't even want to imagine lighting up behind the Dreamwalker's Night-flooded eyes. I took a breath and finished, "But not the way you mean."

I felt the hand on my chest start to move just slightly, the fingers fanning and the thumb rubbing soft circles into the bare skin. I opened my eyes, but Luke wasn't looking into mine anymore—he was looking down, to the point where our bodies were touching. The point where his hard cock rested on my own, a thin layer of soaked fabric the only thing between our erections. "Not yet."

My eyes shot up at that, but Luke seemed completely unfazed by the words he had said. He just tossed them out in passing, like they were as guaranteed to be true as any vision had by a Seer.

I… I didn't know how to feel about that.

* * * *

With a little creativity, I'd managed to get out of the bathroom without embarrassing myself further or taking any more sidelong glances at Luke's tight body. In the hall I'd somehow dragged together enough magic to dry off my clothes, but the missing shirt was a different story — the Dreamwalker had muttered sullenly that I could wear one of his, though I noticed there was a distinct lack of an apology for vaporizing my old one. Luke stayed in the shower while I went to root through his closet.

I knew what I needed to do, and if I stayed near Luke much longer I was going to cave and just let him do what we'd both been wanting for days now. My body burned everywhere his skin had been touching mine, and my Mark still tingled with the ghost of the Dreamwalker's lips, and against my better judgment, I pressed a kiss to the same spot reverently.

If sex was what it would take to get the Night out of my system, then I would do it. It couldn't be that hard, right? I'd done the cop. The produce guy and his roommates, too. Yes, it would hurt, feel like I was cheating on the one person whom I really wanted, but if I did it once, I could do it again.

You sure about that?

The voice in my head mocked me with dripping cynicism, and I tore a random shirt from its hanger in frustration. As soon as I'd tugged it over my head, I was practically running out of the door, shouting over my shoulder to the towel-wrapped Luke that I'd see him later.

If this didn't stop soon, I wasn't sure I'd survive it. The Night needed to end now, and things would go back to a semblance of normal, and if Luke would let me, I'd spend as long as it took to patch together the pieces of the friendship that I'd shattered when that damn vial had first touched my lips.

I wasn't going to let my Dreamwalker down. Not again.

Chapter Seven

Common sense stated that I should probably go to Seethe to try to work off the Night. Last time I'd checked, I didn't have laser lights, strobes or glow sticks in my bedroom. But the Seer in me railed against that argument, insisting that any vision was just of a possible future, the most *likely* future, but not necessarily an assured one. I could make my own future. End the reign of the Night here and now, before I might somehow be lured into finally ruining everything with Luke once and for all. There would be no foreplay, no making out and gentle touching. Just fucking and orgasms, a Night-draining workout that would be free of emotion and completely impervious to efforts for romantic validation. Yes, I needed a good fuck, like Luke had said, which was why a few minutes later I found myself escorting a lovesick-puppy-eyed neighbor I found in the lobby into my apartment.

I fought so hard to keep it clinical, emotionless. He kept trying to interact with me, talk to me, touch me, make it all real, and I'd had to shut him down every time because it wasn't something I could handle. It had taken every mental block I possessed just to finish, and after ten minutes of fighting my own conscience tooth and nail, I was rewarded with a climax so unfulfilling I was almost able to convince myself that any sexual aura I had *must've* been eliminated.

I practically expected a professional handshake as I opened the door to lead him out into the hallway. I couldn't help but think it was better that way, that that made it hurt a little less when I realized just how deep I was digging the hole—Of course, the only thing that *really* made it better was the hope that if I dug far enough I'd come out on the other, Luke-inhabited side. But somehow, the thought of fucking nameless guys to keep the man I loved in a platonic role in my life… It was starting to ache in the most sensible way anything in my life had for the past week.

The door swung closed behind him, and I breathed out a sigh of what I imagined had to be relief. I was already exhausted, and that was anything but encouraging. I reached for my threads, trying to feel for the sickly heat of the Night, to see how much was left, to see how many more soul-draining sessions I was going to have to suffer through before this all could just finally end—

"I thought he'd *never* leave!"

Arms clasped down tight around my chest, hugging me tight. I squirmed away, twisting and shoving against the person until they finally backed up enough for me to get a look at them.

"What the *fuck?*"

Jake stared back at me, eyes hungry with something that made my stomach churn painfully. He reached forward to grab me again, and my threads twisted sharply as magic I barely managed to focus in time steamrolled out of my body and pushed my roommate backward until he fell back onto the floor.

I tried to catch my breath, tried to say something else, but the words and the air wouldn't come, and Jake beat me to the punch, a devious smile spreading across his lips as he looked up at me adoringly.

"Does this mean you like it rough, Cole?"

The rational part of my brain took that moment to note that I'd gotten conclusive evidence that one hadn't been enough, and the Night was clearly still working. At the same time, every other fiber of my mind threw itself full force into the execution of the only act that seemed to make sense at the time — that being, to grab Jake by the shoulders, lift him back to his feet then shake him so hard I thought his head might snap clean off.

I opened my mouth to say something, but before the words could even really form I was cut off by a moan so loud it seemed to echo endlessly off the walls. The eruption of sound from the man I was shaking freaked me out so badly that I dropped Jake completely, a move that sent him crumpling to the carpet again in a way that was so overdramatic it would have been funny if I wasn't so pissed.

"What is *wrong* with you?"

I knew the answer — it was the same thing that was wrong with every single person I came into contact with now. But I couldn't help but ask anyway, even if the reply I was given was an arching of Jake's back as he shoved his pelvis as far up into the air as he could.

Brown eyes, glistening with blatant need, opened and looked up at me.

"*You...*"

Fuck.

Of course I was what was wrong with him. There was no other way to put it, no one else to drop the blame on, not anymore. I was the problem, and damn if I wasn't going to fix it. I had to do it, had to do *him*, before the Night could recover again and make this even worse. "Get up." I tried to sound strong, or at least emotionless like I had just a few minutes before, but I think I fell short on both counts. It was all I could do not to shudder at the way Jake scrambled to his feet as fast as he could, arms already outstretched toward me.

"*Don't!*"

Jake froze, his hands less than a foot away from me.

"Go…into your room—" I struggled to think of how I wanted to handle it, where it would happen, how fast, who doing what. My brow furrowed as I tried to figure out what to say, and I saw from the look in his wavering eyes that Jake was hanging on my every word. My every command. "Lie down on the bed, and…uh…*shit*…, close your eyes…"

He was biting down on his lip so hard it was turning white, but the groan he let out didn't have anything to do with pain. His eyes fluttered closed for a second. "*Then what?*" he eased out breathily.

Then I fuck you with no emotional attachment because I'm just using you, as if I haven't done enough horrible things in these twenty-three years.

The unspoken words echoed in my heart thrummed against a darkness that I had spent my life trying to keep locked down tight. I grabbed my arm as tightly as I could, digging my fingers in until I could feel bruises forming, squeezing my eyes shut tight. "Then, you *wait*," I growled out. "Wait for me." I focused on the pain, focused on the marks of burning and stinging and aching that I twisted into my own bloodstream. I swore I wouldn't let the black win out again. I *couldn't*—I had to stay in the here and now and do what had to be done. "*Go!*"

Jake rushed out of the room in a blur, and I stumbled into my own bedroom, grabbing the side of my desk to keep from falling over. The cold air that burned my lungs was helping to drive away the shadows in my chest and my mind, and I let the spells of suffering drift out of me, their job done for the moment.

I was determined to fuck Jake. I knew I *had* to, had to go over there and screw him into the mattress until we blew, and that would be the end of it, and *Jesus Christ,* I was *not* going to think about Luke right then, and I was *not* going to think about the way I felt sick at the thought of burying myself in another man's embrace when all I *really* wanted was—

Stop. God, for *once*, just *stop!*

My eyes were already closed, but I pressed the heels of my palms into them until stars burst behind my closed lids. I could feel my Sight prickling at the back of my mind, like what had happened in the shower with Luke but much weaker this time—more like a suggestion than anything being forced. Desperate for anything to focus on other than the sickness and the hurt, I twisted at my threads sharply, forcing the magic to ring out in discordant echoes. The spell-song of Foresight built up in my veins, resounding loudly in my ears as I let the ice wash through my body again.

I'd rushed it, and my magic made sure I knew that. Hot needles bore down into my mind, aching pain that I knew would leave me with a headache long after I stopped the vision, but I steeled myself to the burn and kept my Sight fully open as images rushed across my thoughts. Spells of focusing, tightening and clarity poured seamlessly out of my mouth like ephemeral smoke that swirled up around me and grappled at the floodwaters of the time stream, dams and levees that channeled it down from near infinity into only the most likely futures. I let the magic bend how it wanted, racing through the possibilities until it latched onto one of them and unfolded it into my mind. That was when I was supposed to focus in on the person or thing that I wanted to See, but before I could offer my own opinion the spells took over again, honing down until the Sight crashed to a halt in a room I recognized easily — the room just across the hall.

Boxes were stacked everywhere, overflowing with clothes and belongings that had clearly been thrown in them with careless speed. I half wondered if I'd somehow slipped into a vision of the past, to when we'd moved in, but Jake's meticulous nature had meant his boxes were flawlessly organized, every piece of clothing folded, every box labeled clearly. This was more like a train wreck, and as the view of the Sight panned back a little, I saw from Jake's fervent shoving of an armload of pants into one of the boxes that this was definitely a move *out*, not in. One that was done with the panicky speed of someone who seemed to have a lot to be afraid of.

My stomach tightened. It was *me*. Jake was afraid of *me*, and he was getting out of the apartment as fast as he could. He kept glancing at the door as though he worried I might step in at any time and ask him what he was doing — or, more likely, that I would suddenly storm in and try to fuck him again. Clearly in that timeline the Night had worked itself off, but the collateral damage hadn't.

Moisture welled in my eyes in real life, and it fuzzed over the Sight so that Jake's actions became little more than blurs of color. I let my threads go, unraveling the spells that held my mind in the time stream. I didn't want to wait and see if the vision would cut itself off — if I would actually walk in and say…whatever it was I might say. I fell back into reality with a quiet gasp.

My knees gave out, and I slammed to the floor with a muffled bang. My mind churned with the knowledge that, even if I could get the Night out of my system, it was too late to stop the damage I'd done. Jake was going to be terrified of me. I could only imagine what would happen to Aaron. And what about Owen, or Two-A or his girlfriend?

And even then, with all of the *everything* going on inside my head, I still couldn't forget that I had a roommate a few dozen feet away waiting for me to screw him, and an Incubus God only knew where waiting to kill me if I used the Night again. No matter what I did, Jake was going to move out, I was sure I hadn't seen the last of Gavin and after everything I'd already done with Luke…

If there was one thing in the world that I was more sure of than anything, it was this — I was *not* going to get through this. Not in one piece. Not when everything I touched turned to ash, and the one man who had sworn to stand by me was the one person I couldn't go near, the one person I'd never be able to be close to again.

A few more seconds or minutes or hours passed before I realized I could hear the radio filtering in from the living room, background noise that I hadn't noticed until the music had paused for some words from the show's host.

"And that was our number one request for the week! Next on tonight's playlist is one of our older favorites — let's see if you still remember the words."

Bass that I only just recognized crackled out of the radio, made tinny by the bad speakers and the closed door. But something about it was familiar, something I couldn't quite place until the smooth voice began to flow out into the stifling air of my room.

'I'm not Snow White, but I'm lost inside this forest...'

My eyes snapped open in an instant.

'I'm not Red Riding Hood, but I think the wolves have got me...'

It was the song I'd listened to on that first bus ride with Blaine and Hot Guy, a time that felt like it was years past. Back then, the Night had all just been flirting, a fun little bout of attention. Now it was something dark, something horrible that was about to destroy the life I'd finally been getting used to. The echoing lyrics served to remind me of just how wrong it had all gone, how unfair it all was, thrown back in my face with a throbbing Top 40 backing track.

I twisted my fingers into the carpet, too exhausted to try and fight the black I could already feel coiling in my chest, ready to strike. More images of Luke and Aaron and Owen and Gavin stormed through my mind, passionate kissing and hands groping and *pain*, and *this wasn't how any of this was supposed to be!* I thought I might have been shaking because I was crying, but there weren't any tears, not anymore — just fury, crimson rage to match the black, twisting up in bloodied columns of fire in my heart. In an instant I was on my feet, my vision practically seething holes in the door as I stormed toward it.

I'd always drowned my problems in booze, or men, or work — anything to keep every minute of every day occupied so I wouldn't have time to think. But I didn't want to internalize anymore. I was pissed — and it was about damn time someone knew it.

I cranked the dial on the stereo, letting the pounding music rattle through the airwaves louder than I'd ever dared before. The synthetic beats roared out of the speakers, glided under my skin, tightened in my muscles and refused to let go. Shadowed numbness was blanketing my thoughts, muffling the voices of the past and the future and focusing in on the present instead, on the music floating around me and in me.

'Don't watch the stilettos, I'm not, not Cinderella, I don't need a knight so, baby, take off all your armor…'

My arms drifted up into the air as I rolled my hips, spinning a slow circle in the middle of the room. I danced to the rhythms warming the air around me, closing my eyes as the music flooded my body. It was just like the last time in so many ways, as if the song itself was imbued with magic, but this time it wasn't coercion and force. This felt like escape — a trip into the bittersweet darkness inside me that I knew I'd never lose entirely. I let the black steal over my mind completely, surrendering myself to the sound.

'You be the beast, and I'll be the beauty, beauty. Who needs true love as long as you love me truly…'

My right arm spun outwards, sweeping across the top of the mantle and hurling everything we'd placed there across the room. Picture frames and trinkets flew into the far wall, shattering on impact with a smash to mirror the sudden blast in pitch from the speakers.

'I want it all, but I want you more. Will you wake me up, boy, if I bite your poison apple?'

I spun on my heel even as I kicked out with my other leg, slamming into an end table and knocking it over. The lamp that had been sitting on it crashed against the tile, the glow that filtered out of its wrecked shade throwing the entire scene into a disarray of lights and elongated shadows flickering across the walls. I barely noticed.

'I don't believe in fairy tales, I don't believe in fairy tales, I don't believe in fairy tales...'

Magic prickled at my fingertips painfully, and I didn't bother to try to contain it, letting the electricity burn its way out of my body and lance through the air. The lights in the apartment flared brighter, blinking in and out as they surged with energy. A high-pitched whine filled the air, singing out in counterpoint to the throbbing music pounding my ears. Just as the scream peaked I slammed the air with another wave of power. Every light bulb in the room exploded at once, flames bursting to life in the hollowed sockets even as the fire roared brighter in my own body.

'But I believe in you and me. Take me to Wonderland, take me to, take me to, take me to Wonderland...'

Images of Luke seethed across my eyes as I walked through the wreckage of my own life, ignoring the way a picture frame crunched underfoot. Nimble fingers rolling up his latest paper-wrapped escape, fire burning it away with a smoke-choked crackle as those bottomless green eyes sealed shut in relief, never knowing I was a few seconds away from falling into their depths once and for all. I stepped up onto one of the dining room chairs then onto the table, kicking some vase Jake's mom had left there with the same motion. The glass shattered and water flooded across the wood, but I ignored it, spinning tightly on the crowded surface.

'Take me to, take me to, take me to Wonderland. Take me to, take me to, take me to Wonderland, Wonderland, Wonderland...'

My heel slammed down onto a plate, shattering it and grinding the broken pieces into the table top. I danced across the surface, smashing another one to dust and kicking a bowl so hard it exploded on impact. In my mind, Luke's arms were wrapping around me, bands of warmth and comfort in the terrifying haze of the dream world, keeping me safe from Gavin like he had always tried to keep me safe from everything. But he hadn't been able to save me from myself, from the dark thoughts inside that had bided their time until they could do the most damage. I worshiped the green, but some little part of me loved the black, too.

'When I lay my head down to go to sleep at night, my dreams consist of things that'll make you wanna hide...'

I grabbed onto the chandelier, a cheap little thing the landlord had put in to help drive our rent a little higher. I pivoted out over the edge of the table, keeping just enough of my weight on it to keep the light fixture from tearing out as I swung around in a slow circle. The tread of my boots tried to slip in the water, but I caught on the shattered remains of our plates, using the dusted shards to get better purchase as I swung again.

'Don't lock me in your tower, show me your magic powers. I'm not afraid to face a little bit of danger, danger...'

Gavin's hands on me, fingers dancing across arcane symbols of power that twisted my body, forced me into motion—spells rattling around in my head and my heart, trying to make me feel things that I knew I never would while his hands reached lower and lower —

'I want the love, the money, and the perfect ending. You want the same as I, I, so stop pretending...'

I tugged downward viciously, tearing the chandelier out of the ceiling in a spray of drywall and sparks. The twisted metal slammed into the tile and I fell to my knees on the table, crushing more flatware and soaking my jeans with water and what I assume was blood, judging from the pain in my legs and the swaths of shattered porcelain and glass underneath me. Luke's hands were on me again, chasing away the dark memories of the Incubus as he traced the broken trails of magic on my chest. He felt so warm, so perfect, and I would've sacrificed everything I held dear if he could have felt just a little bit of what I felt for him in that moment, as his healing hands held me close.

'I wanna show you how good we could be together. I wanna love you through the night...'

"We'll be a sweet disaster..." The words stumbled out of my mouth, matching the singer's cadence, but she had nothing on the torment in my voice. I settled back onto my heels, looking up at the hole in the ceiling as dust settled down around me like a swirling cloud of smoke, tumbling down from full, smirking lips.

You're my friend, Cole, and I care about you —
'I don't believe in fairy tales...'
God, you're beautiful —
'I don't believe in fairy tales...'
Don't you love me — ?
'I don't believe in fairy tales...'
I always be there when you need me —
'But I believe in you and me. Take me to Wonderland...'

Memory and magic crackled through me like the light bulbs I'd destroyed earlier, shorting out my mind. I fell backward, laying down flat in the ruined remains strewn over our table. My arms were splayed over sharp-edged glass, and dust and broken shards caught in my hair, but my unseeing eyes didn't notice, and the messages of pain were getting caught somewhere between the cuts and my brain, dulling them. I let the darkness seep out of my exhausted body, finally burned away.

I lay there till the song ended, and in the pause before the next, I heard the quiet sound of a door swinging open, followed by soft footsteps.

"Cole?"

My eyes focused in on the face swimming in front of them.

Jake.

Night.

Chapter Eight

I rolled over slowly, never breaking eye contact as I did. Debris cascaded off the table, but Jake refused to look at anything but me, one hand already in his jeans.

The Night inside me flickered dimly, weakened, but still hanging on—not unlike my sanity. The warm glow was responding to Jake's pleasure, growing stronger through its sickly vampirism, and I knew there wasn't time to let it build, that I couldn't give it a chance to recover. I stumbled forward on the table, trying to crawl close enough to pull Jake in for a kiss.

Stinging pain exploded in my hand so suddenly that my arm gave out, and my shoulder cracked against the table top as I fell. Something snapped underneath me, and the leaf of the table pivoted downward, dumping me onto the floor in a spray of dust and glass.

"*Ow, fuck!*" I tried to hold my aching shoulder, but as I brought my throbbing hand in close the pain tripled. My fingers scraped against something sticking straight out of my palm, but the white fireworks slicing across my vision didn't give me a chance to see what it was.

In the next second Jake was rolling me over onto my back, pulling my hand out so that he could see it. My eyes opened to thin slits and I could just make out the jagged piece of glass jutting out of my skin before he bowed forward, hiding it from view. I felt his fingers delicately wrap around the bloodstained shard, and I couldn't help the sharp cry that rang out as I felt it jerk under my skin.

"*Shh*... It's okay, it's all right..." The pain wasn't really helped by his reassurances, but I appreciated them anyway, especially when he ripped the glass out of my palm with a flurry of motion. I gritted my teeth to the stinging and tried to pull my hand back, but Jake held tight, raising his head just enough to place a soft kiss against the cut. I closed my eyes so I didn't have to see it.

I knew I couldn't think about it, couldn't think about him. There wasn't time. If I messed this up one more time I didn't know how I was ever going to get through it, but damn if the thought of it didn't make me sick. I opened my eyes again to meet his adoring gaze.

"If we do this...there's no going back." I didn't bother to hide the plea in my voice, the desperate hope that somehow there was enough of the real Jake left to know what I meant, to say that this was wrong and that he didn't want this. But I knew it was too much to hope for even before the words came out of his mouth.

"I don't ever want to go back..." Jake's lips brushed against mine, and, as he did, I felt my threads twinge, then strum against one another. The Sight was building in me, singing louder, and I was too tired to stop it. Jake deepened the kiss, running his hands gently over my jaw until he'd coaxed my mouth open. I kissed back, the charge of the Night warming my muscles and breathing strength back into my body, but I was losing focus, trying to concentrate on the way my lips were moving, and the pain in my hand, and the beckoning flow of the time stream roaring in the background. There were spells I needed to cast, wards to focus my powers and keep the timelines in check, but they weren't coming to me like they always had, and I couldn't make the marks form in my mind.

Jake pulled me in closer, deepening the kiss, and I felt the Sight try to rush over my eyes — but the magic hadn't formed properly, and my vision swam for a second before clearing...mostly. The center line of my gaze was flickering and jumping with static, trying unsuccessfully to bring together the two different universes each of my eyes was trapped in. With my left, I saw reality, my apartment and Jake moving against me. My right was some future, but I could only just recognize the room staring back at me. An ache was already starting to form in the front of my brain as I tried to make out two worlds at once, one dark and broken, the other bright and well lit. I stumbled backward in my confusion, and Jake's arm wrapped around my side, holding me up.

"Thank—"

"What, did you think I wouldn't find out about him, you *pig?*"

The word caught in my throat as a woman's voice pierced my right ear. A half-second later, she stormed out of the center line of my vision and flipped her blonde hair off her shoulder furiously as she tore open the top drawer of the nightstand, scooping up what I assumed were her clothes.

"Nicole, I—"

The woman spun to face the side of the room I couldn't see, extending her arm threateningly at the man whose voice I was now painfully aware I recognized. "Don't come near me! God..." She shook her head, rubbing her temples in frustration. "I knew dating a cop was a bad idea, but I figured that was 'cause you might get *shot*, not cheat on me with some fucking *guy* you pull over!" She shoved her clothes into her purse, and I tried to follow her as she moved farther into the room, but Jake's lips were sweeping up my neck and my head naturally bent in toward him.

My right eye's view of the future panned with my head, showing me the side of the bedroom I'd been dark to before just as Aaron swept across it, following Nicole. I hadn't thought the six-six cop had it in him to cower quite like that, but he was practically chasing after her on hands and knees. I tried to look to the right so I could follow him, but that made the ache in my head sting so bad I had to shut my eyes just to remember how to breathe.

"Baby, I didn't—I mean, I don't— He—"

I covered my left eye and tried to delicately open my right. My head still felt like it was splitting open, but I tried to look around even though the vision was getting hazy now.

"Do you honestly think there is *anything* you could say that would make this okay?"

I dug my feet into the carpet to stop Jake's slow procession toward his bedroom. I couldn't make out Nicole or Aaron anymore, but it wasn't because of the cloud forming over my Sight—they had moved into the adjoining bathroom. Jake was asking me what was wrong, why I had stopped, but I ignored him, trying to hear more from the time stream.

There was silence for a few beats more, followed by a sigh.

"I didn't think so."

The sound of something metallic bouncing off the ground echoed through the room, and a silver blur came skidding across the floor out of the haze to bounce off my shoe. I bent down to pick it up. I squinted hard and brought it close to my face, even though I already knew exactly what it was before my fingers had even touched it.

A diamond ring, thrown away like it meant nothing. And, thanks to me, now it *did*.

I dropped the ring, standing to my feet as I did. Knives stabbed into my mind as the Sight blacked out completely, lightning cracks warping my gaze until it finally began to clear. I could feel the time lines realigning themselves, trying to reconcile my reality without their guiding magic, but there was still too much to reign in—the Sight started to materialize, but there were holes in the vision, like tiny ink blots scattered across my retinas. In the gaps I could see the real world, but time was moving differently. Jake's motions seemed incredibly slow, but the vision was moving at normal speed.

When I finally made out exactly what I was Seeing, I couldn't help but gasp—it wasn't the *future*. It was the past.

I was on the beach, but not the real one. It was the dream world again, where Luke had taken me after the fight with Gavin. What threw me most about the scene wasn't even so much the content, as the *view*—I wasn't reliving it through my own eyes, I was standing a few feet out and looking at Luke and me like a bystander. It had happened to me a few times before, but it wasn't exactly common, and it was made that much more nerve-racking by the intimacy of the scene.

The image flickered and jumped, and with the holes it was like looking at an old film-reel home movie that had seen better days. The sound of the crashing waves was tinny in the background, filtering in sporadically. I slowly walked closer.

We were both kneeling in the sand. Luke's hand moved over my body, tracing patterns through the blue that was still staining my chest from the glow sticks. Marks danced around his fingertips but the magic in them had broken, and Dream Me was shuffling forward, trying to get Luke to keep touching. There was a need, a plea in my eyes that was unnerving to see as I stared up at the Dreamwalker, silently begging him to make me whole again.

I squirmed uncomfortably and tried to look away, but no matter how I moved my head in reality the view of us on the beach was solidly locked over my eyes. Luke was talking—the sound was too distant to make out properly, but I knew the words he had said by heart, and they rang out clearly in my mind as I watched his hand move down to Dream Me's arm.

Are you ready to wake up?

In the dream that had been the last thing I'd wanted. Now, I'd found myself praying to wake up from this nightmare almost every minute since that Night had crossed my lips.

My Sight tightened in on the scene, coming in close as I kissed Luke. I pulled him down on top of me and rocked my hips against him, and in the real world I almost cried out in relief when the vision started to cloud again so I didn't have to watch anymore. Jake was pulling me along by the hand, and I tried to focus on that with everything I had so I could kill the Sight that much faster. I dug in my heels and held my ground so that I could focus, and I felt his hand slip out of mine and he headed into the room.

The edges of the vision burned away, seething with white light as I shoved my power deep into my core again. My Foresight railed against me, carving a rapid-fire string of images and thoughts into the grooves of my mind before I could completely lock it down. Owen, staring into the darkness of the parking lot, waiting for me to appear and pick him up again, not knowing I'd never come. His straight roommates, shaken by the things they'd done, moving away and effectively writing off the friendships they'd had since grade school. And all the others, Blaine, Hot Guy, Two-A, each future fundamentally damaged by the hand I'd played in it.

I didn't even know what to think, much less what to do, so I did the only thing that made sense—I kept walking, stepping into Jake's dimly lit room.

My roommate was splayed across the bed, completely naked with his arms and legs outstretched. His tanned body shone under the soft glow of the floor lamp, the only lighting in the room, and I could see his muscles tensing and flexing in anticipation, his eyes closed and lips just begging to be swept up in a kiss. I looked for a few seconds more, then let my eyes fall shut.

Five seconds later, I was out of the door to the apartment, stumbling into the hallway and down the stairs.

* * * *

195

I didn't know how I'd made it down three flights of stairs in my haze, but somehow I'd managed. There were no words, no thoughts, just a black vacuum in my head and my heart as I wandered away from what I'd once thought was my only hope of salvation.

It was late, and there was no one in the building to see me or try to fuck me, and if I'd had any thought processes going on I'm sure I would've found it in me to be thankful for that. As it was, I moved on autopilot, taking each step with mechanized care as I made my way down the stairs and into the lobby.

The door seemed to swing open of its own accord, and I walked mindlessly out into the night, ignoring the roaring in my ears as I stumbled out onto the sidewalk and kept going. The sound was getting louder, and the lights dancing in front of my eyes were getting brighter, and I closed them as I stepped down off the curb.

A blaring horn cut through my stalling thoughts, and I realized in that second that I was in the street.

Two headlights flew at me, and there was no time to do anything but shut my eyes. In the next instant, a hand was fisting my shirt, pulling backward with inhuman force. I vaulted onto the sidewalk next to the street, my shirt tearing to pieces under the strain as I was thrown to the ground.

I rolled over onto my hands and knees, trying to catch my breath. I looked up, trying to see who had saved me, when a burst of pain exploded across my ribs as someone kicked me as hard as they could. Something cracked, the force of the hit flipped me over onto my back and I cried out, unable to stop myself. I clutched my arms to my chest, trying to breathe around the barbed grenade of ache that was already tightening my lungs.

My vision cleared just in time to see Gavin bearing down on me, fury lighting a fire behind his bronze eyes. His face twisted into a scowl, and my world went white as his black leather boot flew into my side again. I rolled over, my arms pinwheeling pathetically as I crashed to a halt in the grass in front of the apartment building. Pain rocked my body as I uncontrollably coughed up what I prayed wasn't blood onto the cold ground beneath me.

The Incubus's fingers dug into the fabric at my back, tearing what was left of my shirt off me violently. He stepped away from me and I felt magic course through the air — probably some spell of blindness so no one would be able to see us. I dragged myself to my hands and knees, trying to crawl for the door to the apartment complex.

Gavin's hand wrapped around the back of my neck, dragging me to my feet. His fingers tightened, and he whispered into my ear with disturbing calm, "You just couldn't help yourself, could you?"

Something so evil shouldn't have been allowed to have a voice so smooth and collected — it was supposed to grate and cut as it lashed out at you, not hide its vicious nature behind a mask of silk. But I didn't have much chance to think about that. In the next second, I was too busy being thrown face first into the brick wall of the building.

My legs crumbled underneath me, but before I could slide down the wall I was spun back around, Gavin's hand crushed tight over my throat again, and he hoisted me back up till my toes barely reached the ground. I clutched at his wrist with both hands, but his supernatural strength was beyond anything I could've fought even if I wasn't exhausted and in so much pain.

"I should just kill you right now…" The words were growled into my ear as he twisted his hand, tightening his grip until I couldn't force any air down my throat. I tried to think of a plan, something I could do to get away, but the only things that would come to mind were the images of Aaron and Owen, vignettes of lives that I'd wrecked. Just like when I'd let my dad die, and when I'd let my mom die, and when I'd let *anything* bad happen to *anyone* else, when I could've stopped it if I hadn't been so fucking *useless*… The burning in my ribs and the choking pain at my neck were nothing compared to the things I'd done to other people. To the things I was going to *keep* doing to people as long as I was alive.

For one tiny, gut-wrenching second, I let the thought slip out. *Maybe I'd deserve it…*

What did you just say?

If my eyes hadn't already been bugging out from the strength crushing down on my windpipe, they would've flown open even further as that silken voice rang out in my mind in reply. I tried to focus in my blacking-out vision on Gavin's face, at the confusion floating around in his features behind the fury.

My magic was boiling inside, warming and sparking against the answering aura radiating out of Gavin. The Night had filled me with *his* magic—his unique, Incubus energy that gave him control of sex. Now that we were finally together in reality again, with magic burning through the air and emotions so high, our auras were trying to reconcile, trying to become one again. I could feel Gavin in my mind, racing through my thoughts even as I finally put it all together. After only an instant to pause, he dove deeper, and I couldn't stop him as he raided down into the misery and guilt that was poisoning me inside, the darkness that I'd only ever given other people peeks at. He scoured through the painful memories that had taunted me for years in a matter of seconds.

Not knowing what else to do, I thought the only thing that came to mind — the one thing I wanted more than anything else in this world.

Please, just...make this all stop.

I felt Gavin come to a halt in my mind, his body completely motionless as seconds passed. The lack of air was blacking out my vision, drawing it in at the edges until all I could make out were his lips, which slowly curved into the barest of smiles.

"I intend to."

Magic roared to life in the Incubus, twisted spells of malice that warped and flexed inside him so strongly I could feel them in the air between us. Marks started to form along his arms, racing trails that lanced across tanned skin and begged for a final spell to release them, marks of crushing, sealing and ending, all waiting to bear down on their target — my throat. I only had a few seconds to realize that now, with death only a few inches from my face, that wasn't what I had meant, that I wasn't ready — images of Luke, evasive for so long, finally exploded over my mind's eye, shots of us laughing, and playing video games, and talking, and even the ones I knew I should regret, the dreams of sex and the real kissing and touching, and I couldn't die then, not when the last memory Luke would have of me was of using him, not when he didn't at least know exactly what he meant to me —

Answering spells tore out of the infinity and formed in my mind, rushing so quickly through my body that I couldn't even tell what the marks were before they were stringing themselves together into chains of power, coiling in my chest and rocketing upwards.

Erik Clarke

Gavin's final spell took hold at the same moment, and I felt the magic flying down his arms and into his hands, reaching my neck just as my own did the same.

Heat, beyond any that I could even conceive of feeling, burst into life at the point where the spells collided. My neck burned so badly I was sure that the skin must have caught fire, and my vision went from choked black to blazing white faster than I could track. A colossal boom sounded, and the Incubus and I were hurled backward—but I was already being held against the wall. My skull cracked against the brick so hard that my world immediately went black again, and I fell to the ground in a heap.

I tried to open my eyes, and did so with surprising ease. I was staring out across the street, the lights warping and bowing like the entire scene was melting somehow, but I could just make out Gavin on the far side, struggling to climb to his feet. Cars flying past cut out my line of sight intermittently, but in the gaps I managed to see him brush himself off and turn to look at me. My eyesight was too wavering to make out the look on his face, but in the next moment he'd turned away, and with another rushing car, he was gone completely.

Hitting a wall that hard with my head... I would've thought it should hurt. But I felt almost numb, just a warm, prickling sensation at the back of my skull. I reached back haltingly to try to feel the damage, and my hand caught in hair that was already matting with blood.

That... That's not good.

My head fell back against the wall, and even though my thoughts were already going fuzzy I was sure that I should have felt some kind of pain there. But cement was cooling in my mind, slowing down all thought as it eased into dulling gray, and I could feel myself slipping into unconsciousness as the ringing in my ears started to reach a fever pitch.

I tugged at my threads, trying to force out a healing spell, but they were slow to respond, as sluggish as my brain. The magic started to form, but the darkness had already claimed my mind before I could be sure if the spells had even set.

* * * *

Luke's fingers traced my jaw line, curving under my chin to tilt my mouth up to his. I opened up for him and let his bourbon-flame warmth ignite inside me, a fire that burned a path down to my groin. My dick throbbed against his thigh and I trailed a hand down from his chest to my own waist, trying to get a hold of the button to my jeans.

Wait.

The Dreamwalker's hands were on my face and in my hair, coaxing my mouth against his — one of *my* hands was on his shoulder, and the other was trying to get my pants undone, so...why was there another set trying to help yank down my zipper?

I tried to push away, but the hands that were now starting to feel a *lot* less like Luke's on my head held tight, trying to force the kiss. The ones at my crotch tore at my jeans, tugging them open and trying to pull them down my legs.

With light bulb-above-the-head intensity, I suddenly realized my eyes were still closed. I forced them open, biting down on the lips moving against me as hard as I could and kicking out violently at the same time.

Oh shit.

There was a man in front of me, clutching his now bleeding lip, and a woman holding her stomach where I had kicked her a few feet out, and I had absolutely no idea who either of them were. My head snapped around like a bobble-head on crack, taking in every detail of my surroundings at lightning speed.

Night. Gavin. Almost getting killed.

I shoved the business-suit-wearing creep as hard as I could and struggled to my feet, trying to tug my jeans back up at the same time. The sun was up again, so I must've been lying out in front of the apartment building all night—it was a fucking miracle I'd managed to not be groped until morning. Or maybe I had been. It was amazing that I was even awake so soon after what must've been a pretty serious concussion, so there was no telling what might have happened while I was out. The only positive note I could think of, was that the healing spells must have worked at least somewhat, since I was alive and standing, and only had an *agonizing* headache rather than an *excruciating* one.

The nymphos in front of me were starting to get to their feet, and I could see people in the distance on the sidewalk and at the bus stop that were starting to look over, undoubtedly picking up on the sex I was still venting. I pushed off the wall and stumbled for the door to the apartment complex.

I couldn't go back up to my apartment—Jake was there. If our other run-ins were any indication, Gavin could be practically anywhere, waiting for me. There was blood in my hair, cuts on my arms, bruises on my sides, and I just didn't know what in God's name to do anymore. I practically fell into the bathroom in the lobby, locking the door behind me and slumping against the sink to catch my breath.

My Night-sense was already tingling in my chest as I felt people moving into the lobby, their sexual need drawing them into me like moths to a flame. The handle jiggled and I banged my fist against the door as hard as I could. "*Fuck off!*" I knew they heard me, but that didn't stop the crowd I could feel gathering out there.

Two mirrors hung above the sinks in the bathroom, and I walked over to them, trying to steel myself for what I might see. Even so, I couldn't stifle the gasp at the reflection staring back at me.

I was a fucking *wreck*. My hair was a rat's nest caked with dried blood at the back and dotted with broken glass, and my lower lip had cracked open. A criss-cross lattice of cuts traced up and down my arms from lying on the table, my palms were shredded from falling to the concrete and my chest... Let's just say Gavin didn't half ass anything. Ribs had broken on both sides, and, though my healing magic had set them back in place, I'd passed out before I could try to fix any of the aesthetics. Dark, livid bruising painted my sides, black and blue reminders of just how hard a pissed, magically fueled Incubus could kick. A thin, scabbed line traced from just below my collarbone to my right shoulder where the sharp edge of a brick had caught me as Gavin had spun me around on the wall. Two swaths of raw skin on my back coming down from my shoulder blades finished off the image, the effect of a quick slide down the rough wall when I'd cracked my head against the brick.

Nothing in particular hurt all that much, with most of the internal damage having been healed by my spell while I was knocked out. It was more of a full-body ache, a nagging pain in the back of my mind to remind me that, without my magic, it could have all been so much worse.

The sound of the door rattling brought me back to the present, and I patted at my pockets, praying my phone was still in one of them.

If I had to see Luke in person again, he would try to come onto me, and I didn't know how much longer I could resist taking the one thing I'd been wanting most as it was offered to me on a silver fucking platter. If I was going to have any prayer of not destroying what was left of our original friendship, I needed to stay as far away from him as possible until it all blew over.

Unfortunately, he also happened to be the only person who would know why the Incubus was so determined to kill me, and what it would take at that point to make the Night stop. *Because God forbid something in my life be easy.*

When I felt the familiar rectangle outline in my back pocket, I pulled it out and swept away the lock screen. The garbled image on the screen jerked and shuddered as I realized a spider web crack had fractured the screen, bleeding its LCD fluid along each of the fault lines and leaving most of the display unreadable. I mentally cursed the Incubus for what felt like the hundredth time since I had woken up as I struggled to make the unresponsive touch screen follow my directions. I slammed my finger into the screen again and again while I tried not to glance up too often at the shuddering handle.

The Call menu finally lit up, and when Luke's number appeared I threw my unscathed shoulder against the door, stilling it for a second. The phone rang twice before a sleepy voice on the other end of the line picked up.

"Hello?"

I breathed a sigh of relief and ran a hand through my hair. "Luke?"

"Well, that depends... What are you wearing right now?"

I slammed my palm against my forehead, groaning in disbelief. "*Seriously?* Even over the phone?"

Luke laughed softly in my ear, a sound that was welcome no matter how patronizing. "That's what happens when you're a sex god, babe." I opened my mouth to argue when he cut me off, "But really — what are you wearing, hot stuff? If we're gonna do this, we gotta do it right."

I gritted my teeth and rubbed at my temple with my free hand. *Jesus Christ.* "You've got to be kidding me."

A sigh. "Cole, if we're gonna role play, you should go for someone who's a little less skeptical, or we're *never* gonna get to the part where we touch ourselves."

I almost dropped my phone right then and there. "Yo— *What?*"

The Dreamwalker laughed again. "I know, that's just stupid. I'm totally already jacking it..." The last word trailed off with a groan that I *really* didn't want to be thinking about right then.

"Oh *God*, Luke!"

"Nonono, say it *slower*. Oh...*God*..."

I twisted my hand into my hair, trying to ignore the fact that, as horrendous as the situation was, my dick was already rock hard after talking to him for less than a minute. The door jiggled more forcefully behind me and I slammed my hand into the handle, surging the metal latch with spells of flame and molten heat. The steel melted into slag immediately, effectively welding the door shut, but at a price — nausea shot through me, and for a second I almost lost it and threw up all over the floor. I was still too drained to be doing that kind of magic, and my body intended on making me well aware of that. I took a few moments to breathe through it until the urge to puke subsided. With that problem dealt with for the moment, I could then focus on the other pressing issue—well, the issue *other* than my throbbing erection, but damn it, I was *not* going to have phone sex with Luke! *No matter how appealing it sounds…*

"Luke, would you *please* zip up for a second so I can talk to you about something *important?* Something like, oh, I don't know, a crazy-ass Incubus who wants me *dead?*"

"Can't. Nothing to zip up. See, *I'm* naked. Now it's your turn—what are *you* wearing?"

I thought I was going to tear my hair out. "Would you *stop that!*"

The Dreamwalker just started laughing again, and if I wasn't facing imminent death, I'll admit, I'd probably be laughing too. It *was* pretty funny. But as it was, I really didn't have time for banter, especially considering that the crowd in the lobby just seemed to be getting bigger. I sighed and ran a hand through my hair in frustration. At least when I was with Luke in person I could usually get him to focus enough to get some answers—this was going nowhere. I bit my lip and shot a look up to the sky, half prayer, half "Fuck you, powers that be." Even as I said it, I knew it was the worst possible idea, but I couldn't think of any other way to find out what I needed in time. "Look, can I just come over?" The Dreamwalker started to reply and I immediately cut him off, "And I swear to God, if you say 'that depends, what are you wearing,' I will *find* a way to *strangle* you through this phone!"

"Fair enough. But for the record, I'm not that big on choke-play. Blindfolds and a little bondage are my thing."

Don't, don't, don't *think about Luke tying you up or you really* are *gonna touch yourself while talking to him...*

"Look, just..." I scrubbed at my face. "Put on some clothes, I'll be there in a few minutes." I hung up before he could reply and prayed he'd actually listen. And that his idea of "some clothes" didn't end up being something sexual.

Just one last time—I'd only have to fight off the temptation one more time, long enough to find out how to stop this mess without getting killed, then I'd keep out of Luke's line of sight for whatever amount of time it took to fix the situation. Then we could go back to the way we were before the mess started.

I turned around to leave and saw...the door I'd welded shut.

Well, shit.

* * * *

If girls really did sneak out of bathroom windows as often as sitcoms made it sound, then you'd think those fucking building designers would have made them a little bigger. I wasn't a *ninja* for God's sake, I could've used a little wiggle room.

The window had dumped me into the alley behind the building, and from there it was a quick sprint to the parking lot on the west side. I could feel the crowd moving, trying to figure out where their would-be idol had gone, but I was far enough away that the Night seemed to be wearing off, and I managed to get into my car without any trouble.

The trip across town went by a lot faster than it legally should have, but I didn't intend on risking being near anyone long enough for the Night to somehow put their already-dangerous-enough-devotion on a vehicular scale. My car was enough of a shit-box—I didn't need to get into an accident thanks to a lovesick psycho plowing into me so we could fuck in the wreckage. *Thanks, but no.*

I swung into a spot in front of Luke's building and threw it in park, grabbing the jacket I'd tossed in the back seat a couple of days ago and tugging it on—the last thing I needed was to run into Luke without some kind of top on, and God only knew what had happened to what was left of my shirt after Gavin tore it off me. I knew that if I tried to actually heal the bruises and cuts I would pass out again—I just didn't have the strength yet. I kept the sleeves down and zipped it up all the way and pulled on marks of simple illusion, setting them in place over my hair so that anyone looking at me wouldn't see the blood and the glass. It was an easy spell, much easier than healing, but even so I had to close my eyes as my stomach turned. I stepped out and took a look around. There were a couple of people in the lot, but I figured I would be fine getting to the door as long as I walked fast.

* * * *

It turned out I was wrong. Very, very wrong. One shield spell, three punches and a kick to the shin later, and I was standing in the elevator more or less unscathed, unlike the path I'd had to carve to get into the building. It was like I was in some kind of zombie apocalypse, but it wasn't exactly brains they were hoping to eat—though heads certainly were involved. *When did this shit get so* potent?

I reached the fourth floor and made my way down the hall, not bothering to knock once I reached Luke's door. He'd left it open like I'd figured, and I let myself in.

"Hey there, handsome."

I kicked the door closed and glanced up to see him grinning at me from the table, his head just visible from behind the island. My stomach tightened and I quickly ran a hand over the fabric covering my arms before thinking better of it. "Why do you keep calling me things like that?" I couldn't keep the exasperation out of my voice, but I kept the disappointment to myself for the most part—the more pathetic *"Why can't you call me things like that* without *Night?"* held at bay.

I rushed past where he was sitting without really looking over him, storming into his room and snagging another long-sleeved shirt from his closet. I pulled it on and threw my jacket over my arm and headed back into the main part of the apartment.

I stepped into the living room and tossed my hoodie onto a chair, and when I turned back my feet came to a stop so fast I almost fell over as the air caught in my chest. Now that I was around the edge of the island I could finally see more than just Luke's head.

He's shirtless. Oh fuck, *why does he have to be shirtless?*

That lopsided smirk of his flashed up at me coyly as he took a moment to run a hand through his hair, leaning back enough to give me a glimpse of his cut pecs and subtle abs. Luke wasn't ripped, but his muscles were defined and his body fat low enough to show it, and damn if I didn't have to resist reaching out to touch them. Knowing eyes stayed locked on my own. "I called you handsome because you *are* handsome." Luke lifted the joint he'd been rolling to his lips, his tongue tracing a line with tantalizing care along the edge of the paper. He teased me with a smile, flashing his white teeth as he bit down just the slightest bit at the corner. My breath hitched, and his smile spread wider for a second before he bowed his head to finish rolling it tight.

"You—uh... Why... W-why aren't you wearing a shirt?" I shifted uncomfortably, trying to figure out a way to hide the tightness in my jeans without being totally obvious. I was pretty sure I failed completely.

Luke set down his lighter and took a long drag, then closed his left eye and held up his hand like a gun. His thumb came down onto his index finger just as he opened his mouth, letting the smoke roll out of it. "Bang." Magic lanced out of him at the same time, rushing across the room faster than I could track to blast my shirt into wisps of trailing blue mist with a rush of warm air, just like he'd done in the shower. The Dreamwalker smiled brightly. "Now we're even!"

"*Luke!*" My arms flew across my chest and stomach as I hunched over, hiding as much of my body as possible. I made sure I'd covered all the bruising as best I could before Luke saw any of it—the dissipating cloud of what was left of the shirt was helping for the moment.

The Dreamwalker opened his mouth to say something, but his joint slipped from his fingers. In his rush to catch it before it could fall to the carpet, I spun around and grabbed my jacket, holding it against my body since I didn't have time to pull it on. Sure enough, when I turned back around, Luke was already raising his head to look back up at me, smiling again as he took another drag.

I managed to force more illusion spells over my arms, since they were the one part I had to have showing to hold the jacket in place over the rest. I choked and my vision went white for a second, but I gritted my teeth and shook it off. "That was *your* shirt you just vaporized, you know."

Luke chuckled, a warm sound that eased into my heart faster than any magic could. He leaned back and shrugged, trailing a hand into his hair. "What's love without sacrifice?" He smirked. "Besides, a peek at that body is worth way more than some cheapo shirt."

I glanced away, holding the jacket a little tighter to my chest.

"This shit is *way* less effective when you're around, you know that?"

My brow furrowed and I turned to look back at him. Luke was staring at the joint in his hand like he'd stared at the Night when he'd first offered it to me, transfixed. I shook my head. "What?"

The Dreamwalker twirled the joint in his fingers. "When you're not around me and I get high, I can almost feel normal."

For a moment, I let those words wash over me without much thought — if this was any other situation, they wouldn't have meant much anyway. Then my brain snapped in half.

In an instant, my mind raced so fast that you'd have thought the fucking thing was a bullet train. If Luke could fight the effects of the Night with weed when I wasn't around, did that mean Normal Luke was aware of what I'd been doing with Night Luke? What did that mean? What had he thought? He probably would've run away like Jake was going to as soon as he came back to himself — but he was still there, and I didn't see any boxes packed up. Maybe Night Luke had unpacked them all again as soon as the high had worn off? He couldn't stay baked twenty-four-seven. But nothing looked out of place, like it had been moved either way. And did Night Luke really have the mental fortitude to realize he should unpack the boxes? Did Normal Luke have the cognition to know how wrong what we had done was? Did —

"'Course, I still think about *you* every second, but that doesn't have to do with the Night."

And just like that, the bullet train derailed.

My mouth hung open like some kind of moron, just staring at Luke's lips as though they somehow held the answer. "Uh... You..." I shook my head and swallowed, hardly daring to think about all the possibilities that were making my stomach clench painfully. "Wha — What do you mean?"

The Dreamwalker looked up from his joint, setting it down on the table and shrugging with an easy, open smile. "What I said. I think about you." I opened my mouth to push him for more when he leaned back in his chair, yawning. Luke's hands wound together at the back of his head as he stretched backward, drawing the muscles in his arms, shoulders and chest tight. My half-hard dick tried to rise to the occasion, and I knew I should've been looking away, looking down, looking at anything but the sight of that tight little body that... *Fuck* if I didn't want to just touch every inch of that smooth skin and never stop. But I couldn't, not without wrecking even more things than I already had, so for the moment I contented myself to just look at the movement of taut muscles while I shifted the jacket to try to hide my raging erection.

Luke pushed his chair backward and rose to his feet. I fell back a step, but he was already turning to the kitchen, heading for the fridge with a gait that had just enough sway in the shoulders and hips to show that the Dreamwalker knew I couldn't look away. The jeans he had tugged on were slung low and at risk of falling even lower with each step, the gentle slide of dark denim exposing tantalizing skin millimeter by aching millimeter. I ground the heel of my palm into my crotch trying to keep my screaming dick from tearing straight through my pants. Luke opened the door of the refrigerator, and I forced my eyes to snap to the blank wall to the right before he could bend over to pick something up.

"I'm, uh… I'm gonna go grab another shirt," I mumbled, walking backward toward the hall so the jacket would still be between the two of us.

Luke stood up straight and turned around, leaning back against the refrigerator door to close it. He crossed his arms with a smirk, a can of soda in his hand. "Taking without asking isn't very nice, you know," he teased.

I cocked my eyebrow and leveled his gaze incredulously. "Neither is *obliterating* someone's shirt, last I checked."

The Dreamwalker's grin pulled wider, playful as ever. "You know I'll just do it again."

I felt magic stirring in the air as he went to prove his point, and I didn't have time to do anything but say "Don't!" before the spell had reached the jacket I was clutching.

The fabric fell away from my hands as every thread unraveled into a cloud of black dust that hovered in front of me for a moment before fading away completely. I let my arms fall to my sides, closing my eyes in defeat. There was nothing else to hide behind, and I was still too tired to even think of healing the wounds that fast. I let the spells on my hair and my arms drift away — there didn't seem to be much point.

Silence stretched through the room for a moment, then two. I couldn't make my eyes open. I didn't want to see the look on Luke's face, didn't want to see that the bruises and the cuts looked bad enough to override even the power of the Night. I opened my mouth to say something, some kind of apology —

"*Oh my God...*" The words were growled out on a whisper, and before I could even open my eyes in surprise, Luke was in front of me, his gentle hands trailing over my skin, skating delicately around the worst-looking parts. His breathing was coming fast, and I couldn't look away from the sight of his hands on me. "Cole..." The Dreamwalker cupped my face. "*Cole.*" The strength in his voice pulled my eyes up from the bruises to meet his gaze. His face was set firm with determination, but I saw the way his jaw ticked. Cold fury kept his voice barely held in check. "Who did this to you?"

The words were caught up in my throat, and I couldn't hold off the emotion I felt rising up inside. It didn't make sense, and it was making it damn hard to talk, but I tried anyway. "I... I was trying to finish it. Finish off the Night. But i-it didn't work, and... Gavin..."

My breath hitched, and Luke's hand on my face loosened, sliding down my neck to rest on my good shoulder. "*Incubus...*" The Dreamwalker's hands stayed gentle and warm, but his face was twisted with frustration and anger like I'd never seen in the entire time we'd been friends. Luke shook his head, running his free hand through my hair with a rush of magic that chased away the blood and glass. "I should've followed him into the waking world," he growled through gritted teeth. "Finished what I started. He won't be so lucky next time."

I shuddered in relief, not sure if it had more to do with the magic or just knowing that I was finally safe again, at least for a little while longer while I was here with Luke.

The Dreamwalker's right hand stilled on my shoulder, drawing my eyes back to his, even as he diligently worked his marks of healing into the bruising at the base of my throat with the other. "Why did you try to hide these?"

Heat flushed my cheeks, and I didn't know what to say. *I didn't want to seem weak? I was scared of how you'd react?* They both held pieces of truth, but to admit them was even worse than to just think them. "I-I'm fine, Luke. They don't really hurt, I—" He took a step backward without taking his hands off me, turning me to the side and lifting up my arm to better see my sides. Luke hissed out a breath as he finally really saw the gravity of the damage. I turned away, trying to pull my arms out of his grasp so I could wrap them around myself, but he held me still. The Dreamwalker moved in close and blew softly on the bruises, washing away the black and blue with a flurry of marks that made my head go fuzzy with warmth and soothing.

Luke roamed his hands over me, finding every scrape and hurt and chasing them away with magic and the soft murmur of words on skin. The haze of healing buzzed my hearing, and I couldn't make out what he was saying, but his tone was warm, comforting, and against my better judgment I fell forward into his embrace. The Dreamwalker pulled me into his arms, encouraging me to rest my head against his shoulder so he could more easily reach the scrapes on my back. I was already lulled halfway into sleep when I finally made out a snatch of Luke's words as he healed away a long, jagged cut that traced my spine.

"*I'll kill him...*"

I gripped his shoulders and pushed backward, trying to put a little space between us.

Luke's arms firmed, holding me in place. "What's wrong? Does something else hurt?"

I shook my head, which didn't really help the cloudiness of my mind, but I forced my eyes to snap open anyway. "No, I-I'm fine, but..." I pushed back again, less urgently this time, and the Dreamwalker let me lean away enough to meet his gaze. "Luke..." I shivered in his arms. "W-why does he want me dead? Yeah, I stole his aura, but it wasn't on purpose, and I'm... I'm *trying* to stop the Night..."

Luke's hands trailed down my chest to rest on my hips. He frowned. "Incubi are volatile. Secretive." He sighed with concession. "They're not all bad, but they're *serious* about keeping their magic under wraps. When they're done playing with a human, they wipe their memory. They don't run around turning stadiums into fuck-fests." The Dreamwalker's hands started to drift upwards again, fingers tracing delicate patterns across my warming skin, but I focused in on Luke's words, not his motions. "They don't want the publicity Vamps and Weres get." His green eyes flashed up from my body to my face. "You're sort of ruining that."

My brow furrowed, and I leaned in a little closer to Luke's touch. My hands began to draw paths of their own, sweeping up between his pecs to play across his collarbone. "What—" I blinked, and suddenly realized what I was doing. I snatched my hands back, but Luke didn't follow suit. Without really knowing what else to do, I continued, "What do you mean?"

"You're a Seer, not an Incubus. You can't contain the magic leaking out of you, can't stop from turning every person around you into a lovesick psycho. That's bound to piss off the Incubi Council. They won't be able to wipe *every* human's memory when this is over. There's gonna be collateral damage." Luke scowled, glancing away. "That concerns *Gavin*," he intoned with disdain, "because the Night came from him—you're mimicking his aura, so the Council will think he's the one doing it all."

Fuck. If I was in his place, I'd probably be freaked out, too. But that was still no excuse to *kill* a person. "Can't he just explain that it wasn't his fault? That it was an accident?"

Luke smirked grimly. "You've seen how *understanding* Incubi can be. Do you think they'd bother listening to him?"

Fuck 2.0.

I shook my head, pulling away from Luke's arms so that I could pace off some of the nervous energy building up in me in the wake of the healing magic. "I have to get rid of the Night so that Gavin won't kill me. But the only way to do that is to have sex—and if I have sex, Gavin will kill me." I wound my fingers into my hair, tugging firmly at the roots. "What the fuck am I supposed to *do?* There's got to be magic, or some kind of—shit, I don't know—*loophole* out of this." I rounded on the Dreamwalker. He stared up at me through his lashes, looking so innocent but at the same time so alluring, shirtless and flushed with the magic he'd used to heal me. I scrubbed at my face. "I've fucked this up so many times... What would it even take to finish the Night at this point?"

Luke's brow furrowed, and he ran a hand through his hair as he mulled it over. "I... The Night has been building for so long... I can't be sure, but it would be a *lot*." He rubbed at his lip with his thumb. "We could do it, since I know what you need, but it would still take a while." The Dreamwalker looked up into my eyes again. "Long enough for Gavin to find you before we were done."

I opened my mouth to counter with the fact that no matter what I did it wasn't going to involve sex with *Luke*, but a thought steamrolled into my mind before I could bother — something that I hadn't even thought about since the night this whole thing started. *What if... No, it couldn't be that easy — could it?* Was there time? Would they go for it? In an instant my mind was racing around like a slot car flying off the track, whirling so fast I couldn't even follow it all. I spun to face the far wall, staring at the clock hung there. Two thirty-seven p.m.

"What if I burn it all off at once?"

I could practically feel the confusion roiling off Luke as he came around in front of me, sliding his hands onto my waist again to pull my eyes away from the clock to meet his own.

"All of it at once?" He cocked his eyebrow with a look of disbelief. "You realize you'd practically have to be powering an *orgy*, right?"

I grinned unabashedly, feeling something close to true, guilt-free happiness for the first time in what felt like years rising up inside me. "That's the plan." I grabbed both sides of his face and kissed his forehead excitedly before rushing out of his embrace to pull my phone out of my pocket. Luke was still staring at me like I was insane, but I ignored him, unlocking the screen and flying down my contact list. I pressed the one I needed and put the phone to my ear.

It rang once, twice, then three times, and I couldn't help but bounce on my feet nervously. What if he didn't answer? It could work, I was sure of it, but if I couldn't get a hold of —

"Cole? This is a surprise. What do you need?"

I turned back to face Luke, letting the smile creep onto my face.

"Hey, Will. I've got a favor to ask…"

Chapter Nine

I walked across the empty interior of Seethe, its dance platforms and stage, bar and floor all devoid of any life. In a matter of hours the place was going to be completely transformed, a grinding, screaming pit of booze and sweat and throbbing bass – the eerie silence belayed the power of the four walls and the rampant sexual explosion they would soon have to contain. I squeezed with the hand Luke had grabbed onto and refused to let go of since we'd left his apartment, taking comfort in having his reassuring presence there. I didn't fear the emptiness or the Vampires I was about to meet. God knows I'd worked with them long enough to get over any lingering tension in that regard. But the last time I'd been in the club – or at least, the last time I had been in a dream-version of it – I'd faced off against Gavin, and I'd lost miserably until Luke had stepped in to save me. I felt better knowing he was there for me again, even if he wasn't quite as unnervingly powerful here in the waking world as he was in dreams.

Luke was on edge, looking around into every corner with a diligence and speed worthy of the Secret Service. He'd been to Seethe with me more than once, so I knew it didn't have to do with the location or its occupants. Like me, he was worried about Gavin. But where I was nervous, he seemed practically furious, staying so close and using any excuse to touch me that you'd think he was an animal guarding its territory. I chalked it up to the Night and only protested when I felt like I was enjoying the possessive touches a little too much to say I was being objective about the whole thing.

We moved off the main floor and into the hallway at the back that led to the private rooms of the club. The Vamp's office was the last door around the corner, and I knocked twice before stepping inside.

"So what'd you fuck up this time, Cole?" Adam's grinning face immediately greeted me, and I couldn't help but roll my eyes at him.

"Love you too, asshole..." I muttered as I shoved him out of the way, walking in deeper to the office with Luke in tow. The Dreamwalker shot me a look at my choice of words, but I didn't meet his eyes, focusing instead on the Vampire smirking ever so slightly from across the buffed-cherry monster of a desk between us. Will leaned forward, steepling his fingers.

"I have to say, you did get yourself into a rather *interesting* dilemma, Cole. I'm happy to help, but I'll admit I'm still a little...confused by some of the details of your plan."

"I know, I was kind of rushed on the phone in the apartment, then my—" Arms wrapped around my waist from behind me, sweeping me into a tight embrace as Luke abruptly nuzzled into the side of my neck. Not knowing what else to do, I grabbed onto his arms with my own to keep from losing my balance, inadvertently tightening the hug in doing so. I glanced over at him, but he wasn't looking at me. Instead he was casting emerald daggers across the desk at Will. "...hands were *occupied* in the car..."

I kept looking from Luke to Will, both men staring each other down, in William's case with curiosity, and in Luke's case, defiance. I could see Adam doing the same, tensing just like I was as I felt magic stirring in the space between the two men—no spell in particular, just a growing strength like a warning.

Will sat still for a few beats more, then leaned back in his chair, the mercury of his irises never blinking out of view. "Rest assured, Luke, I'm not trying to challenge your claim. I just want to help, as a friend." I glared at the Vampire in confusion. *Your claim?* Will spared me a glance, then turned back to the Dreamwalker. "Our kind's power is based nearly as much in sex as that of Incubi. That leaves us spared of their influence. No one in this room will try to take Cole from you."

Take me from him? Like I was some kind of property? If the idea of "belonging" to Luke didn't make my dick ache so much, I would have had the sense to be pissed at the objectification. As it was, I was more confused than anything. I'd known the Vamps were immune to Night, but I hadn't exactly been expecting Will to all but promise Luke he could have his way with me. I decided to stay quiet for the moment, though, at least until I was content that the Dreamwalker wouldn't jump across the table and try to throttle Will.

Luke stared William down unwaveringly for a few moments more, and for a breath or two I thought he really might pounce—and to be honest, with as much barely-caged Night in his blood as there was, I honestly wasn't sure who would win the fight. But in the next instant the point became moot, as the Dreamwalker finally blinked, pulling back enough that his hands rested on my sides rather than wrapped completely around me. "Good," he muttered, and I felt the magic in the air dissipate.

Will broke a small smile again, and that helped put me more at ease. Adam shot me a look that I couldn't place, some kind of piercing stare that looked like he was trying to dig into my soul. I didn't have time to worry about that, though. "Well, uh... Like I was saying, I know I didn't explain very well, but basically, my plan is this. Tonight is Halloween." I gestured toward Will. "You guys are going to be throwing a rave big enough to draw in half the college kids in town. I've tried to burn off the Night and failed every time, so now my only real option is to push a whole group of people over the edge fast enough that the Incubus stalking me can't do anything about it. Everyone will come, and the Night will finally vent itself, and Gavin will leave me alone." I rushed it out on one breath, praying that if I said it fast enough it would sound a little more sane than it did in my head.

There was a pause where no one said anything, and I felt my stomach tighten painfully. Then Will tilted his head slowly, leaning back in his chair again. "But...as I understand it, isn't this basically the same formula, just on a larger scale? Wouldn't the result be the same as your other attempts?"

Shit... I squirmed in Luke's hands, not quite meeting Will's gaze. That was the part that I had been hoping no one would mention, partly because I was trying to pretend it wasn't valid myself. But even more so, it was because my only assurance that my plan might work *despite* the scaling issue was a vision that I shouldn't have been able to See in the first place.

"It'll work," I said with a lot more confidence than I felt. "I'm not exactly sure how, but...it will." Will's eyebrow remained cocked, and I stared into those unwavering eyes for a few seconds more before finally muttering through gritted teeth, "I Saw it."

The room stayed silent. I hardly dared to breathe as my gaze stayed deadlocked with the Vamp's. After what felt like hours, he finally took a deep breath and furrowed his brow the slightest bit. "You *Saw* it? Saw *yourself?*"

I started to nod, but Luke was already leaning over from behind me, holding me a little tighter as he did. "Yes. I Saw it, too."

Will blinked. "You *both* had a vision of it?" The Vamp ran his hand through his hair before squeezing at his temples. "I don't suppose I need mention that one of you is, in fact, a Dreamwalker without Sight? And that Cole can't See anything about himself?"

I could tell that Luke was about to snap off a response, and, given the tension in the room, I wasn't about to let that happen. A brief squeeze of his hand caught him off guard enough to steamroll over his impending rant. "It's a long story. Suffice it to say, it was a one-time thing, but the important part is the plan will work." For all I knew I was lying through my teeth, but I didn't know what else I could do at that point except to trust the Sight that had been stabbing me in the back since I'd turned thirteen. I squeezed Luke's hand again. "Please, Will."

The Vampire steepled his fingers and stared at the point where they met intently. I leaned back into Luke's embrace and tried to let his warmth chase away some of the gnawing fear eating away at me. That vision—even if it had been real—was just one possible outcome. What if Will said no, it was too dangerous? What if there was some piece I was missing, and the plan just made the Night so strong that I would never be able to beat it?

Will looked back up at me, and I realized with his flash of that I-know-this-is-a-terrible-idea-but-I-guess-I-have-to-do-it look that I was safe from at least one of those endings.

"Long or not, that's a story I intend on hearing when this all blows over. In *detail*." He licked his lips and sighed. "But you've never been wrong before... I can't imagine you would be this time."

Oh, I sure as hell could imagine it. I could imagine every fucking way this train wreck could go incredibly wrong. But the last thing I needed was to show that, so I settled for a breathless "Thank you" instead.

Adam stepped forward, crossing his arms. "Burning off the Night is all well and good, but why worry about timing? We have four Vamps, a Seer and a Walker here. I say you take as long as you need, and when that Incubus fuck tries to bust in we blow him back to the hole he crawled out of."

I liked the sound of that, and from the growl of approval Luke gave off from behind me, it seemed he did too, but Will shook his head. "While I'll admit it's what he might deserve given what you've said he's done to you, Cole, it won't work. Letting you use a Vampire club to burn off the Night is one thing, but if we so much as touch that Incubus it would be out and out war. You know the kind of animosity that exists between our race and theirs. The Councils would break down overnight."

Adam opened his mouth to snap back, but I overran him. "He's right, it's not worth it. I just need to burn off the Night and get out. I've caused enough collateral damage as it is." God knew the images of Aaron and Owen were more than willing to remind me of that fact if I ever tried to forget it.

Will grinned up at me, blindingly white fangs flashing under the warm lights of the room. "Well then, it looks like we have a rave to plan."

* * * *

By the time we'd hammered out the details it was already getting late, and people were starting to filter into the club, staying close to the bar for now. The music was still at tolerable levels, but I knew as it got later it was going to get louder, *much* louder, then the lasers and strobes would really start to fly. The countless-gigawatt display going on now would seem absolutely tame by comparison in less than an hour.

Luke still refused to let go of me, though I'd managed to get him to settle for just holding my hand again. I wanted to tell myself that I didn't like it, that I was just letting it happen because it easier for him, but fuck if that wouldn't be a blatant lie. I wanted him, wanted to touch him like that every day and do so much more, but if I was going to have any prayer of getting back even the casual touches we'd shared before the Night, I had to be strong. He'd always tried to tell me I was brave, and I'd be damned if I wasn't going to try to be that for him.

Dana and Troy, the other two Vampires in the clan, had come in during the planning process just long enough to figure out what they needed to do before leaving. They were siblings, and I'd never really talked to them much—they hadn't been nearly as interested in me as Adam had been, probably because Troy was straight and Dana... Well, I didn't really know. Either way, they walked past Luke and I, offering only a short wave to show that they knew the plan before moving to tend the bar. Truth be told, private as they were, they freaked me out a little, but I needed all the allies I could get at that point.

Will came up beside me, staring out across the floor of his club. For a second I thought he was going to wrap his arm around my shoulder like he often did, but he seemed to think better of it when Luke shot a glance at him and lifted our linked hands to his mouth so that he could brush a chaste kiss across my knuckles. I squirmed, but neither of the other men seemed to notice. I tried to deflect as best I could.

"Thanks again for this, Will."

The Vampire looked down at me with a soft smile. "It's nothing. Your financial Sightings have never been anything but extraordinary since you began helping us here—and you've also become a good friend of mine, Cole, which isn't easy to find in my..." He seemed to taste the words in his mouth before choosing them. "My line of work. I meant it when I said I was happy to help."

I saw William as more of my friend than my boss too, which, though it was nice to know was reciprocated, made it a damn miracle that I could even still do the Seer work he needed. But then I guess it would be a little self-aggrandizing to think that a friendship with a guy linked our fates enough for me to be blocked from seeing changes in the stock market that might indirectly affect the prospects of said guy's business with which I otherwise wasn't involved. It seemed I was only blocked from Seeing things that *really* would affect me as well—so I probably wouldn't be able to see if Will was going to be in a horrible car accident, for example. But seeing as he was an immortal Vampire I guess that point was moot anyway—

"Besides, I do feel slightly...responsible, for what has happened to you." Will's words snapped me back to reality. My brow furrowed, and Luke squeezed my hand.

"What do you mean?"

The Vampire shifted his feet uncomfortably. "Luke gave you the Night with good intentions. The man he got it from had...*less pure* reasons for creating it. *And* he happens to be on my payroll."

My stomach somersaulted as I tried to wrap my head around what he was saying. "He *what?*"

William had the good grace to appear at least mildly ashamed as he pointed over at the entrance to the club. People were starting to stream in now, but I could make out a man by the door—a guy who was admittedly hot, but other than that didn't seem to have anything unique about him. Average height, average build. "Max York. He's my bodyguard. Doubles as a bouncer." I did a double-take, making sure there wasn't anyone else he could be pointing at.

"*He's* your bodyguard?"

William cocked an assessing eyebrow at me. "Don't let his appearance fool you. When he shifts, he's the largest wolf I've ever seen, and I've met plenty. And his precision with that shifting magic is truly astounding." I looked him over again, but other than the pissed-off look on his face, I couldn't figure how the guy could ever be intimidating. "Unfortunately, he's also a colossal 'man-whore'."

I looked over at Will like he'd gone nuts. "Man-whore?" I was amazed enough that the club owner even used contractions, his speech was so polished.

The Vampire smirked. "To quote Adam, Max invented Night as a way of finding even more sexual partners. As a result, I've had furious Incubi beating my door down for weeks." He ran a hand through his hair, and, not for the first time, I caught one of the contradictory glances into the true age of experiences Will had faced as it clashed with the youthful body he wielded. "But rest assured, the Night you received was the last batch he produced." I couldn't help but look at him with disbelief. That just made him grin. If he hadn't just said I was more or less adopted family of the clan, I would've been a lot more unnerved by the barely contained power in that self-assured, fanged smile of his. "Let's just say he's *learned his lesson*."

Adam came up from behind us, chiming in happily. "Not being allowed to come for three months and counting will tend to do that to a guy. Especially when you're as crazy-horny as Max is."

I glanced over at Max again. Once I knew what to look for, the guy did look pretty miserable…staring at each of the lithe, tight bodies slipping through the door with a predatory gaze that was doomed to be unfulfilled tonight. As though he could hear my thoughts, Max turned and noticed me from across the room, and, after a moment of staring, proceeded to check me out in a way that made me immediately want to shower. In a flurry of motion Luke changed our positions so that he was firmly placed in between the two of us, and I found myself forgetting rather quickly why I'd felt sorry for the Shifter in the first place.

Will clapped his hands together to break the awkward silence—or as close to silence as it could be, when the music was already climbing in volume. "Well, I have a door I need to attend to for some of our more...*interesting* clients." He smiled at me more gently this time, then patted my shoulder, which Luke let happen with only minimal death-glaring. "We'll be ready when you are, Cole." In the next moment the Vampire was swept up into the growing crowd and I lost sight of him.

Without Will there to talk me through it, I couldn't help the fear coiling in my chest, cementing my feet in place even as it made my blood rush that much faster. The more I thought about what I was going to have to do, the sicker I felt, and my eyes flicked from Adam to Luke in the hopes of some kind of respite from one of the two of them. Luke took pity on me first, rubbing slow circles into my wrist with his thumb.

"So what do you want to do until it's time?"

I wanted to hide. I wanted to curl up with Luke somewhere and pretend I didn't have to go up on a stage and make a room full of people have sex so a crazy Incubus wouldn't kill me. I wanted to pretend for a little while longer that I would be okay and this might end well and I wouldn't lose my best friend. But that didn't seem to be in the cards, and it brought home a point I'd been thinking about since Luke had first insisted he come with me to Seethe.

"Luke... I-I don't want you here when it happens." He immediately opened his mouth, and I pressed a finger to his lips and kept talking. "I want you at your apartment, where I know you're safe."

The Dreamwalker wrapped his fingers around my wrist, pivoting my hand so that my palm rested on his cheek, where he held it in place so he could kiss it. I tried to pull back, but he wouldn't let me. "I'll be safe *here*, with you. You need me to be here."

I sighed emphatically, barely resisting the urge to roll my eyes. Fuck if he wasn't making it hard enough for me, because no, damn it, I didn't *really* want him to go! He was the only thing that made me feel like I was even still alive and not just playing out some sick nightmare for someone's amusement. I wanted to stay with him every minute of every day. But he couldn't be here for this, because then what he'd said might come true, and he might be the one to end the Night, and I'd never be able to live with myself. So I tried to put up my walls and act frustrated and fall back into the cynical ass of a role I'd painted for myself since I was thirteen, even if it had never worked on him. "I can take care of myself, Luke, I don't need a *babysitter*. Besides, Adam and Will—"

Luke shook his head, throwing his hair down onto his eyebrows again in his fervency. "No, that's not what I mean! Adam!" he called out over the rising music.

The Vampire turned and walked back over. "Yeah?"

I glanced from Luke to Adam, clueless as to what the other man had to do with this. The Dreamwalker pulled the Vampire in closer so that we could hear each other, never letting his hand fall from mine. "William assumed we were together, didn't he? Like a couple?"

Adam's brow furrowed as he scratched at his hair. "Well, yeah. So did I, although it *did* kinda confuse me, since before you guys never seemed to—"

I cut him off, shaking my head and raising my voice to be heard over the bass as it dropped in an auditory explosion that threw the ravers in front of us into a frenzy. "So he misunderstood, who cares?"

Luke squeezed my hand tightly. "You're going to be fueling those people with Night. But they're going to need *your* orgasm to push them over the edge." I shrugged, about to reply that I knew that, that I'd always assumed I was going to at least have to blow on my own even if the vision of getting screwed didn't have to come true. The Dreamwalker continued before I could say any of it. "This is going to be an entire *rave*, Cole! Some little come shot from jacking yourself off isn't going to be enough. It needs to be deep, strong. Enough to push the others over the top!" We were practically shouting to be heard now, and I prayed the song would end soon so we'd at least have a few seconds' respite.

"So I'll fuck someone random—whoever's close! It doesn't matter."

But now it was Adam's turn to shake his head, not in frustration, but in slow-coming realization. "Actually...it will."

The song finally faded away, and in the sixty seconds tops that I had before the next song had built up to its first drop and drowned out everything, I rounded on Adam furiously. "What?"

The Vampire shrugged, speaking fast to get it out before the music ramped up to full power again. "Night is powerful stuff as it is, and yours has gotten so out of hand. You'll have to be with another magical being to balance you out, or else there's no telling what could happen. It could kill you, or someone else!"

My mouth opened and closed blankly. *No, that couldn't*—but fuck, when I'd been with Aaron and Owen, before this shit had really even got strong, I'd already had enough trouble reigning in my power. I wanted to argue, because I knew where it was going and there was no way in hell I was letting that happen after working this hard, but there just weren't any words.

Luke filled in the gap, already having to shout again to be made out. "You can't screw one of the Vampires, because they'll be in the crowd, acting as amplifiers to make the aura reach everyone. Max is going to have to leave, so that he doesn't shift and kill someone! *I'm* your only option!"

No. No, I was not going to let this all fall through. I was too close. I was grasping at straws, but I would've rather done that all day than admit that I really did have to do what I'd promised myself I'd fight since it all started. "This town is *filled* with magical beings! I'll be able to find at least one here!"

Those green eyes stared into mine with an assurance that I refused to take solace in for once. "One who you'll actually find attractive enough to come the way you need to? Someone who will *know* what you need?"

I turned away, staring at the floor as orange and purple lasers trailed across the cement surface. There was another way. There always had been before—I was a fucking *Seer* damn it! For once in my *God damn life* couldn't I use my power of seeing twelve *billion* different futures to find just *one* that didn't end in everything going wrong?

Adam cocked an eyebrow, glancing from Luke to me and back again. "Cole, I don't really see what the problem is—"

Aggravation bubbled up inside me, energizing my limbs again, a welcome relief from the exhaustion. I pushed Luke aside, stepping closer to Adam until I was leveling his gaze with my own building anger. "You don't see a *problem?* Believe it or not, I don't think it's right to *guilt* my best friend into *fucking me* just to save my own ass!" I shook my head furiously. "There are plenty of magical people out on that floor. Fuck, I'll call up *Derek* if I have to—"

A steel hand gripped my arm and spun me around again. The fire in Luke's eyes was practically boiling over now. "Do *not* call that *fuckhead!* You don't need him, I'm right *here!*"

I tried to reply, but Adam cut me off. "Seriously, Cole, I don't understand why you won't just do Luke. He obviously wants to—" The Vampire finally met my eyes, but his brow only furrowed at the pain I knew had to be showing on my face. He stumbled, clearly trying to figure out what could be scaring me so much. "I mean if you're that worried about it, we can just wipe his…mem…" Adam's voice trailed off as dawning realization finally lit up behind the mercury. I buried my face in my hands, not wanting to have to watch as he finally put it all together.

"You love him."

"*Shut up*, Adam." My voice was shaking with emotion no matter how hard I tried to keep it level. I was pissed, so far beyond pissed, and I couldn't figure out why, but hearing him say those three words no matter how many times I'd said them in the privacy of my own mind just made my blood boil.

"You do?"

The quiet voice at my side was Luke's, but I couldn't look over at him, couldn't see the hope that would be glowing out at me from the Night that had stolen over him. I bore into Adam, refusing to look away. "*Please* don't do this…"

In a rush of motion too fast for me to track, the Vampire had hold of my arm and was pulling me farther down the hall, looking even more furious than

I had been. Luke took a step forward to follow, but Adam rounded on him. "*Stay.*" Magic roared through the space between them, washing over the Dreamwalker with a strength that made me flinch. Luke took a half-step forward, his face twisted in concentration, but in the next second his foot went back to its original position, rooting him firmly to the spot. Adam pulled me a few feet deeper down the hall, then immediately spun me around so I was trapped between him and the wall.

His voice was low, but still buzzing with the strength of the spells he'd just let loose. "You love Luke, but you've been running around fucking anything that *moves*, just because now you *can*?"

I wanted to feel hurt by the accusation, rightfully snap back that it was *because* I loved Luke that I'd tried to screw other people instead of taking advantage of him. But I was too mad to be anything but defensive, and the warm crimson of aggression was too alluring in comparison to the numbness I was so used to at this point.

"Since when were *you* a Goddamn moral compass?" I hissed. "You suck the sex out of anyone that comes through those fucking doors!" Adam opened his mouth, but I overran him, reveling in the aggravation that was fueling me. "And don't even tell me it's to survive, because we both know *damn well* you don't need a fucking fifty-course meal every night like you get at this place. You would be just fine at one good drain a week!"

Adam's jaw ticked, but he didn't change his grip on my arm. "My situation is completely different. *I* don't know who my mate is yet!" He frowned. "I would never run around with my dick hanging out the way *you* have when you *know* Luke is your—"

I shoved at his chest, not that he moved. "*Fuck* you, Adam!"

The Vampire cocked an eyebrow with infuriating calm. "I'm surprised you haven't *tried* to yet."

That did it. Something snapped inside me. Marks of power crackled into life at my wrists, and without a second thought I let the spells of power burn out of me and into Adam, flaring the hallway with blinding light. Caught off guard, the Vampire was thrown to the far wall where he only just kept from crumbling to the floor. I was shaking so hard it was all I could do not to fall, too, but I still found the strength to point at Luke's still form.

"He's fucking *straight!*"

Adam was at my side again in an instant, turning me so that I was facing where the Dreamwalker was pushing against the magic keeping him in place with everything he had just so he could be close to me again. I tried to close my eyes so I didn't have to see it, but Adam grabbed my chin and didn't let go until I opened them again.

"The man *salivating* for you over there is straight? Couldn't possibly be bi?"

I held down the urge to cry and tried to push his hand off, but Adam wasn't letting me, and with his Vampire strength there was nothing I could do about it. I settled for slamming my hands into his chest—it wasn't nearly enough to actually push him away, but at least he could feel how fucking *pissed* I was. "It's only because of the Night!" I shoved against him again, and when that didn't work I tried to squirm out of his grasp, not that that was any more effective. I finally slumped into his arms, resting my head on the other man's shoulder in defeat. "It has to be…"

Adam tilted my chin up until I was looking into his eyes again. The kind of concern I'd only ever seen from Luke before softened his features, and I felt his hands fall away from my body. "Why does it have to be because of the Night?"

I stared at Luke in silence, praying that that would somehow give me the answer, because I needed to know why, too. My mouth opened then closed, and when it opened again, the words came out as if they had a mind of their own. I was as much a listener as the speaker.

"Because if it isn't… If he really *could* be…" I shook my head, staring transfixed at those full lips frozen in place. "If he really is, then…" I swallowed. "Everything I thought I knew about the only person left who I really care about—it was all a lie. I really could have had him at any time, if I'd just been strong enough to say it."

I felt Adam's hand on my shoulder, and for all I know he may have said something, but I was deaf to any voice but my own, even as it dipped into nearly a whisper. And still, I couldn't stop staring at Luke, like his body was the only thing in this world that I could see. "I always told myself it was wrong to think of him like that. Fucking me. Loving me. Wanting me like I've always wanted him—" I tried to look away, tried to see what Adam was doing, but my mind refused to let go of the thread it was unraveling, not until a sharp voice echoing down the hall pierced through my reverie.

"*Seer!*"

I blinked heavily, turning to the sound. For one gut-wrenching second I thought it might be Gavin, until I recognized the figure at the end of the hallway as Troy, running a hand through his wild blond hair.

"Your aura is already affecting the crowd. Half of the club is trying to get in this hallway!" He glanced over his shoulder, and I saw Dana there as well, holding a group of ravers at bay with what I assumed had to be magic. Troy turned to face me again. "If the Incubus doesn't already know where you are, he will very soon. It's now or never."

Now or never. The butterflies in my stomach that had been staying still for the moment roared into a flurry, and I only just stopped myself from dry-heaving. It had to be now. I had to get up there and end it once and for all, banking on some half-baked vision and Luke—

As if on command, Adam released his spell with a wave of his hand. Luke slumped for a moment, then blinked a few times as full control of his body finally started to return to him.

Now. Go now. Do it before you get too scared and ruin everything again. Go!

I rushed forward, throwing my arms around Luke before he could do anything more than blink. I slammed my eyes shut, losing myself for one tiny second in the warmth of my Dreamwalker's embrace as his arms wrapped around me. I turned just enough to whisper into his ear. *"Whatever happens... I'm sorry."*

Luke's hand gently palmed my chest as he pushed me back enough to look into my eyes. A calm I wouldn't have expected to be there filled his features, and I wished I could share the same assurance. "Don't be."

I pressed my lips to his, ignoring the screaming voice in the back of my head. I had already gone past the event horizon of my own damnation. It was far too late to regret a single kiss.

I pulled away before the Dreamwalker could try to do anything else, rushing out of his arms and into the pounding bass of the laser-lit darkness with the Vampires at my heels.

* * * *

Adam hurried me along the wall, keeping himself and plenty of distance between the clubbers and me. After a few tense seconds, he led me through a door and down another short hallway, and in the next second I realized I was at the back of the main stage. A few feet forward and to the right, and I'd be on display for the entire club to see. The limelight was currently filled by a DJ mixing the screaming music filling the room, but with a flick of Adam's hand he'd leave the stage and I'd be up. Shielded from the speakers by the walls around us, the Vampire took advantage of the relative quiet to finally talk again without having to scream.

"Are you gonna be okay?"

I ran a hand over my shirt, smoothing the creases that had formed there. It didn't really matter—the ravers weren't going to give a damn what I looked like, just the Incubus energy I was going to be flooding their bodies with—energy that was obviously already starting to work, seeing how many of them were trying to press their way even closer to the stage.

"Ask me again when it's over."

The Vampire smiled sadly, and I looked around for something to distract myself with so I didn't have to see his pity. A box of glow sticks sat on a table in front of us, and I reached over to grab one. I accidently caught two, but I held onto them both anyway, cracking them to see what colors I'd gotten.

Two glow-stick wristbands smoldered eerily in the darkness, pink and orange…

Oh fuck.

I hesitated for a moment, then checked to see that the link was at the end of both of them to complete the circle and make two bracelets. I felt like a criminal having to slip the noose over his own neck, but I couldn't resist the urge to snap the two lines of fluorescence down on my left wrist. I lowered my arm, watching as the bands of color glowed up at me brightly from the shadows of the hallway.

God, I wish Luke was here…

I didn't have a chance to think any more about that, as the DJ's song was already starting to come to an end. My stomach clenched tightly at the realization, and I prayed again for a strength I didn't think I was capable of. Adam signaled the DJ and handed me the headset mic, clipping the receiver to the waistband of my jeans.

"We'll be in the crowd reflecting the aura, so they won't rush the stage. It's gonna be fine." He smiled weakly, patting me on the shoulder. "It'll all be over soon." I nodded, trying to quell the shaking in my hands long enough to get the headset on properly. Adam squeezed my arm briefly and was gone, no doubt to blend into the crowd and signal the other Vamps to be ready.

The song came to an end, my headset beeped plaintively to confirm that it had hooked into the audio system and the DJ disappeared into the darkness at the other side of the stage.

I was up. It had to be now.

I took a step forward, faltered then promptly threw up all over the floor. I fell to my knees, barely able to take in a breath. The metallic tang of vomit burned in my mouth, and I scraped at my lips with my hand to wipe it away.

It wasn't going to work. I'd missed something, some clue, and the vision wouldn't come true, and the Night was going to be too strong to ever stop it. And Gavin... I wouldn't be able to escape him this time...

Get up. Get up!

I dug my fingers into the wooden column to my right as I dragged myself to my feet. I'd never so much as taken a public speaking class, much less walked out in front of a crowd of hundreds and worked them up until they all *came!* But damn it, Luke needed me, and I had one last shot. My fist flew into the wall, hitting the wood so hard I heard something crack, and I couldn't be sure if it was the wall or my own knuckles. The pain stabbed up my arm like electrified needles, and my nostrils flared as my lungs dragged in a frigid breath. My vision swam at the edges, but I blinked it away and stormed out onto the brightly lit stage before I could lose my nerve.

* * * *

Music still pounded out a beat behind me, an instrumental clusterfuck of beats that was quiet enough for me to talk over but still pulsing with enough volume to keep the crowd moving against one another. A sea of jumping, grinding bodies swam in the black in front of me, looking more like waves crashing against the base of the stage than actual people. That was good—if I had to really see them, had to really think about what I was doing to them, I would've thrown up again in no time flat.

The laser lights at the base of the stage swung wide to the beat of the song in the background, playing across the crowd before spinning back in tight to point straight up. The spotlight that had been whirling around the room snapped into place pointing firmly at my body, and I knew it was time.

"How're you guys doing?"

My voice was stronger than I would have expected — more confident, assured. Apparently it was good enough for the crowd, as they roared out some kind of affirmation, reaching their hands to the ceiling frantically.

All right, Cole, come on. You can do this. You pretend to be things you're not all the time, this is no different.

I had zero knowledge of what a striptease was supposed to be like. All I knew was you needed to end up pretty much naked, and you had to toss out some innuendos along the way. With enough Night in the air, I knew it really wouldn't matter what I said anyway.

After only a few seconds under the spotlight I could already feel sweat starting to bead up on my skin, and I pulled the front of my shirt out and back in a few times to rush some fresh air over my chest. The relief cleared my head a little, and with it left an idea. *All right – we'll go for campy.*

"Is it just me, or…" I blew out a breath, wiping at my brow with an exaggerated sweep of my arm while I flexed my biceps. "Is it *hot* in here?" I set my feet a little farther apart and fanned at myself with my hand while I peered out into the crowd with a look of ease I wished I could have actually felt.

The ravers screamed out their affirmation, furiously jumping to the beat of the music and my little show. I fanned out my shirt again, making sure that when I let it go the deep V neck of the collar was seated as low as possible. I could already feel the Incubus aura radiating out of the crowd, flowing out of me and reflecting back off them. I reached for my threads, finding the fever-hot glow that was the Night inside me.

Let's see what this stuff can really *do…*

I trailed one hand into my hair and the other slid down to my crotch, where I squeezed my hardening cock with a flare of the Incubus aura. The clubbers cheered again, grabbing hold of one another as their sexual need spiked furiously. I looked out into the darkness with feigned innocence. "You're hot too?" I intoned breathily. They roared wildly, and I let a smile tease at the corners of my mouth.

"Well, let's see what we can do about that…"

My fingers gripped the hem of my shirt, and I closed my eyes as I vented more Night into the roiling air. I could feel the four Vamps in the crowd, burned outlines in my mind that were taking in my power and reflecting it back out, making it stronger and less focused in on just me. Scattered across all four walls, they were more than making sure that no one would be free of my influence. I surged the Night again, pushing it as hard as I could, and was rewarded with a colossal moan from the crowd as the cheering broke away into more primal sounds. It felt like I was letting loose a monster into the air, one that swallowed their every desire and used it to grow larger, to feed it right back to them magnified tenfold.

I sucked in a breath and clenched every muscle as tight as I could as I pulled the shirt up my body at an agonizing pace. With every inch of exposed skin, I felt the white heat of the aura burn brighter, crackling away at the edges, and the cries of bliss rang out so loudly there was no mistaking them over the pounding of the music. I pulled the shirt off completely, running a hand down my chest and abs, already slick with perspiration. My head lolled back, and with my other hand I played across my collarbone, making my pecs tighten and jump.

My eyes drifted open lazily, and I smiled again. "That's better, isn't it?"

Night rocketed out of me like heat-seeking missiles, detonating throughout the crowd. My breath hitched as I realized I was losing control of the aura, that it was being dragged out of me whether I directed it to or not. For a second I almost let my face fall, barely tamping down the urge in time—I had to keep up the act, couldn't let it show how much it was starting to terrify me to stand up there and practically ooze sluttiness onto the stage. I had to pretend I was in control for at least a little while longer, until I could get them all hot enough to...

To what? Come? I was going to have to blow for that to happen, and for that I needed someone with magic. I could feel the power in some of the people in the crowd, but it was fuzzy, washed over with the Night coursing through everyone's veins. It was hard to pin down any one source.

My hands still moved over my body, swirling and squeezing like I wasn't in the middle of an internal crisis to rival any DEFCON code. The aura was working, making the ravers grind against each other and move their hands to places that would normally call for a lot more alcohol than they'd consumed, but they needed more, so much more if it was going to work, and I knew I had to be running out of time. Gavin could break in at any moment. I needed to start sacrificing what few morals I had left, and *fast*.

I tugged at my belt buckle, letting some of my assured finesse fall by the wayside in favor of speed.

My left hand wasn't dexterous enough to do it by itself so I reached down with my right, but I misjudged the distance and cracked my knuckles on the metal. Pain bloomed into fire tipped knives under my skin, but I forced out another wave of Night to distract the crowd into a rush of moans while I clutched it to my chest.

Magic crept its way through the thick air to wrap around my hand, healing the ache with familiar grace. My eyes flashed open as I stared out into the darkness, trying to make out where the spell had come from. More of the Incubus aura tore free, charging the crowd with molten need, but in the flurry of movement and strobes and lasers, I could just make out one person front and center, seemingly unfazed by the urge to dance that had captured everyone else in Seethe.

The air locked in my throat, even though I'd known it long before I'd seen him.

Luke.

The remnant marks of his magic trickled away into the crowd as he stared up at me, that little smirk playing across his lips. Laughter bubbled up in my throat, an expression of relief in the middle of the insanity I was trapped in, this nightmare that was almost worse than Gavin's, because in this one the Dreamwalker couldn't save me. But knowing he was here, no matter how hard I'd tried to get him to leave — somehow it surged my body with the energy I needed. The bass pounded out behind me, and I reached down into my jeans, squeezing the base of my cock with a confidence that made the corners of my vision go black.

I moaned into the mic, closing my eyes and breathing in the sex pouring off the masses in front of me. The monster inside me answered their call,

Erik Clarke

roaring into a flame that ignited in my bloodstream and pumped raw voltage into the rave. The music peaked, the crowd screamed and I clawed at the button of my jeans, tearing down the zipper.

"I always wanted to do this for you... Wanted to show you what you do to me..." My words graced out through the speakers, silken honey that dripped out of the cracks in the beats of the song. I couldn't stop looking at Luke, my strength in the middle of this laser-cut hell, and without a word we both knew this was for him, that everything I was saying may have been heard by everyone but was really for his ears alone. The Dreamwalker stared up at me with a kind of adoration that made my chest ache, and I closed my eyes as I saw him reach into his jeans.

"I need you so bad..." I wrapped my arms around my chest, hugging myself as I rolled my hips toward the floor in tune to the music. Radioactive heat pulsed out of me then back in, reverberating smut that already had most of the club shirtless, but they needed more, always needed more, and I pushed harder, flushing the Night to new heights I'd never dared reach in a way that made my teeth shiver and ache. "I tried to show you, but I knew you didn't feel the same way." I bit down on my lip, scraping a hand across my chest in a move that left faint red trails across the skin. "But now I've got you." I swallowed hard. "And I'll be damned if I let you go now."

The crowd screamed out in a fury, and I could see some of them trying to rush up onto the stage, held at bay only by wards of shielding that one of the Vamps must have set in place. I could just make out the Vampires in the black, each sporting their own crowd of ravers desperate for a touch, a taste, a peek. I caught sight of Dana, men crawling across her skin like it was their lifeblood, but she had eyes only for me, staring up hungrily with a hand down in her cut-offs. Silver eyes burned out across the darkness with molten fire, closing only when her shirt was torn from her body in her worshippers' fervency.

I looked to Luke again, panting up at me furiously from a few dozen feet away, and I groaned as I rolled my hips into my waiting hand again and again, slowly stroking my cock closer to the edge.

The bass dropped and so did I, sliding down to my knees. I kept squeezing and stroking, refusing to give myself or the Night a moment's respite. My free hand ran through my hair, and I stared the Dreamwalker down with need so bad it hurt. "I want to know what you look like when you come." My voice shook, but I couldn't stop, didn't want to stop, and I cried out as my dick pulsed so hard I thought I might lose it right then. I gritted my teeth and closed my eyes. "I want to see you lose control. God knows I've dreamed about it—I see it every time I shut my eyes, but I want to see it now, the way you'd tense up..." I was out of breath, barely able to moan out what I needed to say, but I wouldn't have stopped for anything in the world. "The way you'd hold onto me like I was the only one who could save you from just *drowning* in the ecstasy." My eyes flew open and I let the aura explode, burning so hot I felt it seething its way into even the Vampire's resistant blood. As they gave in to my power, I lost sight of them, blending into the static-pulsing grind of the Night-flooded crowd.

And still Luke stood there, staring up at me desperately while everyone else in the room was falling to the floor, pressing against the walls, tearing off pants and shirts and any piece of clothing that could get in the way of their desire for one another. I fell forward onto my hands, crawling toward the edge of the stage, closer and closer to the only thing left that I still needed. My fingers dug into the headset at my ear, ripping it free and tossing it aside, throwing the receiver to the crowd as well. I reached the edge of the stage and stared into Luke's eyes, smoldering emeralds in the sex and the black. My arms shook and so did my voice, but I didn't care—all that mattered was the man in front of me, held away from me by so much more than the shield spell between us.

"I want to see what you would've done if I hadn't stopped you..."

Luke shuddered, and I clutched at my chest, where my threads were pounding against each other in rampant discord. For a second I thought it was the Night, finally tearing itself out of me even without an orgasm to trigger it, but this was something else, something that burned so bad I coughed up bile onto the floor below me. My wrist was on fire, and when I looked at it, my Mark was quivering along the skin, pulsing and jumping in ways I'd never thought possible.

I looked up to Luke's face, but he didn't have any answers for me, not in time. Lightning crackled along my skin, and I screamed as my eyes stung so badly I fell to the stage floor. White light flashed out, and in the next second I felt the time stream tear open in my mind, sweeping me up in its raging floodwaters.

* * * *

Gavin.

The Incubus flew across the parking lot with arcane speed, bearing down on the main door of Seethe with furious determination. The human bouncers had already caved in to my control, which was for the best, as I'm sure he wouldn't have spared them on his path of destruction. Magic twisted out of his hands so fast I couldn't track the marks, spells that obliterated the door as he smashed his way into the club.

He flew through the crowd, throwing fucking couples left and right as he stormed up to the stage, where two men were—

Oh God.

Chapter Ten

The Sight ripped free of my mind, sealing off the rush of the future and leaving me broken on the stage.

No...

I hadn't Seen a clock, or anything to indicate how long I had until the Incubus broke in, but it couldn't have been long — the fading traces of the vision burned at my mind so strongly that it could only have been a matter of minutes.

Night still gunned in my veins, and the sexual fire it offered was the only thing that gave me the strength to drag myself to my feet, staring out into the crowd with clouded eyes. Every person was in the throes of passion, either fucking or being fucked, sucking, tasting, losing themselves in the people around them. The aura filled the room so completely that marks of longing and need were literally dripping from the walls, panted out on every breath, too strong to be taken in anymore by the saturated air of the club.

Now. You need to fuck someone now!

I reached out with my waning strength, letting my magic call out for an answer in the crowd.

Nothing happened.

I pushed again, harder this time in a move that made my stomach turn, but still nothing. Night was raging through everyone so completely that it was acting like a veil, dimming any magical being's signature under its own pervasive strength. I tried it again, and again, desperate, but there wasn't anything I could do — the Night was showing me one last time the kind of power it held over me, and there was nothing I could do to stop it.

I scoured the mass of fucking bodies, trying to make out one I recognized — Adam, Will, hell, *anyone!* But it was too dark, and everyone was moving too much, and there was no way to make out any person in particular now that they had finally lost themselves to the moaning, grinding passion I'd forced onto all of them.

I spun around wildly, not knowing what else to do, until my eyes came to rest on a single man, standing shirtless on the edge of the stage, encircled by a shroud of swirling marks of power. It was like a vision from a dream, and my breath hitched in my chest as the still-spinning spotlights raced across his body and onto his face.

"No…" I shook my head, falling to my knees on the hard stage floor. My fingers twisted into my hair and tugged with all the pain of my misery as my heart sank down into the pit of my stomach. "No, I-I can't…"

Gentle hands wrapped around my wrists, pulling my fingers out of my hair and coming to rest on both sides of my face.

"Cole — Cole, look at me."

I couldn't breathe. I tried to push against the hands moving over me with such concern and kindness, tried to shake my head and back out of his arms, but my Dreamwalker held on tight and wouldn't let me run away. Salty tears burned paths down my flushing cheeks, and Luke brushed them away with his thumb, urging my face upwards with a hand on my chin. The vision of him swam in front of my eyes until I could blink away the water enough to make out the grave seriousness painted across his features.

"Cole, we have to. There's no time."

"No!" I knocked his hands aside, climbing to my feet and stepping away from him with my arms wrapped tight around my chest. Air wasn't moving into my lungs properly, and I gasped with each breath, trying to drag in more than the tiny rush my throat would let pass. Luke stood as well, but I held him away, pressing my hands into his chest and refusing to let him push his way any closer. I couldn't do it. *Not now. Not ever!* I *wouldn't* do that to him.

"Cole—"

"No. No, no *God-fucking-damn-it, no!*" I was crying, and I hated that I couldn't stop, couldn't even try. Luke shook his head furiously, throwing his hair into disarray as the laser lights twirled maniacally around us, catching us up in beams of boiling red and seething purple in tune to the still-throbbing music. The Dreamwalker shoved forward, forcing my arms to bend so that he could grip both of my shoulders.

"The Incubus—"

"I don't care!" I was shouting above and beyond what was needed to be heard over the beats, but I couldn't stop myself. "I don't *fucking* care anymore, Luke. I'm not going to do that to you!" I choked.

The Dreamwalker's eyes bore into mine with an intensity that made me turn away. He pulled me back to face him with a hand. "Listen to me." I tried to shake my head and push him away, but Luke knocked my hands aside and shook me. "No, *damn it*, listen!" Air shuddered out of my chest. It felt like something inside me was crumbling, breaking down and sealing off all the parts of me that kept me stable. I shook in his hands, and the tears burned in my eyes as I tried to be strong enough to hear what he had to say.

Green burned in the darkness, two irises that boiled with molten heat. Luke's fingers softened in their death-grip on my body, but only slightly. "I know you think that everything I've done has been the Night, that there isn't any of the real me left in here." He shook his head. The Dreamwalker's voice quaked with overflowing emotion, but his face was strong, his jaw firm. "You're wrong. More than you could know. But, Cole, you have to know that, Night or not, I could *never* let you die if there was a way I could stop it."

If there was anything left of my heart, that was the moment that it broke once and for all.

I clawed at Luke's arms, falling to the stage as all feeling left my limbs. He followed me down, hugging me close to the warmth of his body. I slumped into his shoulder, holding him as tightly as I dared, knowing in that moment more than ever that the safety I felt in his arms could never last. The black hole inside me tried to stir into life, but I kicked it back down into the pit it had crawled from and sealed the locks with my agony and my frustration. There would be no numbness, no shield holding the pain away—I deserved every second of it, and I would drown in the flood if I had to.

"We can't... I-I..." My words ghosted across Luke's feverish skin, the strength in them broken, the fight long gone. It was too late, just like I'd always been too late.

The Dreamwalker squeezed me closer, running his hands over my shoulders and my back, marks of soothing and calm riding the trails his fingers left until they could ease under my skin and take hold. I tried to fight them, tried to resist the comfort because I shouldn't have been allowed it, but Luke knew how to get through all of my defenses, just like he always had. He leaned in close, brushing his lips across my ear.

"Let me save you one last time."

I wanted to stop him. I wanted to do what was right. I wanted to push him away and know that, even as Gavin choked the life out of me, at least Luke was going to be able to live—that he would find other people, ones who weren't poison, whom he didn't have to take care of. I wanted Luke to find a place where he could just *be*, without my past and my forever-uncertain future sucking him down to the depths. I wanted to be the person Luke deserved to be with, not the person he was stuck with. But what I *wanted* didn't matter. It never had before, and as far as I was concerned, it never would.

"I'm sorry."

I fell backward to lie flat against the stage floor, the trails of my tears the only sign that some small part of me wasn't as soulless as I knew I really had to have been to let this happen.

* * * *

Luke's hands trailed up my stomach, tracing heat across my frigid skin in a way that surged my cock with the blood it had lost in the panic of my vision. I grabbed blindly for his shoulder, dragging him down on top of my body with a groan as the force of his hips grinding into mine caused black stars to burst across my eyes. There wasn't time for toying and teasing, just action—God only knew how long we had until Gavin showed up. I thrust upward into his body, forcing my pants and boxers farther down my legs. The Dreamwalker helped me get the jeans the rest of the way off and did the same with his own, but he hesitated as his fingers dipped under the waistband of my boxers. The sensitive skin there jumped, tightening at the warmth of his fingers on my body. His eyes met mine.

"You should be the one to—"

I shook my head, already knowing what he meant. He thought I should fuck *him*. My stomach turned at the idea, and my fingers dug into his shoulder harder. "No."

Luke sighed, his fingers starting to swirl on my skin. The feeling was driving me insane, a simple touch that fueled the flames of desire into an inferno that easily outranked anything the Night had caused. I shut my eyes as I tried to suppress the urge to slam my hips up into his again and claw away the thin layers of fabric that now stood between the me and the body I'd been longing to touch for so many years, if only it would've longed for me the same way. "Cole, it's your orgasm that'll push everyone over the edge, mine doesn't mat—"

My hand clamped down over Luke's mouth. "*No.* I won't take that, too."

I thought if I drowned the guilt and the self-loathing in my anger, it might be enough to let me actually go through with it. My dick was more than willing to play along—I was disgusted at my own weakness, but that didn't do a thing to stop the throbbing ache at my groin, where I could already feel my erection pressing up tight against Luke's hands. The Dreamwalker nodded against my hand solemnly, staring down at me with a kind of understanding that was so poignant it burned the edges of my mind and forced me to look away.

His fingers tightened and tugged downwards, and the rush of cold air washing over my cock as it sprang free caused a shiver to rock down my spine. My head lolled back and I closed my eyes, desperate to not have to see the look on Luke's face. I didn't want to see the artificial desire, the Night-patented look of lust that just days ago had so intoxicated me on the faces of Aaron and the produce guy and anyone else who had paid me half a glance. To see it in those eyes would have just hurt too much.

Oh fuck, who am I kidding? My heart was already wrecked beyond any kind of break that could've been fixed. The least I could do was watch it happen.

If I pretended it was all just one of my dreams, one of the little fantasies I'd played out so many times in the night when I was alone and lost, then maybe the raw wound ripping itself open inside me would sting a little less. If I could imagine that this was only as mildly wrong as they had been, and that it wasn't the one thing in this world that was about to finally destroy any relationship I might have with Luke — maybe then I'd be able to lie to myself long enough to revel in his touch until I came and brought the future down on all of us.

It was the only chance I had. I tuned out the voices screaming in the back of my mind, the conscience, the morality and whatever goodness I had left, drowned them out with the music still pounding through the air and the bass vibrating the floor and the chorus of moans and gasps from the orgy swimming in the dark around us. My world was strictly sounds and touches, smells and sights. The misery could wait—it *had* to wait. It was the only way.

Luke's warm breath fanned across the head of my cock, and I only just stopped myself from thrusting straight up into his face. Instead, I shoved my hips down into the wood floor of the stage, moaning without restraint. The sound made the Dreamwalker growl out his approval, wrapping his hand around my erection and slowly stroking up to the tip. White-hot needles twirled in my bloodstream at the sensation, and in the next second his mouth had captured mine.

The Dreamwalker's tongue seared its way past my defenses, urging my lips to part and sweeping me up in the strength of his need. My eyes were squeezed shut, but the sickly glow of an orange laser burned across my closed lids, and I pulled Luke down even closer, deepening the kiss in any way I could. His hand gripped the base of my cock and tightened in time with the roll of his hips into mine, and I matched his speed, pressing myself into his grip every time. My fingers clawed at his boxers blindly, catching the waistband and forcing them down his thighs.

My fingers found his aching erection and with eyes still closed I wrapped my fist around it and stroked gently at his overheating cock. Luke pulled away from the kiss to cry out, a shudder going through his body so forcefully that his arms gave out, bringing our bodies down flush on top of one another's. I finally opened my eyes, using the pause to take a gasp of air. I reached around with the hand trapped between us, catching both of our cocks and squeezing them tightly, stroking both of them a few times in a move that made a shiver rocket down Luke's spine. His fingers dug into my shoulder, and I moaned as I shuffled upward, pushing the Dreamwalker down my body just enough that his dick was out of my reach and lined up between my legs.

Luke pressed a kiss to my collarbone, then raised his head enough to catch my gaze. I nodded silently, gripping his hips tightly and sliding my legs farther apart.

The Dreamwalker shifted a little, getting into a better position. I could feel magic twisting around me at his command, but I didn't try to watch the marks. My head fell back flat against the stage as the spells worked their way into my skin, ones that warmed me and helped ease some of my vaulting panic. Luke's lips caught mine again, and I opened my mouth just as the pressure at my entrance shot through the roof.

I bit down on the Dreamwalker's lip and hissed out a breath. *Fuck, fuck, fuck...* Luke pulled away just enough to brush my hair back up higher on my forehead then set his hand at the side of my face, stroking the line of my jaw with his thumb. "Relax, baby," he whispered, catching me up in the strength still floating in his eyes around the Night. I could feel the aura still pouring out of me, flooding into the bodies that were crying out in more and more desperation around us, and I let the warmth of the energy take hold in my own body. The electricity of the Incubus power burned through my veins, forcing my muscles to tighten then fall languid as I let the desire work into my bones. I crushed my lips to Luke's, flaring the Night white hot so quickly that I immediately felt him thrust into me.

My breath hitched as the pain managed to override even the strength of the Night, but I couldn't stop the moan that tore out of my throat to rise into the chorus of the room, sounding out in counterpoint to the answering one from the Dreamwalker. Luke Cowen, the man I loved more than anyone else in this world, was finally inside me. That thought alone turned every barbed ache racing through my body into a blessed sting, a relief and a promise and a damnation all in its own right. He rocked his hips, working himself back out then back in slowly at first, and I shoved myself down onto him, tilting my hips so that every move the Dreamwalker made pushed him in a little deeper.

If there was a Hell, I was damn sure I was going to it. But fuck if I wasn't going to take every ounce of pleasure I'd fought so hard to avoid on the way down.

Luke's mouth burned molten kisses down my throat, points of fire that flared brighter than even the Night in my mind. My hand tangled in his hair, the glow sticks I was wearing boiling in the dark. Luke pulled back and thrust forward desperately, and I arched my back hard. His cock collided with a spot inside me that made the world of my sight explode open with the force of a supernova.

Colors stood out with almost blinding vividness, liquid beauty that melted and pooled as lasers traced the air, and the flushed tones of Luke's body moving on top of mine seemed to swim across my retinas. I dug my fingers into the Dreamwalker's arm and I forgot how to breathe, writhing between the hot body above me and the cold floor beneath. Luke rushed into me until our hips were pressed tight together and I squeezed myself around him as tightly as I could, my cock throbbing so hard I knew I couldn't have long until I broke.

As if he could hear my thoughts, Luke's hand wrapped tight around my erection, stroking firmly in time with his thrusts. I rolled my hips to the rhythm, banking the angle of my pelvis so that each one made tiny points of white prickle at the corners of my vision.

"Cole…" The Dreamwalker panted my name out with such breathless determination that my stomach jerked, but I pulled my mind down out of the infinity he was thrusting me into to focus in on the wavering image of his face.

The sex had flushed blood to his cheeks, and desperate seriousness kept the smirk that was second nature to him completely out of play, replaced with tight-jawed need. His hair was wrecked, his lips red from the kisses, and, locked together there in the orgy hell of Seethe, I didn't think I'd ever seen anyone look more beautiful than he did in that moment.

"Come for me…"

Luke's words eased out into the pounding airwaves, a command that was so much more powerful than any magic could ever have been. My muscles tightened, my cock surged with raw Night-laced voltage and I screamed out his name as oblivion came crashing down.

Pleasure went off inside me like a grenade, a violent explosion of sheer force as I blew in his hand. The flames chained upwards, burning through every sinew in my body, and I arched my back so high that my head rolled completely back as throbbing shadows washed over my eyes. Orgasm lanced into every square inch of my crumbling strength, hurling me to the vaulted ceiling so high above and promising me it would never let me fall.

It was perfect, just like I'd always imagined and so much more at the same time. And to think—I'd only had to lose everything that mattered to me to finally get it.

I heard Luke cry out my name, felt him lose control deep inside me, and all across Seethe there was a tremendous roar that shook the walls themselves as every single person was thrown over the edge of sanity at once.

My body suddenly bucked and seized violently, and I screamed as something inside me crackled with overloading voltage. The Incubus magic rippled under the surface of my skin, quaking under the sheer force of so much passion erupting in one tiny moment. Searing ice stole over my lungs and rocketed up my throat, twisting my threads sharply and refusing to let go as the barbed tendrils of the Night tore themselves out of my body. Marks of power beyond anything I could have uttered bubbled up in my mouth, effervescing into a cloud of white smoke that dragged itself out of me and into the air in a swirling vortex of spell-work. Turbulent magic was stripped from the bodies of everyone in the room, shooting invisible fireworks of power to the ceiling, and the spells detonated like mortar shells in the air above us, rampant energy that rushed into the lighting and sound systems so quickly that the breakers surged and blew in an instant, throwing us all into darkness.

My body was numb, taken too far into ecstasy to be dragged back yet. But my mind had already long-since returned, and it launched into overdrive as Luke slumped down on top of me.

Somehow, I'd been right. It had just been so much backlash, so much power *blasting* back into my body when I'd never been built to wield sexual magic—it must've short-circuited the aura, scaling issues or not. If the black hole in my chest was anything to go off, it probably could have done a damn sight more than that, too, so I probably should've been thankful. After all, it was over. I'd finished it, vented the Night out of my body and freed us all from its influence. On top of that, I'd also finally been fucked by Luke, which I had been dreaming about for seven years.

I closed my eyes, letting the tears stream down from them in silence. I wasn't *going* to hell—I was already in it.

The sounds of realization were already rising up into the air, cries of "What the fuck!" and "Who are *you?*" and "Oh my God!" and everything in between. If I'd ever prayed for some tiny moment that people might not remember what they'd done thanks to the Night once the effects wore off, I was immediately proven dead wrong. And now I had two seconds at best before Luke stirred, sat up, looked at me and knew what I'd done, what I'd made him do, what I should've stopped and regretted and never have allowed in the first place. This time I really would have to watch the disgust form in his eyes, the hatred, because there wasn't any magic left to save me. Even if I'd had the strength, I couldn't make myself wipe his memory so that he would have to walk around each day, never knowing the sick, fucked-up things I'd—

"I love you."

The words were whispered against my skin, spoken into my chest with a softness that had almost made me miss them.

Minutes seemed to stretch by, but I couldn't even breathe, much less move. I blinked dimly at the ceiling, so shocked that I didn't even have the capacity to try to think.

What!

I scooted backward, leaning up and grabbing Luke by the shoulders so that I could look him in the eye.

He couldn't have said what I thought he'd — *the Night was worn off, I was sure of it, but how could he — why — he — I —* Luke's eyes opened, and for one tiny instant I stared into the crashing emerald oceans in front of me.

Then everything went horribly, *horribly* wrong.

Faster than my eyes could track, Luke flew out of sight, ripped off my body with inhuman speed. The Dreamwalker tumbled into the roiling mass of people panicking in the darkness, thrown from the stage by the monster looming over me.

"Luke!" I screamed out his name as loud as I could, but a half-second later Gavin's hand was crushing down tight over my throat. Rage like I hadn't thought possible seethed in the Incubus's eyes, but I felt no fear at the sight of it — just untameable fury.

Gavin had hurt Luke. He was going to *pay*.

I flew my fist up into his face, smashing against his jaw hard enough to knock him off balance. I kicked out with my leg, trying to roll the Incubus over so that I would be on top of him, but I misjudged how fast he'd recover and he grabbed my wrist, slamming it down to the stage floor so hard that I thought it might have broken. I cried out in pain and he grabbed me by the throat again, choking off my scream and lifting me to my feet.

There was a second of air rushing past my ears before my head smashed hard against the far back wall of the stage, cracking the wooden paneling there. My vision swam and I clawed at Gavin's arm, but he just pulled me forward and slammed me into the wall again, harder this time.

"You couldn't *fucking* help yourself, *could* you?"

I stared into that face so full of hatred, framed with quaking black as I started to run out of air.

"Fuck...*off*..."

The words escaped through my gritted teeth, and they just made Gavin scowl harder as he slammed me into the wall again.

"You thought this little stunt would save you? That you could hide behind your little blood-sucker friends?" He moved in close, his black hair falling down to his molten copper eyes. "You were *wrong*. The Council will make me do the time for this little orgy of yours, yes, but I'm going to make *you* pay first." He squeezed tighter, almost completely blocking off my airflow.

"If you kill me...the Council...will—"

Gavin smiled grimly, flashing white teeth that somehow seemed infinitely more dangerous than any Vampire's fangs. "Charge me? Lock me away? Probably. But don't worry about imprisonment, *Seer*." His smile twisted into a look of disgust. "You should be so lucky, you fucking *waste* of magic. It's time you learned what suffering *really* is, Turner." He looked over his shoulder into the darkness, then turned back with the beginnings of a smile forming again on his face. "Starting with what I'm going to do to your little Walker friend."

Anger so true and pure that I hadn't known it existed blossomed in my chest like a nuclear explosion, a devastating wash of energy that forced the darkness at the edges of my vision back like a shot of epinephrine straight to the heart.

Luke. He was going to hurt Luke.

I would *never* let that happen.

"Touch him...and it'll be...the last thing...you ever do." My fingers dug into Gavin's arm so strongly that I felt muscles and tendons twitching under my strength. The Incubus's eyes flickered to the point where I was death-gripping him with the briefest moment of uncertainty, but it was quickly pushed away in favor of self-assured contempt.

"What are you going to do about it, *Seer?*"

You're about to fucking find out.

The way he tossed out my title like a challenge, an affirmation that I was only a *Seer*, and not a race with any real strength—it was nothing less than what I would've expected, but it was also the last time he would ever make that mistake again. Gavin had tortured me, tried to kill me, and now he planned to do the same to the only person whom I truly cared about in this world. It was time he saw exactly what a Seer could do.

Marks formed in my mind, bright shining stars that were beyond any magic I'd ever tried to control before. In a normal situation the spells would have torn me apart, flooding my threads with so much power that I would have literally been burned into dust by the sheer energy at hand. But in my mind the image of Luke flooded my thoughts, memories of the laughter and the tears and the touching, and of what Gavin would do if I gave him the chance. Steel cooled in my blood, locking my muscles down tight as I wove the master spells together into a roaring symphony of strength that hummed across my threads and rang out in the air around me. He was going to hurt Luke. I couldn't let him hurt Luke! Marks surged over my skin so quickly that Gavin couldn't even try to follow them and I bore into his eyes with all the fury I could dredge up.

There was a reason I was one of the most dangerous races on this planet. Gavin was about to learn that first-hand.

I let go of the Incubus' arm and plunged my hand into his chest, seething magic pushing my arm out of our dimension and into the one where his threads of power, his connection to the magic of this world, resided. Gavin cried out in pain as I gathered them up in my fist and twisted as hard as I could, but I refused to slow down. Icy whiteness formed at the corners of my mind, the beginnings of Sight magic that gathered strength with exponential speed. The Incubus' threads hummed out discordantly, unused to the power I was shunting into them but powerless to stop it.

Gavin's grip on me loosened, but I didn't follow suit. If anything, I gripped even tighter as I let loose the spells that would open the time stream in my mind. The familiar rush of the boundless number of futures began to slip through my threads and in turn, into Gavin's — in a normal vision I would focus the power, call on spells to dam up the waters and give me only what I needed. This time, I fired magic into the current to stir it to tsunami strength. Futures exploded in my mind's eye, a nearly infinite number of potential ends to a nearly infinite number of potential causes. In a millisecond, I watched the birth and destruction of cities, countries, *worlds*, every plant and animal and rock and molecule, Seeing them all but without having to truly *see* them. With a twist of his threads, that became Gavin's job.

Let's just say he wasn't suited for the position.

In an instant, hundreds of timelines became thousands, then millions, billions, so many that there weren't even names for the amounts. Gavin dropped me outright, clutching at his chest, but I wasn't anywhere that he could stop me — I was *inside* him, inside the very thing that he'd used to harm me and I'm sure countless others — the core of his magic. His threads of power quaked violently in my hand, unable to take a load that was only ever meant to twist sex, not the infinite modulations of the flow of time itself. I pushed harder, slamming more and more realities into his threads. With a colossal crack that was audible even in the physical world, one of them finally snapped under the strain.

Like a chain of dominoes, one after another the rest of the Incubus' threads of power broke in half, each suffering more and more relentless magic as there were fewer strings to share the load. I pulled back into reality, sealing away the forces of the time stream. I fell to my knees, screaming in pain as magic that was stronger than I was cut its way out of my body, its work finally done. Smoke drifted off my skin, tiny marks floating in the gray haze.

Gavin collapsed to the ground in front of me, unconscious. I blinked through my pain, making out two figures dressed in black suits approaching from the far end of the stage, but my attention turned back to the Incubus in front of me. My senses were so burned out by the spells that I couldn't tell if I just wasn't sensitive enough to pick up on his magical signature, or if the chain reaction I'd set off had actually snapped every thread inside him, leaving him as devoid of magic as any human. I couldn't find the strength to regret what I'd done even if it were the latter. Either way, Gavin would have hell's own time trying to hurt anyone else.

I reached backward to touch the back of my head, and immediately pulled back with a hiss at the spike of pain that caused. I could feel blood there again, and my vision swam for a moment before I suddenly felt a warm hand on my wrist. I looked up in confusion and was greeted with a calm but serious pair of copper eyes, flecked with silver.

"You are Cole Turner?"

It took a second to assure myself that it couldn't be Gavin, somehow recovered and with a different pair of eyes holding onto me. But no, whoever he was, he wasn't Gavin, although he certainly was an Incubus. And dressed in a suit? The realization served to confuse me and remind me that my pants were still halfway down my legs, so I hurried to pull them up and zip them. The Incubus didn't break eye contact. He clearly expected an answer.

"Y-yes?"

He turned my arm so that my wrist pointed upwards, and his thumb briefly tapped my Seer's Mark, which prickled for a second. He met my eyes again. "Our apologies, Seer." He looked over his shoulder to the other man in the suit, who was currently weaving spells of binding to keep the unconscious Gavin locked down tight. "Lucien! It's Turner. He's injured."

My mind was buzzing from the pain and the confusion, and I wasn't sure which was worse. The first one was solved a moment later, though, as the Incubus holding my arm released a wave of healing marks to course over my body, warming me and chasing away the aches and the bruises. I fought the immediate urge to fall asleep, grabbing onto the Incubus by the shoulder to keep myself grounded. "W-Who are you?"

He cocked an eyebrow as he continued to vent healing magic into me and pulled me to my feet. "My name is Damien. Lucien and I are members of the Incubi Ruling Council." That was enough to make my eyes open fully, and I balked as I looked from one of them to the other. *Two* Council members were here? The arrival of *one* was enough to make every magic being in a fifty-mile radius get their act together, and fast... Which probably meant I was in *deep* shit.

Damien must have seen the way I tensed, because he took a half-step backward and continued. "There is no need for concern. We are not here to charge you, Seer. The extenuating circumstances of this"—his face twisted uncomfortably, and he gestured noncommittally with his hand—"*Night* are grounds for substantial leeway." The barest of smiles teased at the corner of the Incubus's mouth. "I must say, your little show actually made our job of tracking this Rampant much easier. He was a problem long before the Night was created, but that certainly was a...turning point."

My head was still too fuzzy from the healing and the fighting to really make out all of what Damien had said, but I'd gotten enough to know that I probably wasn't going to be charged by the Council, at least for now, and that was saying something. My brow furrowed as I looked at the slumped Incubus on the stage floor, currently being lifted to his feet by Lucien. "Did I...break him?"

Damien glanced over his shoulder at Gavin, then turned back to face me, straightening the sleeve of his suit. "His connection to magic is not completely severed, though that may change after our ruling." Silvered-copper flared with interest. "But I must say, that was a truly incredible display of magic, especially so soon after venting the Night." He looked me over with a surveying eye. "You cannot be more than twenty-five years old—how did you channel such powerful spells?"

It had been easy, once I'd thought of what Gavin was going to do to...

Oh my God.

Erik Clarke

My stomach turned violently, and I gripped Damien's arm as strongly as I dared, staying on my feet only by leaning against the wall. The healing magic had blurred my mind, forced me to forget the very reason I'd done what I had.

"Where's Luke?" I looked around desperately, trying to make out anyone in the crowd, but there weren't any people out on the floor anymore—even in the dim lighting I could see that everyone had left, no doubt trying to leave the scene where through methods they couldn't understand they'd been forced to have sex with anyone nearby. I still scoured the walls, determined to find him. *He couldn't have left, could he? What if he was hurt?* Gavin had thrown him into the crowd, there was no telling what had happened to him... I shook Damien's arm. "Where is he? Where's Luke?"

Damien looked at me like I'd gone insane, shaking his head. "I—I apologize, Seer, I don't know who 'Luke' is—"

I fell to my knees, shaking my head. Tears stung at my eyes, and I only just kept them at bay. "Where is he, I—I need to know he's okay, need to know he didn't—that Gavin didn't—" My voice trailed off, my mind racing too fast to put my thoughts into words.

Damien's brow furrowed as he thought it over. A moment later the warmth of a hand on my shoulder drew my attention. "A moment."

The Incubus disappeared into the darkness, and I crawled my way back up the wall. My chest was aching, hurting worse than it ever had in my entire life. I had known Luke would hate me for what I'd done, known he would leave me—but I needed to hear him say it, and, more importantly, I needed to know that he was okay, and that Gavin hadn't hurt him. If he wanted nothing else to do with me, like I knew he should, then I at least deserved to know he was safe before I lost everything.

Damien reappeared just as suddenly as he'd left, and I looked up at him desperately, but he just nodded to the side as Adam stepped up from behind him, scowling. As soon as the shirtless, sex-mussed Vampire caught sight of me his eyes went wide, and he flew forward to grab me by the arms, running assessing hands over my body to check for any kind of injury. His eyes scoured my face protectively. "Cole! What happened? Are you all right?"

I opened my mouth to reply, but no sound came out. Damien's clear voice rang out in the quiet of the abandoned club, a carefully measured tone that told me he was talking to Adam. "You'll take care of him?"

The Vampire's face twisted into an expression of contempt, and the mercury of his eyes smoldered with annoyance as he shot the Incubus a glance over his shoulder, nodding in Gavin's direction. "Can't do any worse than your *friend* there did."

Damien stood stock still for a moment, the only physical sign of any response being the slightest tick of his jaw. He turned away a second later expressionlessly, moving to help Lucien stand Gavin up.

Adam turned back to face me, his eyes flashing across my face again. He closed them a second later, letting out a calming breath as his fists clenched at his sides. "Incubus!" he tossed over his shoulder.

Damien paused, turning back to look at the two of us guardedly. He cocked his eyebrow just minutely enough to show he was listening.

The Vampire rolled the words around his mouth for a moment before finally forcing them out. "Thank you...for helping Cole."

Silence met him for a second that seemed to stretch like minutes. Then, finally, Damien gave a brief nod and turned away. In a flash of magic, all three Incubi disappeared, and I dug my fingers into Adam's shoulder again.

"Adam, where's Luke? What happened to him? Gavin threw him into the crowd and I—I don't know if he's hurt, or...or worse..."

The Vampire's brow furrowed. "I don't know. I haven't seen him since before you started. I assumed he left like you told him to."

The breath caught in my throat, and I felt my fingers going cold. "He didn't. He stayed, and he—he's the reason the Night stopped." Adam's eyebrows practically shot up to his hairline, but I didn't have time to explain any more than that. "When Gavin showed up, he threw Luke into the crowd and I don't know what happened to him after that."

Adam ran his hand over my arm gently, and I shivered. *No. Don't say it, please don't say it, Adam —* The Vampire shook his head.

"There's no one else here, Cole. Just the clan. Luke...he must've just...left."

I shook my head, and I would have fallen to the floor again if Adam hadn't held me up. *That can't be right — Luke wouldn't have just left.* I knew him better than that. He might hate me, sure, would definitely be disgusted by what I'd done, but he wouldn't just up and leave. He'd confront me, make me explain who the hell I thought I was to have taken advantage of him like that. He would demand closure. He *had* to!

He had to let me explain, even if I never got to see him again, he had to let me tell him why I'd been so weak!

Tears were pouring down my face, but I didn't even try to stop them now. I shook Adam, shook him *hard*, beat my fist against his chest.

"He can't have just *left!* He... He can't... I-I— I have to... Have to tell him..."

Adam held me close, rocking me gently as I sobbed into his shoulder. "I'm sorry, Cole."

Luke had run away. I'd chased away the one person who had always stood by me, and it was all my fault. Not Gavin's, not Max's, *mine*. I didn't even get to explain why I'd done it, not that that would have helped. I'd always destroyed the lives of the people near me, and this was no different.

Before I went on stage, Adam had asked me if I was going to be okay, and I hadn't replied to him. But I knew the answer now.

I was never going to be okay again.

Chapter Eleven

I stumbled down the street Seethe's parking lot backed up to, a creeping numbness putting a film over my thoughts and barely offering me enough direction to help me stagger over to the bus stop. It had to be after two in the morning, and I could only imagine what I must've looked like, still shirtless, smeared in my own cum, with wrecked hair and glow sticks on my wrist. Adam had tried to help clean me up, but as soon as he'd left to find me something to wear I'd wandered out into the night.

Luke was gone. My *life* didn't even matter anymore, much less my clothes.

Another man stood at the bus stop already, late twenties. He wasn't wearing a costume, and he didn't look like he'd been partying. I fell in line next to him reflexively, waiting for the bus to arrive. He gave me a quick glance as I approached, then went back to looking at his phone. My brow furrowed.

No wink. No suggestive smile. No blatant groping, unsolicited kissing. *Nothing.* I almost started to panic before I remembered that, without the Night in my system, I was just any other weirdo on the streets of Kelvin in the middle of the night—maybe with a little more excuse because of Halloween, but not enough to really matter.

Damn.

I was...*normal* again. An odd realization, when I'd never felt more *not normal* in my entire life. I was a Latent Seer who'd just turned an entire Vampire club into an orgy, then had sex with my Dreamwalker best friend to vent out an Incubus aura, at which point I'd been attacked by said Incubus and used my ability to See the future to sever his connection to magic. There was nothing fucking *normal* about me, but the man next to me had no way of knowing that, and if I'd been capable of feeling anything more than the inky darkness choking off my heart, I would have been envious of his blissful ignorance.

The bus came to a stop in front of us, and when the doors swung open I climbed inside and found a seat as far away from the other man as possible. We were the only ones on the bus at that time of night, and I closed my eyes, dropping my head back against the window.

It was over. Luke was gone. I'd dodged one bullet and taken a shotgun blast to the chest in return, and there was nothing I could change about that now—so why did this numbness inside me still hurt so damn much?

* * * *

I practically fell into my apartment, only just staying on my feet as the door I'd been leaning on swung open. It was dark, which made sense considering the time of night, but even in the shadows I could tell that something wasn't right. My fingers fumbled blindly at the wall, catching the switch and flicking it upwards, but nothing happened.

Oh yeah. You blew them out when you tried to fuck Jake.

The voice in my head dripped with soulless sarcasm, and I swallowed down the bile that started to rise at the base of my throat. I was exhausted, but I managed to throw out just enough magic to let marks of lighting drift into the burned-out sockets of the living room. In the warm glow of the spells, I could finally make out the wreck I'd left in my wake — and the fact that nearly half of the items in the apartment were completely missing.

In any other situation I would have assumed that we'd been robbed. Unfortunately, I happened to know exactly how every broken plate or upturned piece of furniture had ended up in its place, and exactly where the missing items were — probably halfway across the state by now. Jake's room would be completely empty, I was sure, stripped of anything that could be taken quickly enough. My roommate was already long gone, cutting his losses and running as fast he could manage before I found him and tried to fuck him, no doubt.

I traipsed through the wreckage, the shattered picture frames and broken glass, the lamps knocked to the floor, the countless trinkets smashed to dust in my twisted dance of destruction the night before. My feet carved a path through the debris and finally came to a stop in the middle of my room.

How had everything gone so wrong so fast?

The warning signs had been there, sure, but in the space of less than a week everything I had left in my life had imploded like a dying star, stripping away anything that mattered. Jake thought I was going to attack him and had run away. My apartment was almost beyond repair. I'd ruined one man's marriage, broken the heart of another and God only knows who else I'd hurt on my path as I drilled my future into the ground at light speed. And Luke—

My stomach churned, and I leaned forward onto my nightstand for support, faltering to a stop as my eyes caught onto a tiny glimmer of light flashing up at me.

I gripped the vial in my hand, glass that had lost the fire inside that had once caused it to heat up my fingers like a furnace. I twirled it in front of my face, staring at the way the light reflected and refracted across its curves with sick fascination. My entire life had come down on top of me, and all because of this one tiny vial.

Who'd have thought?

I hurled the glass at the far wall as hard as I could, watching with visceral relief as it exploded into thousands of tiny shards that spread to every corner of the room. My legs shook then gave out, and I fell to my knees. I thought I was going to cry, but no tears came to my eyes—it was too late for them. I'd spent them all hours ago. What was done was done, and I couldn't go back in time and change any of it even if I would've had the strength to do something differently.

I couldn't even see *forward* in time when it came to my own life, so there was no way to know if there was some prayer that I might ever be all right again. I was sure I wouldn't be, but the frustration as my Latency made one last stab at my heart just threw me a little deeper into the darkness threatening to swallow me whole. I just didn't know what else to do anymore. My body ached. The strain of the magic burned in my chest, though it didn't have anything on the pain in my heart. And after everything I'd been through, my mouth still tasted like vomit and the trailing edges of Night-laced smoke.

Like some automaton I rose to my feet, wandering into the adjoining bathroom. My toothbrush seemed to sweep mint-flavored relief across my tongue of its own volition, since I certainly didn't remember having told my hand to do so. Apparently my body decided that that, at least, was a problem it could fix. I wasn't about to argue.

Rapid-fire thoughts still burned through my mind, chasing down every eventuality, trying desperately to figure out the little clue I might have missed, the tiny point of goodness that could be found in the sludge I'd let my life become. I closed my eyes, already resigned to what I'd been telling myself for days—I'd truly wrecked *everything.*

Wait — there is *one thing I can do.*

My eyes flew open and the toothbrush fell from my mouth and into the sink as the realization swept over me. *Could it really work?* It was a long shot, a crazy plan that had the potential to make things even worse if I was right—but I had to try. I jumped back over to my bed and lay flat on the mattress, shutting my eyes as I reached for the magic that was still crackling inside me with raw voltage.

Marks formed over my body, complicated strings that I would've had the intelligence to fear if I wasn't already so terrified at the insanity of what I was doing. The spells wove intricate paths around my body, wrapping me up in magic before plunging deep into my body.

Darkness immediately washed over my vision as I was hurled headlong into the world of dreams, images of Luke burning the path down into the shadows.

* * * *

Rough sand pressed against my cheek, and I stirred sleepily, pushing myself up to a kneeling position as I opened my stinging eyes to the cool rush of salty air. The full moon above washed the beach in pale light that seemed to glitter back up at me from the grains of sand, like tiny diamonds glowing with a luminescence all their own. Waves crashed heavily behind me.

I forced myself to my feet, the ache of over-extended magic burning like acid in my arms and legs. The wind rushed up over me, catching my hair and knocking it down onto my forehead, and I ran a hand back through it as I spun to face the source. A harsh breeze that made me shiver rode across the waves, and I rubbed at my tingling arms.

It was our beach, entering my life for the third time in as many days. But this time was different—it was so cold, and the wind and the waves seemed to know that I wasn't meant to be here, biting into my skin and smashing against the sand with predatory strength. I reached for my magic by habit, but in the world of dreams I was powerless to cast *anything*, much less a ward to chase away the chill working into my bones.

I spun around in the sand, scouring the trees in the distance and the expanses of rolling sand to both sides, but there was nothing—no one.

It couldn't be right. Surely in a dream, where he could face me without the dangers of dealing with me in person again, he'd come when I called him, if for nothing else than closure.

"Luke!" I stared out into the nothingness until my eyes burned, then stared even harder. "*Luke!*"

There was no answer, just the steady crash of the waves and the mocking whistle of the wind. I screamed out his name again and again until my voice was hoarse. *No! It's not possible.* Tears burned harsh paths down my cheeks, and in desperation I turned to the uncaring ocean, scouring the blue-black expanse for any sign of hope.

"*Luke!*" My throat seized and I coughed violently, my vocal chords seething as though shards of glass were being ground down into them. "L... Luke..." I stumbled forward in the sand, splashing into the coming tide and falling to my knees as I clutched at my chest. I let my head drop forward, staring straight down to the water that was coiling around my legs, my tears blurring the image into one that swam and blurred.

"*Where are you?*" My wrecked voice whispered the words to the waves moving over me.

My last hope had run dry. Luke was gone, not even willing to confront me in the realm of dreams, and I was finally, truly alone—just like I'd always told myself I wanted. My eyes burned with the heat of guilty tears, but my limbs were already going cold, losing the strength to hold me up as the bitter ocean plunged icy needles under my skin with each movement of the tide.

Six years ago, after my dad had gone, I had almost lost myself to this water. I'd let the shadows inside my heart grow darker and darker still, until there was nothing left inside but the emptiness and the pain, and when it finally overflowed it had taken everything Luke had to keep me safe. But there was no one here to save me this time, and in a sad little way, I was glad. At least I wasn't going to hurt anyone else anymore.

What would happen if I just let the waves take me this time? If I let go, let all the pain pull me under and make the world stop hurting?

The waves seemed to hear me, wrapping around my waist hungrily and pulling at me as the tide rushed back out to sea. I skidded forward in the sand, dragged a few inches deeper, then a few inches more as the water tugged me again. I closed my eyes and relaxed the muscles that were knotting from the chill. With each pass of the tide I tilted forward then back, falling closer to the surface each time. A few more seconds and I would slip under— Just three more... Two...

Wait.

The sound of the water seemed to be receding, no longer crashing so close to my ears that it blanketed out the rest of the world. And the pull...the force dragging at my legs, tugging me in a little deeper with each second— I opened my eyes slowly, peering out into the moonlit darkness in front of me. My brow furrowed as I flexed my stiff fingers numbly.

The waterline was almost five feet out in front of me, crashing harmlessly against the sand.

What the fuck?

I dragged myself to my feet, standing on shaking legs. The wind rushed over my soaked clothes, but somehow the chill was gone, the frigid breeze replaced by one that soothed my shivering with subtle heat. I couldn't help but run a hand through my hair, too confused to do anything more than just stare blankly at the receding waves in the distance.

How...?

"When I said I love you..."

My heart stopped.

Hardly daring to breathe, I turned full circle to face the sound of the voice behind me.

"It... It didn't have to do with the Night."

Luke stood a few dozen feet from me up the beach, smoothing out his shirt with a hand that I could see was shaking even at that distance. Our eyes met, and for a second I thought he was going to look away until he let a breath ease out from between pursed lips, holding my gaze with trembling strength.

All at once my chest was hammering again, but now it was too fast, much too fast, and I could scarcely even think enough to figure out what in hell I could even say. I had thought I would've fallen to the ground again if I'd ever heard those words from him, but the effect was just the opposite, making my muscles burn and ache like I was a runner poised at the starting line. My mouth opened and closed dumbly, offered no direction by my drowning brain.

"Wha... What do you...mean?"

Luke wavered in front of me, swaying slightly as his one hand seemed to death-grip his other biceps. The Dreamwalker swallowed, glancing down to the sand for a few seconds before looking back into my eyes, a new determination burning there that challenged the rampant tension squeezing the rest of his body tight.

"I mean," Luke took a deep breath, steeling his jaw. "I love you, Cole. I... I want to *be* with you." The air he'd taken in shuddered out of his chest unevenly, but he refused to look away. "I have, for a long time."

Green and blue stayed locked on one another in the moonlit shadows for what seemed like hours, the thoughts that so commonly burned through my mind like a bullet train nowhere to be found. With no direction to stop them, my aching legs took control. I moved slowly across the uneven sand, careful steps that belied the fact that I couldn't spare a glance at a single thing but Luke. I drew closer to the Dreamwalker by inches, dragging out the tension longer than I ever could have had the patience for if I'd had any power over my own motion.

Seconds, or minutes, or days later, I was in front of him, standing so close that there was nowhere to look but up into his eyes, into the green fields that hadn't turned away from me for so much as a second. My hand came to rest on the side of Luke's neck, and I pulled him down into a kiss.

It barely lasted a second, a momentary press of my lips against his. I almost tried to deepen it but immediately faltered, pulling back a half-inch as I realized there was no answering pressure. My eyes flew open.

Oh God, I misunderstood somehow, this wasn't what he meant. I ruined it all over again. How could I —

Warm arms stole around my chest, dragging me back in as Luke's lips swept over mine in a desperate rush. His hands splayed over my back, pulling me in even closer as his mouth captured mine, parting my lips and flushing my body with a glowing heat that felt so much better than the Night ever could have. In the tiny pause as we gasped for air, I couldn't stop the rich, breathless laughter that burst out of me, soul-deep relief that made my limbs shake so badly with released tension that I almost fell to the sand.

"I..." I was so confused, so many unanswered questions burning through my mind, but at the same time, I had to fight the urge to just shut up and revel in the closeness of Luke's body, in his warmth that I somehow was allowed to feel for at least a while longer. Only the desperate need to know if that gift was going to be taken from me gave me enough strength to put a hand on Luke's chest and put just enough space between us that I could look into his eyes again, still wrapped in his embrace. "I thought you ran away?"

The levity that had softened my Dreamwalker's features faded slightly as his face steeled with deadly seriousness. "I would *never* do that to you, not if I had any choice." His arms squeezed me a little tighter, and I couldn't hold back the beginnings of a smile that teased at my lips, even as Luke shook his head in frustration. "It was the fucking Council. When they stormed in to stop Gavin, they cast spells into the crowd, ones to wipe memories and force people to go home." I felt his thumb start to swirl gentle circles on my back. "I managed to stop the first, but it took so much out of me I couldn't stop the compulsion." Luke scowled. "I was halfway home before I could break the spell, and by the time I got back to Seethe you had already left."

Already, the smile had left my face. That was a piece of the puzzle, but that wasn't nearly enough, didn't even begin to explain the parts that really left me so utterly—

"Confused?" Luke offered, the barest of the smirks that I'd missed so much tugging at his lips.

I shook my head, letting my fingers fan across his shirt, still unwilling to allow any more distance than was physically necessary in the panic-fueled fear that if I let Luke step away from me he might never come back again. "There isn't even a word for it." With my free hand I scrubbed at my face before meeting his eyes again. "So...this whole time...*seven years*...while I've just been assuming you were..." My mouth hung open for a few seconds before snapping shut. I just didn't know what else to say, I was so lost in the beginnings of a world that I'd apparently been living in for almost a decade without even knowing it.

Luke's smile held, but it looked sadder for it as he gestured toward the sand, urging me to sit down next to him. We moved to the ground, but I kept hold of his hand, desperate to preserve some form of contact. "It's...kinda a long story."

I snorted, gesturing out to the expanse of the dream world, where the passage of minutes and hours was practically meaningless. "I think we can make time." I had to know why I'd been granted this second—more like twentieth—chance, and I'd be damned if I wasn't going to get every detail.

The Dreamwalker grinned openly before looking down to the point where our hands were clasped together, to the spot where his thumb was tracing patterns across my skin, his smile becoming more wistful. "In high school, before we were friends, I watched you systematically shut down *every* person who tried to get close to you—teachers, students, didn't matter." His smirk spread a little wider, and he squeezed my hand. "Pretty soon, I decided I had to finally find out if you really were that big of an asshole."

I cocked my eyebrow. "How romantic..." I droned sarcastically.

Luke laughed, a deep sound that reverberated in the quiet air of the beach and made me want to crush my lips against his again. "Well, it's true. You acted like a dick—but I wanted to know why. I kept trying to get closer to you until you finally cracked enough to show me the real you." The Dreamwalker scratched at his head then ran a hand through his hair. "That's...kind of where things started to go wrong."

My brow furrowed. By my estimation, that was when everything in my life started to go *right*. "What do you mean?"

"You...misunderstood." He shook his head. "What I called...*flirting*...you just took as friendship. I didn't— I mean... Fuck." Luke rubbed his free hand on the leg of his jeans nervously. He took a deep breath and barreled out the words so fast I had to focus hard just to follow along. "I was pretty sure you were into guys, but I wasn't *completely* sure, and you never really said anything at first to make me think you liked *me*, and you never really asked if *I* was into guys because you just assumed I was straight, and that makes sense and everything since, you know, most guys are, so I just figured I'd come out to you when you told me *you* were gay, but then you never actually *did*, because one day you just mentioned in passing that your last date was a dick, and I didn't know how I could say it because you hadn't and—"

"Luke!" My hand clamped tight over his mouth, catching him off guard. I squeezed at my temples with my free hand, trying to process almost four years of secrets in the four seconds it took him to rush them out. "Just...breathe." After a beat he took my advice, dragging in a wash of air as I pulled my hand away. His shoulders sagged slightly with the relief of a story finally let loose, but all I felt was even tenser.

He liked me the whole time? And I honestly didn't pick up on that? It had been so easy all these years to chalk up everything that had gone down between us as perfectly normal, considering how completely un-fucking-normal our lives were. I had wanted a friend for so long, but always held people away. Then someone was finally even more stubborn than I was, and he fought his way into my life, and I'd thought everything he'd done after that had just been what any true, best friend would do—one of my parents died and I felt like it was my fault, and Luke was there to hold me and get me through it, with his soft words and his warm arms and his healing magic. Then he did the same again. And again. And *had* been doing it ever since we met seven years ago, always keeping me safe, and never pulling back even an inch when I needed someone to hug, or cry on, or bitch to, or play video games with, or—

Jesus Christ.

I couldn't even think of a single time when Luke *hadn't* pushed everything else in his life to the back burner for me. Whatever I needed from him, whenever I needed him, he was there, every single *fucking* time. I wasn't just blind to my future—apparently I was blind to my *present*, too.

I looked up into Luke's eyes, not even sure how I could say all of the...*everything* he deserved to hear. He beat me to the punch, the beginnings of a smile flickering in the moonlight.

"When you kissed me that night—the night that you got wasted... I wanted to kiss you back so bad. I wanted to climb on top of you and show you just how much I needed you." I stared up at the Dreamwalker, transfixed with my lips parted. It shouldn't have been so sexual, shouldn't have made my dick throb so hard in my jeans, but somehow hearing the words I'd been wanting to hear for so long and *knowing* that they were true, that they weren't just the side effects of some fucked-up drug—the thought had me melting, even as Luke shook his head, throwing his hair to the side. "But you thought I was straight, and you'd just lost your dad, and..."

"And you were trying to do what was right." I finished for him. That, at least, I understood immediately — stepping away from something you've always wanted because you know it's wrong to want it at all. Though I had to say, it seemed like Luke was a damn sight better at it than I'd been.

His hand squeezed mine tightly, drawing my eyes back up to his own and away from the distant crashing waves. "But it *wasn't* right." He sighed. "Keeping someone in the dark can hurt them, whether you're trying to keep them safe or not. Case in point." He gestured toward the two of us. "If I would've just grown a pair and told you how I felt, none of this would have happened."

"This isn't your fault, Luke. Just because you didn't tell me you liked me — "

"I *gave* you the Night that started all of this." He smirked slightly. "Even *you* can't honestly say that I didn't have a hand in the shit that went down."

My brow furrowed again. I didn't blame Luke for this — I may have at one point, but everything that had happened after he handed me the Night was my choice, my responsibility. He gave me the tools, maybe, but I dug that hole all on my own. I opened my mouth to tell him as much, but his soft voice stopped the words in my throat.

"You had dreams about me. Sex dreams."

The change in conversation threw me so fast I couldn't do anything but sit in silence as my mouth went dry, my cheeks flushing. I looked down at the sand in embarrassment, and almost started to pull my hand away before Luke's warm laugh pulled at my attention again.

"I'm not *mad*, Cole. It actually was kinda what kept me sane, knowing that you really did like me too, at least a little. I thought it might have just been a weird flash-in-the-pan deal that first time I felt the pull and showed up just in time to see us making out right in front of me." His smirk grew, and his fingers started to trace patterns across my palm. "But then you had another one. And *another* one. So then the next time I felt the dream starting I kind of...jumped in."

The breath caught in my throat, and as ridiculous as it seemed considering everything we'd done in *real* life, I still couldn't stop the panic that churned my stomach. "Jumped...in?"

Luke bit his lip, as much to hold back his grin as to show any sign of shame. "Didn't you notice they were getting a little...detailed? Realistic?"

I ran a hand through my hair, cringing as I thought of all the things I'd done—all the things I'd *said*—in those dreams, in the moments when I'd thought it wasn't *really* Luke, that he wasn't ever going to have to know how bad I wanted him, or what *exactly* I wanted him to do to me...

"*Shit...*"

Luke's hand traced my jaw, lifting my head so that I faced him. He seemed to practically glow in front of me with reassurance, his hand warm and comforting on the side of my face. "It's okay, Cole. I swear." His smile never wavered. "The point I'm getting at is that I knew you liked me, but even then I was scared to tell you that I liked you too, because it would change everything, and if it went wrong..." He licked his lips. "I was okay just leaving things the way they were for a little longer, because at least I knew. But after a while...that wasn't enough."

The Dreamwalker shook his head again, looking out at the ocean. "I don't know why I even got the stuff. It was stupid... But you had no clue that I wanted you like that, and when Max said he had something that could help... I... At first I thought *I* would drink the Night, so that you'd come onto me again in real life and I could tell you the truth." He turned back to face me, the smile faded from his face. "But then you found it, and you were so excited about your date with that Derek guy, and I was so fucking high and jealous that I decided to give it to you." He scrubbed at his face. "I don't know what the fuck I was thinking—and I made it sound like it was gonna help with your Sight..." Luke caught my gaze with the utmost seriousness. "I'm so sorry, Cole. It was never supposed to get this...*big*. But no matter how much I tried to fight around the Night to show you the truth, you pulled away, because *you* were trying to do what was right."

What was right. I shook my head, looking away from Luke. "I haven't done a single thing that was right since this all started." I pulled my hand out of his, standing to try and pace off some of the nervous energy that had reached a fever pitch in my veins. There was a thought unraveling in my mind, an argument I'd buried because I'd never expected to need to voice it, but now it worked itself out of my mouth haltingly. "I've hurt people, Luke. In ways I don't know I can fix, even with magic." I swallowed hard, trying to force some of the determination and strength the Dreamwalker had shown tonight into my own body. "I'll be damned if I'm not gonna try as hard as I can to repair the damage I did anyway, but..." I steeled my jaw, refusing to give any ground as Luke looked up at me in confusion. "If the last seven years somehow haven't already shown you, this has to have made it pretty damn clear that I'm broken. Luke...you've always been there for me, you're really the only reason I'm still *here*, and I love you, but—y-you shouldn't want to be with me. You should be with someone who isn't such a wreck, someone who's better—" I was rambling, running my hand through my hair, but for the life of me I couldn't stop.

Faster than I could track, Luke was in front of me, his hands on my body forcing me to look up into his eyes as he pressed a finger firmly over my mouth. "Hey— Shh." I tried to shake my head, but he wouldn't let me budge, and only when he could see in my eyes that I wasn't going to argue did he lower his hands so that he could run them over my arms, bringing some of the warmth back into my body. His lips caught mine in a brief kiss, just enough heat to remind me how badly he still wanted me, but gentle at the same time. He moved back a half-step, smiling genuinely. "I don't want *better*. I want *you*."

I couldn't stop the answering smirk pulling at my lips as I cocked my eyebrow at his choice of words. "I feel like I should be a little offended at that..."

Luke grinned deviously, a look that made my body tingle in the best way possible. "Well, you *are* kinda fucked up."

I shoved him, pushing him back almost hard enough to make him fall over. As it was, he had to pinwheel his arms like an idiot to stay standing, and that just made me smile even wider. "Thanks, *asshole*."

The Dreamwalker cocked an eyebrow as he shook his hair back up over his eyebrows and began a slow approach back to where I stood. "Cole... I wanted to be with my best friend for years, and instead of just being honest with him and telling him how I felt, I snuck into his dreams at night and had sex with him, then gave him a drug that would make everyone want to fuck him so that when *I* did there would be an excuse." His hands came to rest on my hips, and he looked at me with that knowing stare that had owned me since the first time I spoke to him. "Neither of us is exactly *perfect*."

I wound my hands into his hair, pulling his lips down to mine so I could show him exactly what I thought about all that. He deepened the kiss, racing heat through my mouth and down to my crotch as I lost myself in his warmth. I pulled back just enough to blow a soft breath across his flushed lips. "Feels pretty damn perfect to me."

Luke grinned, lunging forward to capture my mouth again, but in the second before he could, a thought surged over my mind so quickly that my knees almost gave out on the spot. I jerked backward before the Dreamwalker could kiss me, fisting my hands into his shirt so tightly I almost tore the thing off him. His face immediately cleared, all sign of sexual frustration gone the moment he saw the look of sheer terror on my face. "What is it? Cole, what's wrong?"

No, please, please, please, I know I probably don't deserve him, but please don't let this just be —

"What... What if—?" I swallowed hard, trying to force the words to come out even as they burned at my throat. I looked into Luke's concerned eyes imploringly. "What if this is just a dream? A *real* one, not one where you're really here, where...you really feel... What if you're actually—" The words trailed off as the traces of air in my lungs slipped away, refusing to be replaced by any new oxygen.

The Dreamwalker's tension eased out a second later, the panic that had clearly locked his body tight slipping away so easily that I almost followed suit— almost. But I had to hear what he had to say, needed to be absolutely sure that I wasn't going to lose it all again before I could even think of breathing, much less relaxing.

Luke's hand came to rest on the side of my face, tilting my head up enough to meet his gaze. "This is real, Cole, I swear." I started to open my mouth, and he cut me off, nodding. "And I know that's what I'd say even if this was a dream, but trust me — I'm a part of your life, and I'm staying here. In fact..." The Dreamwalker stroked his thumb gently across my cheek. "I'm kinda just a few dozen feet from your apartment door."

My brow furrowed. "What do you mean?"

He smirked. "I'm passed out on the stairs up to the third floor."

What? My jaw dropped, and Luke laughed, but I couldn't stop from sputtering in disbelief. "You just...went to sleep in the middle of the building? What if someone would've... I don't know...fucked with you?"

Luke's smile warmed and he pulled me in a little closer, running his hands over my back possessively. I unconsciously arched into the touch, craving more. "You were calling me. I said that I'd always be there when you needed me, and I meant that."

I ran my hands over his chest, teasing across the edge where the collar met his flushed skin. "Damn." The word slipped out of its own accord, but I couldn't disagree. Just...*damn*.

His lips met mine again for a brief second before he pulled back. "I was going to your apartment to tell you the truth." He smirked again. "*And* to ask you to give me a chance at being more than just your friend."

Luke was *more* than just a good guy. He had saved me more times than I could count, seen me in the darkest hours of my life, and he still wanted to be with me. He knew I had baggage, and he didn't try to brush that aside— instead, he made sure that I knew that he was there to help me through it. Yes, I was broken, but Luke had never believed I was too far gone to fix. He loved me, and he had stayed by me, even after I'd thrown us both into hell and had to drag our way back out of it.

I grinned, powerless to stop the smile that was lighting up my entire being as I reached gently into the magic swirling along Luke's skin.

"I can give you more than just a *chance*."

I tugged at the marks of power floating in the air, warping them into something I could control as I forced spells of awakening to flood my body with white heat.

* * * *

I threw open the door to my apartment, breathless from so much more than the manic blur that was jumping out of my bed to wrenching at the handle.

Luke stood framed by the doorway, his scruffy hair messy from the night at Seethe, the long-sleeved shirt he'd no doubt had to find on the floor looking stretched and hanging limply off his lean body. His jeans were slung low on his hips, and the secretive smile dancing across his lips, that shy little expression that had first made me want him, shone in the dim lights of the hall.

I fisted his shirt and dragged him in, crushing our mouths together with shameless abandon. The Dreamwalker's arms wrapped around me, pulling me in closer as he kicked out to swing the door closed behind him, and I moved backward, letting him pin me to the kitchen counter.

"God, Cole..."

I ran my hands up under his shirt, racing my palms across the tight planes of his abs, sides, and chest. Luke arched into my touch, grinding the hard line of his cock into my own crotch. My hands seized and a staccato cry burned its way out of my throat as I involuntarily thrust even harder into his body.

"Bed. Now," I hissed out through gritted teeth. Luke groaned into my neck, where he was laving nuclear kisses from the edge of my jaw down to the hollow of my throat. I squeezed his hand tightly and pulled us away from the counter and toward my room.

"Did some remodeling?"

I could hear the smile in Luke's voice as we hurried a path through the wreck that was my living room. I stepped over the broken lamp and turned just far enough to flash him a smirk as I pulled him through the doorway. "Went a little crazy. Nothing new there, right?"

There would be a time to talk through what had happened, how close I'd come to losing it. There would be a time to fix the apartment and the gears in my heart that had crumbled over the years, and if there was anyone who would be able to make me whole again, it was Luke. But that moment, after everything that had happened, after learning once and for all that I was going to have him by my side to do all of those things and so much more — right then, all I needed was to be with him. No dreams, no crowds, no orgy, just Luke and I, together. *Finally.*

I pulled my shirt off over my head, tossing it aside. Luke's eyes seemed to flare brighter with each inch of skin I exposed, and I unclasped my jeans achingly slow. I savored the scrape of the zipper on the head of my cock through the thin fabric of my boxers, and I groaned as the pants hit the floor. Luke's breath hitched, and I grinned up at him. Raw magic sizzled in the air like crackling voltage, and I dragged the arcing currents inward until I could shape them into the marks I needed, ones I'd become intimately familiar with over the last few days. Luke watched the symbols tracing paths across his body, and the smirk teasing his lips spread wider.

"My turn." I let the spells go, slamming into the fibers of every piece of clothing on the Dreamwalker's body and obliterating them into a multi-colored blast of smoke. The clouds coiled over Luke's body, drifting off his flushed, exposed skin like venting steam.

In the next second I was kissing him again, rushing our tongues together in a flame-laced fight for control. Luke's hands drifted down from my sides to my hips, and with a surge of heat across my tingling skin my boxers disintegrated into nothingness. I moaned into the Dreamwalker's mouth, digging my fingers into his shoulders hard enough to leave bruises.

God damn!

Luke pushed forward, pressing the backs of my knees into the edge of the bed so that I fell backward onto the sheets. I slid up the bed, making room as he climbed up on top of me, his arching body practically glowing with furnace warmth. Luke set his hands on either side of my head and dropped to his forearms, scraping our aching cocks against one another as he brought his chest almost flush to mine. His mouth captured mine, and with every breath his overheating chest met my own. I arched up into his heat and squeezed the tight muscles of his ass, crushing his hips down on top of mine with a tug that stopped the air in my lungs.

"Cole…"

The word dripped through the thick air, a growl of possession that made my dick squeeze so tight I thought I was going to implode. Mind-crushing gravity drained all blood and thought to the point where our bodies writhed down into one another's, and my vision went black as my eyes were slammed shut by the strength of my need.

I grappled at Luke's arms, crawling my way out of the ecstasy-laced darkness I was falling into long enough to force my eyes open and meet his gaze. His body was already trembling with pent-up power, but he held my stare firmly.

"I love you," I panted out breathlessly. I shook my head, running my hands over the Dreamwalker's shoulders. "No qualifiers this time, no *as a friend—*" I smiled shakily, almost laughing in sheer relief as I brushed my lips across his for a brief moment. "I love you, Luke Cowen."

Luke grinned unabashedly, the genuine warmth of it lighting up the darkness we lay in, washing over me with a purity that chased away any memory of the guilt and the pain that every touch had brought just a few hours earlier. His hand trailed down from the side of my head across the curve of my jaw. "I love you, too." A short bark of laughter cut through the air, and he shook his head as he smiled at me. "*Damn*, I've waited a long time to hear you say that."

I spread my legs farther apart, letting Luke's hips settle into the space between them. I groped blindly in the top drawer of my nightstand, finally pausing when I caught hold of the lube. We could have used magic again like we had at Seethe, spells to relax my body and make it easier, but there was something so much better, so much more personal about the normal way. I pressed the bottle into Luke's free hand and smiled up at him. "Better late than never?"

His green eyes shone in the dark as he pushed himself farther down my body, never breaking my stare. "Amen to that." He smirked up at me, and I let my head fall back against the pillow as his fever-hot mouth wrapped around the head of my cock.

"God, Luke..."

I moaned to the ceiling as his fingers pressed inside me, spreading in time with the slow, torturous movements of his tongue. The Dreamwalker's hand trailed up my chest, and I arched my back, tightening my cock as he swallowed me all the way down to the base. I cried out, and Luke hummed his approval, throwing me dangerously close to the edge of my sanity as I almost lost it right there.

I grabbed blindly at his waist, pulling in a wordless plea. I needed him. *Now,* in every possible way, and I shuddered in relief when I saw that he knew what I'd meant. Luke pulled his mouth off me and replaced it with the warmth of his hand, stroking gently as he moved back up my body enough to capture my mouth. I squeezed my eyes shut and bit down hard on his lip as he moved forward, pushing just enough that the head of his cock was inside.

Without the magic to help me I was skating a thin line, dancing on the event horizon of pleasure and pain, and Luke paused to gently rub his hand into the muscles of my chest and arms that I'd squeezed almost as tightly as my eyes. Without Night to grease the wheels, it was harder than the last few days had lulled me into believing, and damn, Luke was *thick!* I let out a slow breath and forced my hands to release the wrecked sheets and come to rest on the

Dreamwalker's hips. Tentatively, I pulled him forward, an inch farther, then another.

Luke's hand never stopped moving on my erection, teasing me dangerously close to the edge with each stroke, with every scrape of his thumb across my leaking head. I lost myself in his touch, falling into the swirl of flushing skin, flaring green and fluxing shadows. My muscles tensed and tightened in time with his movements, as he parted my lips with his tongue and pushed himself in the rest of the way.

Our hips were flush against one another's, and I held him as close as I could, finally remembering why this was all so much more than worth it. To be here, safe in Luke's arms, two pieces of one whole—I groaned his name, melting down into the darkness waiting behind my eyelids.

He rocked backward then started moving against me to the rhythm his hand was setting, speeding up incrementally as I writhed deeper into the sheets, pressing my hips lower and pushing the angles until he found the exact place I needed. Detonating fireworks crackled through my veins, and I squeezed so tightly around Luke that I wasn't sure my body would ever remember how to relax again.

The Dreamwalker groaned his ecstasy into my mouth, magnetic heat that dragged an answering cry out of my own lungs. He slammed into me harder, and as he buried his face into the side of my neck I bit down on his shoulder, hissing the ache out over his skin. The shadows of the room seemed to arc and bend, throbbing to the silent scream of our passion as it rocked through the molten air.

Luke squeezed the base of my cock, *hard*, and I shouted his name into his neck as I was hurled headlong into another dimension, one of exploding stars that expanded out in each direction into the infinity. My body twisted so tight that even my threads were wrenched out of place, flaring magic so bright that if my Dreamwalker hadn't been there to balance me every item in the room would have burst into flames in a millisecond. The biggest load I'd ever blown in my life shot onto my chest, and my body crumbled underneath me as I finally lost all sense of feeling.

My orgasm threw Luke over the edge, forcing him to lose himself inside me in a throbbing, shuddering detonation that seemed to go on for hours as I held him to my chest. He dragged in a shaky breath, so lost in his own burst of perfection that he had to take a minute to do nothing more than remember how to breathe as his hands moved slowly over my sides.

Fuck what had happened at Seethe. Fuck everything I'd ever done with another person before then. None of it mattered—none of it compared, and I knew that nothing else ever would with an assurance I couldn't even imagine refuting.

Luke laughed softly, breathlessly into my neck, and I did the same, pushing up on his shoulders until he was suspended above me again, smiling down through the afterglow I knew I'd never get enough of.

In that moment, for the first time since I'd turned thirteen, it didn't matter that I couldn't see my future. Because lying there, with Luke in my arms... I didn't need to see it. I could *feel* it, feel the forever running between us, and damn it, it was everything I'd ever wanted. Luke's lips stole over mine and I kissed him back, smiling as I held him close.

Everything and more.

About the Author

Erik Clarke is still trying to figure out how to balance work, school, writing, and the ever—elusive 'social life'. He's also still trying to figure out when the outlandish plots and crazy characters he'd scribbled into the margins of his notebooks for years somehow coalesced into an actual novel.

Born in Ohio and now struggling through the constant love/hate relationship that is living in the beautiful but sweltering Arizona landscape, Erik is thankful every day for the incredible, supportive family and friends that surround him—and for the sheer joy that writing two characters to their happily ever can bring.

Erik Clarke loves to hear from readers. You can find his contact information, website details and author profile page at http://www.totallybound.com.

Totally Bound Publishing